BERMONDSEY
"THE FINAL ACT"

CHRIS WARD

Copyright 2014 Chris Ward

All rights reserved

ISBN - 10: 1505880165

ISBN - 13: 978-1505880168

CHAPTER 1

The couple were strolling arm in arm down Tower Bridge Road as though they hadn't a care in the world. It was mid-October and there was a biting cold wind, the kind that got in your bones if you weren't dressed warmly. The man was in a short, fashionable, expensive dark-blue wool coat. He had light grey chinos on, held up with a wide black leather belt, and his shoes were slip-on black leather loafers. A black shirt completed the ensemble and he looked fashionably expensive and trendy. He also sported a handsome thick moustache and beard plus a good head of brown hair. The thick-rimmed black glasses gave him even more of an arty look. Someone could easily have seen him as a film director or an ageing pop music video producer! The woman with him had an enormous mop of red hair with a man's Burberry-style flat cap perched on top, and her hair was matched with dazzling green eyes. Her long black tailored coat kept her warm and at the same time gave nothing away about the firm and delectable body underneath it.

The man steered her towards a parade of shops, they walked past a small hardware store then a barber's, a bike shop, HSS Equipment Hire and finally Crystal Clean dry cleaners, and they had arrived at their destination. The queue was three-deep coming out of the front door and the couple joined it, rubbing their gloveless hands to keep warm. The woman looked at her escort as if to say "where the hell have you brought me now?". The man just smiled and looked up at the name on the green awning hanging over the front door of the building: 'M Manze, The Noted Eel and Pie House'. Sharon followed his gaze and read the name, saying: "Eels, I am not eating eels."

"Well?" said the woman in a slightly raised angry voice, looking into the man's eyes.

"Well what?" said the man in reply. "I told you I was going to take you for a slap-up lunch and that is exactly what I'm doing." The woman looked through the window by the door, and could see nothing at all marvellous about eating in this dingy establishment.

The queue shrank and soon the couple were standing at the marble counter and being asked what they would like. The man felt he was at home, it was warm and there was a comforting food smell of years gone by, and the serving

The Final Act

ladies resplendent in their green uniforms were smiling just the same as he remembered they'd been doing a year ago.

"Yes guv what can I get you?"

"Double pie-and-mash and a cup of tea please," said the man, giving a huge grin.

"Oh and a single pie for the lady." He had remembered his partner who was looking even more unimpressed as she surveyed the shop.

The man stared as the creamy mash was dolloped on and smeared down onto the side of the plate, two pies were added and then a generous serving of green liquor was poured around the pies. The man was in heaven at the sight and was already licking his lips.

They took their food, picked up their teas and cutlery from the end of the counter and the man led them to the back of the room to the last table. The woman looked at the tables, observing the old fashioned church-pew-like benches, and the marble tables held up with good black painted ironwork. She looked around and the only thing she really did like were the mirrors on the wall surrounded by old but very shiny clean green-and-white tiles.

"The shop's been open since 1892 and the building is listed so nobody can alter anything," said the man whilst splashing vinegar onto his pies and then shoving a huge piece of one of them, accompanied by mash, into his mouth.

The woman had tasted the food and was picking at it. Even though she was hungry, it was hardly a five-star Michelin restaurant she thought to herself.

"Don't tell me you're not going to eat that!" said the man. ogling the woman's food.

"Go on then I don't want it," said the woman as she pushed the plate towards him. He grasped it and scraped the remaining pie-and-mash on top of the food he had left and instantly attacked the meal with a passion.

The woman was just not impressed with anything about Manzies, she kept glancing around and then looked up at the two circular ceiling fans rotating methodically. She became hypnotised with their movement and hum.

Throughout the meal the man had been watching the front door to see who came in. It was unbelievably busy with customers entering on a continuous basis. The man had finished his food and sat back and let out a contented sigh.

"That was so good. Reminded me of my childhood, you can't beat pie, mash and liquor."

The woman came back to life and was about to ask if he was being serious but decided not to bother as the man was obviously besotted with this pie-and-mash thing!

"Can we go now?" she asked in an exasperated voice. "And I'm hungry so perhaps we could pick up a takeaway?"

The man didn't want to ruin the occasion so said nothing and just relished the moment, gazing around him and soaking up the atmosphere. He glanced up at the door once again and stopped dead. The woman instantly sensed the change in her partner as she whispered, "Who is it? What's wrong?"

"A blast from the past. One of Paul's fucking hired helps by the name of Matt."

"Keep very calm and he won't recognise you, I promise it," said the woman firmly.

"Let's see then."

The man and his companion got up from the bench and made their way down the shop. 'One, two, three,' the man was counting the tables to himself, 'four, five, six, seven'. They were near the door. He passed the man called Matt and eyeballed him for a second. There was no recognition from him and he passed the eighth table and the couple were through the door and out into the fresh air.

The man pulled his collar up and smiled at his woman. "So what would you like? Chinese?"

The woman looked at the man and put her arms round his neck and whispered into his ear:

"You are my special one, I told you nobody would recognise you. Now if you get me a really tasty Chinese takeaway I'll show you my appreciation when we get home!"

Sharon nibbled at the man's ear, pulled away and they both laughed as they headed back to their black Ford Mondeo that was parked nearby.

Mad Tony Bolton was back on his manor.

CHAPTER 2

Paul Bolton had been shocked to the core when he heard that not only had his brother Tony escaped from Broadmoor High Security Psychiatric Hospital, but Richard Philips had absconded from HM Prison Long Lartin. He was now waiting for the next shock, as he always found bad news came in threes.

The Den had been turned into a veritable fortress with a complete overhaul of the security systems, new cameras covered all the areas around the building and then fed into a new security operations room, where two men monitored the screens 24-hours a day. All the doors and windows had been replaced with bomb-proof steel and glass. The club was still open six nights a week but it had extra security on the door, and extra guns at vantage points throughout the club's dining and dancing facilities. The entrance to the offices had been completely rebuilt with a two-door system, where you were allowed through the first, which then locked, before the second door would be opened, while all the time cameras were monitoring the scene.

Paul had brought in extra guards and now had Duke, Matt, Pauly and Dave as his personal protection team. Dave was still supposedly looking for the sex tapes that Ryder had sent to London over a year ago, but in reality nobody mentioned it and Paul had given up hope of ever finding them.

Paul's major concern was that Tony and Richard Philips were out there somewhere, almost certainly planning to pay him back for perceived wrongdoings by Paul. Richard had lost half his business when Jack Coombs had joined in partnership with Paul, and Tony knew that Paul had set up the Referee at the Royal Lancaster Hotel in London. Richard Philips had taken care of Jack and almost killed Mary, his wife, at the same time.

Richard could have also guessed that it was Paul who informed staff at Wormwood Scrubs that he was planning an escape, so that was another problem to overcome. Paul was sure that Tony would eventually head back to Bermondsey, he was a man of habit and it was inconceivable that he could be happy anywhere else. Richard Philips was something else, Paul still thought a deal could be done but did not know Richard that well. The former man knew one thing for sure: he could not afford to wait and do nothing, he had to find a way to talk to Tony and Richard, otherwise he would never have peace and would spend the rest of his life looking over his shoulder. To that end he had contacted each of the solicitors acting for Tony and Richard, just in case they happened to hear from their clients. It was a foregone conclusion that they would, because both the solicitors were as bent as nine-bob notes. So it was a case of wait and see when they came back to him.

The one really good thing in Paul's life was his relationship with Lexi, which was now as solid as a rock. Lexi was still studying but took care of the home and did most of the cooking. They ate out occasionally but Lexi was a very homely person and enjoyed spending quality time with Paul more than anything. She was loyal, loving and still knew how to excite him in bed, so it was a marriage made in heaven even though they hadn't legally tied the knot. Lexi was aware of Paul's problems as they discussed everything and all she ever said was, if you want me to do anything to help just ask, it doesn't matter what it is, just ask me. Paul knew he could ask Lexi for anything but wanted to involve her as little as possible, but it was good to know she would be right next to him if it came to a fight. Children had been talked about but Lexi wanted to finish her master's degree in History at City University and Paul could not even contemplate fatherhood until the issues with Tony and Richard had been sorted.

Paul seldom thought of Emma and had stopped drinking Prosecco months ago, but he still remembered what the lady volunteer helper had said at the Hammersmith Hospital that terrible day: "You never forget but time does heal wounds." He would certainly never forget Emma but he had moved on and Lexi was now his partner and he hoped she would be for the rest of his life.

Lexi and Paul still lived at the flat in Chelsea Harbour but were considering a move to the country. Paul kept in touch with Mary Coombs and had taken Lexi on his last visit. The latter had loved the fresh air and countryside around Chelmsford and Mary's picturesque garden. Lexi said she would like to have a vast garden when they had children and Paul came up with the idea of buying a property immediately that they could 'weekend' in sometimes. Lexi was thinking about that and considering all the options.

CHAPTER 3

Karen pushed the key into the lock and turned. She opened the door and was greeted by the same smile as always and the words: "Miss Karen, Miss Karen how lovely to see you." Chau said this as she danced around Karen, and then she kissed her on the mouth. "Come into my boudoir and make passionate love to me."

Chau was always happy. She had been to hell and back at the hands of the people traffickers and was now enjoying life to the full, and they were both laughing as Chau held Karen's hands and danced her into the small lounge and onto the cream leather sofa. Chau kissed her again on the mouth and Karen responded in kind, by sticking her tongue down Chau's throat. They eventually parted.

"Hmm I can smell something absolutely delicious. What is it?" cried Karen.

"That is sweet-and-sour chicken with special fried rice, but the question, Miss Karen, is do we eat before or afterwards?"

"Before or after what exactly?" asked Karen.

"You know Karen, you know!" Chau was jumping up and down with excitement. "Before or after we make love – I want you so much!" And with that she jumped on Karen and started to undo the buttons on the other woman's shirt.

"No, let's eat first," said Karen as she hastily did the buttons back up. "I'm starving so let's eat, then I'll have a shower and then we'll see what happens next." Karen was giving Chau a sexy grin which left her under no illusion as to what they would be doing after Karen had had the shower.

"OK I accept we eat and then you shower and then I stick my tongue up your arse!"

"Chau," Karen screamed, "you are incredible."

"I like to think so," said Chau as she made her way towards the kitchen, swinging her petite sexy little arse from side to side.

The relationship with Chau had become totally exhausting. Every time Karen opened the door it was sex, sex and more sex. She tried to talk to Chau about it

The Final Act

and on most occasions didn't actually mind, but just occasionally she wanted to sit and read a good book, which was difficult with Chau trying to undress her all the time. Chau had told Karen she was terrified that Karen would leave her and go back to men, and that was one of the reasons she wanted to keep Karen sexually fulfilled all the time, as she did. Karen had told her that she had never been happier, she was as much in love with Chau now as when they had first made love on the Isle of Wight over a year ago. Chau tried so hard to keep Karen happy that she didn't realise that her efforts could eventually drive her away.

Karen was now a detective sergeant and Jeff was still a detective constable, but it didn't make a ha'p'orth of difference at work unless Michael the boss was involved; he now always spoke to Karen as if she was the senior of the two of them. Jeff was happy to see his days out at Rotherhithe Nick as he only had three years to go before retirement. He had thoroughly enjoyed the last two working with Karen, and now planned to take it a bit easy as he approached the end of twenty-five years working for the Met.

Karen and Jeff were working on some small cases and seemed content to have a bit of an easy time after their escapades with the Albanian people traffickers. Many officers had lost their lives and Karen and Jeff were eternally happy that they weren't amongst them.

The news that the lunatic Tony Bolton had escaped from Broadmoor was a shock to the system for both of the police officers, as was the news that Richard Philips was on the run as well. Jeff was scathing of the security at the hospital and prison, and blamed Tory funding cuts for the lack of staff and inadequate systems.

It was a typical Monday morning and the two officers met in the canteen as usual for the first of countless coffees they would consume in a day.

"Morning Karen you're a bit late," said Jeff, looking at his watch and raising his eyebrows.

"Are you my boss then?" Karen answered aggressively. "Sorry Jeff—Monday morning blues, you alright? How was your weekend?"

"Great thanks caught some fish and West Ham won two-nil. What more can a man want in life?"

"So exciting," agreed Karen with a fake yawn. "So any news on the escapees?"

"Nah nothing," replied Jeff. "They're both rich, so if I was in their shoes I would be in some far-off country enjoying the sun."

"Maybe," said Karen looking thoughtful, "but you know what? People like what they're used to. I can't see Tony Bolton leaving London for good, and I don't know about Richard Philips so…"

"You see that's why you're now a detective sergeant and I'm still a detective constable."

Karen just looked at Jeff for a second. "Fuck off Jeff, and get the coffees eh?"

Jeff did as he was told and fetched Karen a coffee. "How's Chau?"

"Very well thank you." Karen quickly changed the subject: "So are we getting involved in looking for Tony Bolton and Richard Philips?"

"What's the point? Someone will snitch on them sooner or later, they'll be back inside before long, you mark my words."

"Great. So while we have murderers wandering around our patch enjoying themselves, we sit on our arses drinking coffee all day?"

Jeff smiled. "Yeah, great isn't it? Want a refill?"

CHAPTER 4

Richard Philips was sitting at the kitchen table in the one-bedroom flat he had rented in Basildon, Essex. He was dressed in his usual home attire, which comprised blue-coloured tracksuit bottoms, black tee shirt and a thick black jumper. He was well cheesed off, because he couldn't go anywhere and had been cooped up in the miniscule flat for what seemed like an eternity, even though it had only been six months. He was desperate to go out and have a good time. He remembered the wild sex sessions with Julie, the black girl from the brothel in Peckham. "Oh if only!" he thought to himself.

The parcel had arrived from the solicitors and was sitting on the table. Richard made himself a cup of Tetley's tea and then took a sharp steak knife out of the cutlery drawer. He made a precision cut along the top where it had been sellotaped, and he was excited as he had no idea what it was that was inside. He pulled the brown paper back and eyed the contents: three tapes. He took the top one out and went into the small lounge, then knelt down by the television and placed the tape in the old video player and pressed 'play'.

He sat back down and watched the screen. Suddenly it came to life and there were three people, two girls and a man. "Jesus!" he shouted, and jumped up from the chair and, sitting right in front of the screen, he looked closely. It was that bastard Paul Bolton with two women and they were not playing scrabble! Richard sat back down and watched as the three participated in a catalogue of sexual positions, which ended with the man coming all over the two girls. He sat quietly for a minute and then went back to the box, removed the two final tapes, and found what he was after: a letter.

It read:

Richard,

Sex tapes featuring Paul Bolton his wife Emma and a girl called Lexi from the starlight club. I left them with my solicitor as a form of insurance with the proviso that if not collected within six months then they should be given to you. So if you end up with these then something terrible has happened to me! Do with them as you wish. Ryder

"Bloody hell!" said Richard aloud. If only Ryder had known it was him who was partly responsible for his death at the hands of the Boltons. Richard took the two videos back to the lounge, sat down and started to watch the fun. He watched the entire three tapes and in the end he had to rush to the toilet to get some tissue prior to jerking himself off on the sofa. He hadn't touched a woman for months and the two on the screen were absolutely gorgeous. He gathered up the tapes and put them back in the box, then took the letter and threw it into the kitchen bin. He took a chair, stepped on it and placed the box on top of one of the kitchen cupboards, out of arm's reach. He then sat down and thought about what he could do with the tapes. One thing was for sure: Paul Bolton would have to pay a lot of money to get them back.

The solicitor had also told Richard that Paul Bolton wanted a meeting. Richard had agreed to it, as he was still going to ask Paul for the five million pounds that he had asked for when he was in the Scrubs. Paul had offered a million but Richard thought that was derisory and now he had the tapes…

The only huge worry he had was that if he was caught the authorities would make sure he never saw the light of day again. And he would have to be extremely careful when dealing with that snake in the green grass, Paul Bolton.

CHAPTER 5

Tony and Sharon got home from Manzies Pie and Mash Shop at two-thirty. They were still living at number 34, Brockley Road, Lewisham, the place they had gone to immediately after the escape from Broadmoor. They always entered and left the property through the back door, so scarcely anyone ever saw them. It was an area where everybody kept to themselves and the police were the enemy of all.

Sharon Travis had worked at Broadmoor for a year. She had shocked herself by having the relationship with Tony, but in truth she had always gone for the bad boys. Sharon was surprised by how well Tony looked after her: he actually considered her more than she ever thought he would. She desperately wanted to move from Lewisham, for it was a filthy polluted place to live and they talked constantly about moving to a villa overlooking the sea somewhere in Spain, and then doing some travelling. Tony was adamant that 'things' had to be sorted before they could consider anything, and that meant sorting things with Paul.

"Nice Chinese Tony. Do you want some?" Sharon asked.

"Eh? No thanks," Tony responded. "Who the hell could eat Chinese after a pie-and-mash lunch?"

"Good. All the more for me then."

Tony took a Becks beer from the kitchen fridge and sat at the table next to Sharon. He opened it, took a long swig, and then belched loudly.

"Do you have to do that?" she grumbled. "I'm eating for God's sake!"

"Sorry Sharon. Look I've got some news."

Sharon became interested. "What's that then?"

"I'm going to meet up with Paul to sort things."

"You mean you're going to kill him?"

"No I do not mean I am going to kill him," he said. "I might *like* to kill the fucking bastard but not yet, not until I get what's due to me."

"And what's that Tony?"

"My clubs."

"And then you'll kill him?"

Tony laughed. "You're getting to know me."

Sharon took the last bite of Chinese food and sat back. "You told me the violence would end."

Tony jumped up, knocking his chair backwards onto the floor and started shouting: "Don't fucking start! I told you—after I've sorted Paul we can change our lifestyle, not before! So shut the fuck up, do you understand?"

Sharon was scared, aware that when Tony was in a mood, he was so volatile anything could happen. "Of course I understand. You owe him."

"That's right I owe him and he's going to get it, believe me." Tony picked the chair back up and sat down. He lifted the bottle of beer to his mouth and drained it.

"Get me another beer."

"Yes master," laughed Sharon.

"That's more like it." Tony grabbed her arse as she moved to get his beer.

Two minutes later Sharon's legs were wrapped around Tony's back, and she was digging her nails into his shoulders as he pushed hard into her wet place.

"Harder Tony, yes *harder*, God that's good." Sharon was bucking in time with Tony's pushing; he couldn't hold on any longer.

"Ahhhhhhh!" he shouted as he came inside her. They collapsed apart, breathing heavily.

"That was quick," Sharon commented.

Tony answered: "Yeah well I've got things on my mind, this meeting with Paul for one."

"Where the hell are you going to meet him?"

Tony looked concerned. "I don't know yet but somewhere very safe. Well, safe for me anyway."

"So what else is on the agenda?" Sharon was bored to death.

"I've got to see some people, we need some help if I am going to sort Paul. Remember he has an army of guys he can call on."

"Will that be easy?" Sharon was genuinely concerned.

"I've told you a hundred times: with money you can do anything."

"Yeah I suppose so. I'm going to have a shower. See you in a minute."

"OK, I'm going to make some calls."

Tony was up against it. Paul had his close team around him, all of whom were totally loyal to him, and he could call on probably thirty-odd guns from the clubs if he needed to, whereas Tony would have to hire men he didn't know, which was not ideal at all. He got on the blower and started a round of calls to old acquaintances.

He was on the phone for an hour and had managed to put together a small crew of three that he felt he could trust. Tony was scared of one thing, and that was some bastard snitching on him to the Old Bill. He had to keep ahead of the game at all times and never let his guard down for a minute.

Sharon reappeared, having removed her red wig and the green contact lenses, and she was wearing no make-up. Tony looked up, laughing, saying, "Bloody hell girl I nearly didn't recognise you!"

"Very funny Tony." Wearing the wig all the time was truly horrible for Sharon and she took it off in the house whenever she could. The truth was it completely transformed her appearance, giving her the confidence to feel safe enough to go out.

The hue and cry had eventually calmed down following the escape from Broadmoor, with numerous newspapers suggesting that Sharon had almost certainly been killed by Mad Tony Bolton and buried under concrete somewhere. How far from the truth was that? Sharon had recently read that Dr Gary Thompson had only just returned to work following the trauma he had suffered in the violence during the escape. Sharon could never forget his face when she had picked up the toothbrush knife and handed it to Tony. Whenever she thought of that she couldn't help but smile. That Dr Thompson was a complete wanker who was only concerned about one thing and that was himself, thought Sharon.

Tony had gone into the kitchen and shut the door. Sharon could hear him talking on his mobile but could not pick out the words. Tony had done this once before and Sharon had thought he was talking to his solicitor, so she concluded that perhaps he was doing so again. Tony had then said it was better if Sharon didn't know everything, otherwise she would worry too much. Not knowing was what made her bloody worry, she reasoned, as she crept nearer the kitchen door, trying to hear what was being said.

She heard Tony say: "Speak to you later" and she darted back into the lounge. Tony appeared and looked at Sharon in a strange way, smiling at the same time.

She leaned towards him. "What's happening? Are you up to something?"

Tony just looked at her still smiling. "Something is happening and it will help me get even with my bastard brother." Tony pointed at his nose, saying, "Mind your own business" and then went back to the kitchen. Sharon heard him take another beer from the fridge and open it.

CHAPTER 6

It was the end of October and it was freezing, and it seemed that the rain never stopped. It was also howling a gale, and to cap it all the forecast predicted snow for the weekend. Paul was in his office at the Den looking out of the reinforced window. He had spent the morning mapping out how he wanted to handle the situations regarding Tony and Richard Philips, and now it was time to talk to his trusted lieutenants.

"Come in," he ordered.

First in was Duke, the tall giant who had to pay heavily to get all his suits handmade because of his size. He had started as a driver/bodyguard but Paul had found him to be surprisingly intelligent and well informed on a host of topics, so he was now a very trusted advisor.

Dave was next. He had been with Paul for ten years, managing clubs and doing private projects, such as looking for the sex tapes.

Then came Roddy who had risen to be financial director of all their operations. Roddy knew more about the business in financial terms than even Paul did. If anything big was being planned, Paul always involved him.

Lastly Matt and Pauly entered.

Paul motioned Matt and Pauly to sit at the side of the room while the others sat at the boardroom table.

Bolton took a bottle of whisky and some glasses from the bar and placed them in the middle of the impressive oak table.

"OK so let's get down to it," he began. "Everybody knows the score. Tony and Richard Philips are out and I suspect looking for some sort of payoff from me. What you don't know is that I have arranged to meet with them individually to see if there is a sensible way forward."

"Are you serious?" asked Dave, looking aghast.

"Absolutely."

It was Duke's turn to speak. "This is very dangerous. The two of them are crazies, Jesus we will have to be very careful."

That's what Paul liked about Duke: he didn't say, "No you can't do it", he accepted that Paul had made a decision, and then it was up to the team to offer advice as to how to keep him safe and get what he wanted.

"Two separate meets in two different locations on different days, easy," said Paul.

He looked at the team. "Look listen carefully, I want this sorted without violence. If it can't be done then we will have to take another route, but I want to give it a chance. I am fed up with senseless killing and disposing of dead bodies, do you all understand that?"

Nobody spoke for some time until Dave spoke again: "OK I understand, but Duke is right, both of them are, how shall I put this? Insane is a good word. They are both mad, you do realise that, don't you?"

"Maybe, but everybody has their price, even mad people. Roddy I want to talk to you about finance but I first wanted you to get an overall feeling for what is going on, so that's why you're here. I'm waiting to hear where these meets are going to be, but I have stipulated public places with lots of people so they will probably end up being in local pubs."

Dave butted in before Paul could continue: "We could shop both of them to the Old Bill, easy, get them back inside where they belong."

Paul laughed. "That was my first thought as well but there are reasons why I don't want to do that. First Tony's my brother—if we can reach an agreement somehow, with him maybe going to live abroad I'd be happy with that. Secondly, one, or even both of them could escape again—it's unlikely, I grant you, but possible. Lastly if they go back inside I will never have peace because I'd know that at some time they would get out, so that's why I want it sorted. I don't want to spend the rest of my life worrying about Tony and Richard Philips.

"I agree," Duke answered in a positive tone. "Let's sort it once and for all." He looked round the room and everybody nodded.

"Good. Now as to the detail, as soon as we hear where the meetings will take place I will let you all know," Paul resumed. "Dave, you will be in charge of my personal security at all times and accompany me to the meets with Duke." Paul looked over at Matt and Pauly. "You two will have heavily armed teams outside the locations, so that if something happens it's up to you to get us out in one piece. If that's not possible then you are to kill every living soul who is there, you understand?"

"Every living soul? If it's in a pub there will be a lot of people about,." Matt observed.

Paul gave Matt a hard stare. "You will not know who is involved. I want everybody wiped out, killed, kaput, blasted into pieces, do you understand? Or shall I give the job to someone else?"

Matt looked sheepish. "I understand and it'll be as you say."

"Good, now let's have a drink," said Paul as he opened the whisky and poured the drinks. They knocked back the small whiskies in one. "OK that's it. Roddy you stay behind, I'll talk to you guys when I hear more."

Everybody left the room except for Roddy.

Paul poured whisky into two tumblers and handed one to Roddy.

"Roddy the next three months are going to be scary. I can't tell you everything it's better you don't know, suffice to say problems need to be solved and I intend to do just that." He paused for a moment. "I'm going to give the brothels to Richard Philips."

Roddy was shocked. "You what? Give that shit the brothels? Are you out of your mind?"

Paul just looked at Roddy.

"Sorry Paul but I can't believe you're going to do that."

"Roddy, look at it like this. These brothels were never ours, we didn't build them up from scratch. Jack Coombs brought them into the business and Richard lost out because Jack double-crossed him and he ended up in prison. I don't regard them as ours and, to tell you the truth, I'll be pleased to get rid of them."

"But the money! The profit!" Roddy was shaking his head unable to take in what Paul was saying.

"They aren't and never really were ours, and that's why I will not lose any sleep over getting rid of them. Their loss will also hopefully make Richard happy and keep him off my back. Roddy, I want to concentrate on the clubs, after all we still have a massive business with huge profits, we are not going to starve," said Paul with a laugh and a smile.

"No, of course we aren't but you know accountants—we don't like to see the figures going down," and with that Roddy smiled. "So what about Tony?"

"Simple I'm going to offer him money, cash. How much do we have in Switzerland?"

Roddy looked to the heavens. "About eighteen million in cash. How much are you going to offer him?"

"I don't know yet I'll give that some serious consideration," Paul replied thoughtfully. "I want Tony out of the way and I want him happy with the amount, something that will allow him to be comfortable living abroad in Spain or wherever for the rest of his life."

"Tony's a Bermondsey Boy. Do you really think he could move somewhere like Spain?"

"I've no idea but he would never be safe here unless he had plastic surgery," Paul reasoned, then went quiet.

Roddy broke the silence: "He could do that." There was another pause. "You do realise he's quite mad?"

"I've known that for years," said Paul.

Roddy looked thoughtful. "Look, from a financial perspective the sooner it's all sorted the better."

"Yes the sooner the better. I can feel tension in the club, everybody's on edge it's affecting us all."

Paul heard from Tony's solicitor first via a phone call. "OK I understand," he said, "but it's hardly a suitable venue. I said OK didn't I? Yeah fine."

Paul put the phone down leant back in his chair, put his blue Barclays biro in his mouth and chewed the end. The meet was to be at the Blue Anchor, a famous Millwall football team supporter's pub in Southward Park Road, Bermondsey. That was typical of Tony, to pick a local pub, but a strange choice because he was so well known in that area. Paul had been a regular in all the pubs down the blue and knew the landlords well.

The Final Act

He picked up the phone again and dialled. "Pat it's Paul Bolton how are you?" he said when the call connected.

Pat replied in his strong Irish accent. "Fine thank you Paul. I know why you're calling."

"This meet on Friday. I understand you have guaranteed everybody's safety."

"That's right I'll have a couple of boys here, any trouble and believe me nobody will leave the pub. You do understand what I'm saying Paul?"

"I do Pat, as long as Tony understands as well."

"I've already spoken to Tony and he has got the message loud and clear."

"Good I'll see you Friday night then."

"Look forward to it Paul, look forward to it."

Paul hadn't been in the Blue Anchor for at least two or three years, and in truth he didn't care where the meeting was as long as it was safe.

He briefed the team and everything was prepared for the Friday night. Pauly and Matt would be outside parked up in Blue Anchor Lane with a team of four guns. Paul, Duke and Dave would then enter the pub.

The driver pulled up at the main entrance on Southwark Park Road at exactly eight p.m.; they had already driven past the pub twice to recce it and all seemed normal. Pauly was parked round the corner and was in contact with Duke by earpiece. Any trouble and they would be in the pub in five seconds.

Dave pushed open the front door of the Blue Anchor and was followed in by Paul. He stopped and looked around. Nothing had changed much. There was a huge sign above the bar saying 'Bermondsey's No 1 Millwall Pub', and on the right were some brown leather comfy chairs and a black sofa, a couple of Millwall Flags and the flat screen TVs on the walls. Dave glanced to his left and saw the same snooker table he used to play on years ago. There must have been thirty-odd people in the bar. Paul looked over and saw Pat, and they nodded to each other and Paul made for the back of the bar.

"Paul you made it then?" barked out Pat in his deep Irish brogue.

Paul looked round and saw some hard types giving him the eye. "Let's go somewhere private shall we?"

The Final Act

"Sure. Up the stairs into the private room."

They were trooping up the stairs. "Pat," Paul asked. "Is Tony here yet?"

"No he's late, but he was always late so nothing new there."

The atmosphere was tense. Paul, Duke and Dave entered the private room, and they were immediately pushed against a wall and searched by two huge men who looked as ugly as pit-bulls. "Clean" shouted one of them.

"So what would you fellas like to drink?" asked Pat.

Paul ordered a small whisky and water, while Duke and Dave asked for a beer each.

Pat picked up a phone receiver that obviously connected with the bar and spoke: "Annie, would you bring up a whisky and water and two Becks and let me know the minute the other guests arrive."

Tony and a bodyguard called Steve had been in the pub for thirty minutes and had watched Paul enter. Tony thought for a second that he could easily have stabbed Paul as he walked by. For Tony to be in the Blue Anchor, a pub he used to visit frequently, and to have nobody recognise him showed how good the disguise was. He decided it was time and whispered to the bar girl Annie: "I'm here to see Pat."

Annie picked up the phone receiver and one minute later Pat arrived to escort them upstairs.

Tony pushed open the door and walked into the room followed by Steve, they were searched and the announcement "Clean" was shouted.

Paul stared at the two of them, wondering who they were, studying them very closely, especially the man with the beard and tash. "Fucking hell," he said to himself, followed by: "Hello Tony how are you? I like the disguise. Brilliant."

"Yes," Tony replied. "It allows me to come and go as I please. When I came in the pub even Pat didn't recognise me."

"Yes I'll tell you the truth I didn't recognise him at all," Pat said, laughing, and all were aware of the easing of the tense atmosphere.

Tony and Steve had brought their drinks up with them.

The Final Act

"So look I'm going back down, my two friends here will be outside the door," Pat told them, looking at Paul and Tony: and there was a meaning in the look that Paul and Tony understood. It was simple—if there was any trouble then the two men would kill them all, and that was how Pat guaranteed the safety of everyone at meetings held in his pub.

Tony and Paul sat down at a table while Steve, Dave and Duke sat in chairs against the wall.

The terrifying atmosphere was back and you could have cut it with a knife. There was a deafening silence in the room until Paul finally spoke:

"So first, Tony, we need to forget the past and look to the future."

"The past can never be forgotten," replied Tony, staring hard into Paul's eyes.

The silence returned.

Paul finally spoke again: "We have both done things that need to be forgiven or forgotten. If we don't do that it will be hard to move on."

Tony leaned back in his chair and scratched his itchy beard.

"That's easy to say. You weren't the one locked up in the fucking nuthouse with a load of lunatics."

Paul smiled and Tony was not pleased. "You find that fucking funny?"

"No sorry Tony, it's not funny."

"Look let's get on with this shit," Tony went on. "I want what's due to me."

Paul looked thoughtful again. "And what is that Tony?"

"Twenty million cash."

"What are you, off your fucking head? Twenty million? *Twenty million*? It doesn't grow on trees you know."

"Don't give me a load of bollocks Paul. I know how much money the business makes and most of it is cash, how much is in Switzerland? Tell me then, how much?"

"I don't actually—"

"Don't tell me you're not sure," Tony interrupted him. "You would have found out from Roddy exactly how much, to the penny."

"OK. Give or take a few grand, twelve million in cash."

"You're a fucking liar Paul." And with that Tony made to get up. Duke, Dave and Steve all jumped up from their chairs, but Tony stopped and held his hand out to the three of them. "Don't worry." He slowly sat back down.

"Tony," Paul tried to explain, "there have been setbacks that you don't know about. Two of the brothels were raided and closed by the Old Bill. Nothing stays the same, you know that."

"I want twenty million. You can pay me ten now and ten in say six months' time so let's say April."

Paul was thinking he could do that. "That could be possible Tony. But you realise any funny business after the first payment and you will not see the second?"

Tony threw his arms in the air. "Of course—I'm not stupid. Do we have a deal then?"

Paul was calculating that if he gave the brothels to Richard Philips he would not have the profits from them, but the arrangement would still be feasible.

"You have a deal Tony." And Paul held his hand out.

Tony left it hanging for a second and Paul wondered if he was going to shake or not. Tony opened his palm and spat in it and grabbed Paul's hand. "Deal," he shouted.

Tony was happy. "Let's have some drinks to celebrate, hey Irish you outside?" One of the men stuck his head in the door. "Bring a bottle of whisky and some beers and don't hang about."

The heavy shut the door and went down to the bar.

"So, Tony, where are you living?" Paul asked.

"I'm in Essex. Very nice it is too."

"By the way what happened to the girl you kidnapped from the hospital?"

"You don't want to believe everything you read in the papers."

"So what happened to her then?"

Tony was getting seriously pissed off. "I don't fucking know! I got dropped off and she was in the car with the boys, that was the last time I saw her."

"So Tony," Paul changed tack. "What are you going to do?"

"I'm giving serious consideration to moving abroad, I need some good weather—this fucking rain and cold is no good for me."

"Costa del Sol Spain?"

"Maybe." Tony then thought he would have some fun. "I heard Richard Philips is out."

Paul immediately went on the defensive. "Yeah. Any idea where he is?"

"How the hell would I know?" Tony downed his glass of whisky and banged it on the table. "Time for me to go. Oh you'll need this of course."

Tony handed Paul a piece of paper, Paul read the top line: *Hyposwiss Private Bank—Wealth Management—Zurich*. The rest was the account number and other details.

"So when will it be in the bank?" Tony asked as he made for the door.

"I'll talk to Roddy. Probably Monday."

Tony was smiling. "Monday would be good Paul—don't disappoint me." And with that Tony opened the door, and Steve got up and followed him out.

Paul took a deep breath and stretched his arms. "One down one to go."

Paul was happy that Tony appeared to be satisfied. Who wouldn't be chuffed, with twenty million quid on the way? But as Paul knew from experience, things were not always simple when dealing with Tony. He seemed alright but you could never really tell.

"OK boys let's get going," Tony said.

Dave led the way down the stairs and stopped at the bar; he looked around and all seemed normal. He turned and nodded to Duke and Paul and led them out of the side entrance into Blue Anchor Lane. Matt and Pauly pulled up in the car and the three of them jumped in. They headed straight back to the Den and Paul went to his office and slumped into his chair. He then called down to the bar and asked for a new bottle of whisky. The liquor arrived and he gulped a mouthful. There was one call to make before he did anything else. He picked up the receiver and dialled the number.

"Pat? It's Paul. Sorry I didn't see you before we left."

"No problem, glad I could be of service."

"Look if you're ever in the area make sure you pop in for a meal and a few bevvies eh?"

"To be sure I will Paul, thank you."

"OK, thanks again Pat. See ya."

Paul spoke to Roddy and told him to arrange the first payment for Monday.

It was ten p.m. and Paul was drained, but he picked up the phone and dialled another number.

"Hi how are you? Good. I'm leaving now so see you soon, what's for dinner? Lovely, one of my favourites, love you. Bye."

He was in a good mood and decided he would stop on the way home to Chelsea and get Lexi some flowers, he buzzed through to Duke and told him: "I'm ready let's go."

CHAPTER 7

"Jesus I'm so bored," said Karen as she yawned. She was sitting cross legged at her desk fiddling with her pen and tapping the desk. She was in one of her many dark trouser suits which she found were so much more practical than skirts or dresses. She was looking haggard, which was not surprising as she had been up half the night drinking and having some very dirty sex with Chau.

Jeff was raising his eyebrows and looking to the heavens when he told her: "You can be bored but please stop the bloody tapping on the desk, it's driving me mad."

In response Karen tapped even harder but then threw the pen across the office towards the door. Just at that moment Michael, their boss, decided to open it and the pen hit him on the shoulder. Michael stopped and was looking as if he was desperately thinking what to say, then he adjusted his glasses, took a step back out of the office and shut the door. Karen looked over at Jeff and they both raised their eyebrows but didn't say anything. They heard the door open again, and Michael stepped in once more, at the same time ducking, making a pretence of avoiding flying missiles. It might have been funny at any other time but with the mood Karen was in it just was not. Michael had expected a laugh but all he got was two sour-looking faces. He then straightened up and decided to revert to type.

"Have you two got nothing better to do than sit around chucking pens at each other?" he demanded. Karen and Jeff just sat there, not bothering to respond.

"What's happening with the Gilbert case?" Michael went on.

Karen glanced at Jeff as if to say 'you tell him' using only her eyes.

"Held up in Court," Jeff replied obligingly. "Nothing's going to happen for months. Files have been lost, witnesses have disappeared. It's a pile of shit."

Michael touched his glasses, something he always did when he was about to launch into a seriously lengthy tirade. "It may be a pile of shit but unfortunately for you two it's *your* pile of shit and it needs cleaning up." Michael's voice had gone from normal to apoplectic. "All I ever see is you two drinking fucking coffee, arguing or sitting around twiddling your fucking thumbs. I've had enough!"

The Final Act

It was all Karen could do to stop herself laughing and one look over at Jeff and she could see that he was in the same boat.

Jeff spoke: "What are you proposing then Michael?"

"Proposing? Proposing?" He was turning red and was almost screaming. "I'm proposing you two do some fucking work for a change, that is if you wouldn't mind? After all the Metropolitan Police are paying you very handsomely for your fucking time!"

Jeff and Karen didn't speak, they just looked at Michael. In the end he couldn't take any more, and he opened the door, stepped out and slammed it with a crashing bang.

"Do you think something has upset him, Jeff?"

"Looks like it."

They then both burst out laughing uncontrollably for a full five minutes.

Jeff was the first to recover. "Fuck he's right you know. We need to pull our fingers out and do something spectacular. What about catching some terrorists who are planning to blow up Scotland Yard?"

Karen was already laughing. "We wouldn't stop them doing that for God's sake, it would be manna from heaven!"

They were both in hysterics again, and in the end Karen had to leave the office as her stomach was hurting so much.

"I'm off for a pee," she called out. Unfortunately for her she almost knocked Michael over as he came striding down the corridor, which made her laugh even more. Michael carried on down the corridor, shaking his head in exasperation.

Eventually the laughter died down, fresh coffees were secured from the canteen, and Jeff and Karen sat at their desks contemplating what to do.

"Jeff we need something interesting to do or we are going to go mad."

Jeff looked very serious for a minute and then spoke: "I agree we need something challenging and perhaps something that could give us a fair bit of kudos. And I think I may have come up with something that would fit the bill perfectly."

"*Do tell, please Detective Constable Swan.*" Karen was larking about again, putting on a posh old-fashioned voice.

"Look, those bastards Tony Bolton and Richard Philips are on the loose. Let's see if we can't find one or even both of them. Do you remember you said you didn't think Bolton would be able to leave his manor? Well I tend to agree with you."

Karen was thinking hard. "If, and it's a big if, bearing in mind that they could both be in Spain sunning themselves at this exact moment, but it could be worth a look. And if we got anything out of it, bloody hell we would both get gold stars. Look Jeff, I need a breather from Chau. How about we go to the pub later and discuss it over a pint?"

"Sounds a very good idea to me ma'am."

They were back smiling at each other and both brains were already ticking over as to how and where they would start looking.

The rest of the day was very much a non-event, nothing of any interest took place and anyway Karen and Jeff were too busy thinking about Tony Bolton and Richard Philips.

The nearest pub to the Nick was the China Hall but Karen liked The Ship, at Rotherhithe; it was a very popular pub, with good food, good beer, clean, friendly, everything you wanted in a cracking boozer. They were in Marychurch Street within ten minutes, and found that it was much too cold to sit outside at the wooden tables. Jeff had a pint of lager and Karen was nursing a large red wine. It was quiet and they found a secluded table tucked away in a quiet corner where no one could overhear them.

They both took a sip of their drinks and relaxed back into the comfortable chairs.

"So I think you may have hit the nail on the head," Jeff began. "I've been thinking all afternoon that there is no way Tony Bolton, born and bred in Bermondsey, is just going to leave. It would be too difficult for him."

Karen took a good slurp of her wine. "I agree but where do we start?"

"Easy, we do what we always do: put the word out to all our friends, snitches, pub contacts, everybody in the local area."

The Final Act

"Bolton's an easily recognisable character. He must be holed up somewhere locally but it will be difficult to dig him out."

Jeff leaned across the table. "We know from experience everybody makes a mistake at some time, we just need to be there when he makes his."

"OK. What about that tosser Philips?"

"He's another local so is he the same as Bolton? I don't think so. I reckon he'll be off as soon as it's safe to move."

Karen drained her glass. "My round."

"OK one more. I've got dinner waiting for me at home and I don't want to be late again this week otherwise she'll kill me."

Karen got the drinks and sat back down.

"Christ, Michael was in a foul mood today," she commented, "although he did provide some welcome entertainment."

Jeff just looked at Karen. "You never should have slept with him."

Karen was shocked. "How did you know?"

"It was so obvious. But it was some time ago wasn't it?"

"Yeah. Happened once and I regretted it the minute I woke up in his bed."

"Oh well we all make mistakes." Jeff commiserated.

"OK let's get back to the job," Karen went on. "Why don't we go and see Bolton's brother Paul?"

"Good idea. I wonder what sort of relationship they have now? Tony could never work in any of the clubs, it would be too dangerous for him."

"I agree. Let's give him a call tomorrow, we can visit him at his club—it'll be good to get out."

Karen was knocking back her wine.

"Good job you left your car at the Nick," Jeff said. "I'll drop you at home."

"Let's just have one more, please Jeff?"

"You can have as many as you like, but no more for me—I don't want to get stopped by those traffic bastards."

Karen shot up to the bar and ordered another large red wine; she felt slightly light headed already so knew that she would be pissed with a couple more.

She was beginning to enjoy herself and told Jeff she would get a cab home. Jeff didn't like leaving her but made her promise that she would not take the journey on foot.

Karen was on her fifth red wine and was in a happy mood. Chau had phoned three times and after the third, Karen turned the phone off. Karen was looking at the other people in the bar. There were two youngish girls talking loudly who were both very attractive. Karen was wondering what it would be like to have sex with the two of them. She kept glancing their way, and then needed another drink, so she went up to the bar and forgot them. She ordered a red wine, paid and turned to go, when she nearly bumped into one of the two girls.

"Oh sorry," Karen apologised.

"Don't worry no problem, are you on your own?" the girl asked her.

Karen was slurring her words a little: "Yeah. Drink after work you know, I'm letting my hair down." She laughed as though she had said something really funny.

"I'm Becca." So saying, the girl held her hand out.

"I'm Karen and I'm a bit pissed."

"Let me get my drink and then why don't you join me and my friend Sasha?"

"Hmm OK, that sounds like it could be fun. I mean yeah, great, love to."

Becca ordered drinks and got Karen another red wine, and they walked over and joined Sasha. Karen studied the two girls, realising that they were sexy gorgeous women, not girls. They were dressed well in what looked like expensive casual designer clothes and their jewellery looked nice as well.

"So what do you do Karen?" asked Sasha.

"I'm a copper, or to be precise I am a detective in CID, which is the Criminal Investigation Department."

Sasha and Becca exchanged a look and then laughed. Sasha piped up: "We're in safe hands then."

"You could be if you play your cards right." *Shit*, thought Karen. *Why did you say that?*

Becca was next to talk: "Are you chatting us up?"

"Err Oh God, sorry. I've had too many wines. You must think I'm crazy."

"Not at all," whispered Sasha. "As it happens, we're going back to my flat. Why don't you come with us? We'll pick up a Chinese and I've got loads of wine in. So what do you say?"

Becca put her arm around Karen's back and squeezed her arse.

That feels good thought Karen. "Sounds good but I can only stay an hour. I have to be somewhere."

Karen knocked back the half glass of red, stood up and moved to walk out with the two women. As she did so she stumbled and Sasha caught her before she fell, saying, "You'd better hang onto my arm." Karen did as she was told.

They got to Becca's car: a green Volkswagen Golf. Becca climbed into the driver's seat and Sasha steered Karen into the back with her. Before Karen knew what was happening Sasha was kissing her full on the lips. She hadn't expected it but began to enjoy it very quickly and pushed her tongue deep into Sasha's mouth. Karen then felt Sasha's hand part her legs and slip her fingers up under Karen's skirt. She then felt her knickers being pulled down and suddenly her pussy was being invaded by at least two fingers. She was wet within seconds and spread her legs so she could feel more comfortable as Sasha rhythmically pushed her fingers in and out Karen's pussy.

Becca kept glancing in the rear-view mirror to see what was going on and she was getting excited. "You bitch Sasha!" she muttered. "Trust you to get first go!"

"You're driving for Christ's sake you'll get your turn," was Sasha's hurried reply. "She's tight and very sexy."

"Are you talking about me?" slurred Karen.

"Yes darling. I said you were gorgeous," Sasha replied.

"I know I am." With that Karen sat up and pushed Sasha's hand away. She grabbed the girl's shirt front and ripped it apart, the buttons flying all over the back of the car. Then she lifted Sasha's bra and clamped her mouth round one of the stiff nipples, while her hand then disappeared down the other woman's trousers and found a very smooth wet pussy.

Karen was enjoying it but suddenly had a mental image of Chau. She pulled her hand out of Sasha's knickers and sat back in the seat, away from her.

Sasha was annoyed. "What's wrong Karen? That felt good."

"Stop the car."

Becca shouted: "What the fuck?"

"Stop the car NOW!"

"Karen don't be like that, we're having a good time," spluttered Sasha.

"If you don't stop the fucking car NOW you will be in big trouble."

Becca remembered what Karen did for a living and pulled over to the kerb.

"Good riddance bitch!" shouted Sasha as Karen opened the door and stumbled onto the pavement. Becca put her foot down and sped away.

Karen was confused. *Where the fuck am I?* she thought. It was very dark, and she looked around to try and get some sort of bearing, and saw a road sign saying Tooley Street. *Thank god for that* she thought, I know where I am and I'm not that far from home. Karen started walking back towards Jamaica Road whilst watching the road for a taxi. There wasn't much traffic and she looked at her watch. Shit, she realised, no wonder: it was midnight. Where had the time gone? She continued walking and then suddenly a car pulled up alongside her and someone was speaking to her out of the window, saying: "Wanna good time love? We'll pay you, take care of the three of us we'll make it worth your while."

She kept walking, but the car kept pace with her. "You working late tonight baby? Come on, get in, and we can have a good time."

Karen stopped. She had sobered up very quickly.

"If you don't fuck off in the next two seconds there will be trouble."

The boys in the car didn't like that and the atmosphere changed from pleasant to tense. "Who the fuck are you talking to bitch?" snapped the driver.

The back door of the car opened and a young black guy got out and asked: "What sort of trouble you gonna give us baby?"

Karen reached into her jacket inside pocket. *Shit no fucking badge!* This could turn nasty.

"I am a police officer. Get back in the car and drive off NOW!"

Karen fumbled in her pocket and pressed the on button on her mobile.

A second boy got out of the car and moved to the other side of Karen, blocking her escape. Karen prayed the phone was on and took it out of her pocket. "I have a weapon!" she shouted.

The boys burst into laughter, turning to the driver. "She's got a weapon. Looks like a phone to me." They were laughing so much they didn't notice her press a speed dial.

"What shall we do with the bitch?" one of the boys shouted.

The driver answered: "She should come for a ride with us man."

"Where exactly are we boys?" Karen answered. "I might be able to spare an hour but you'll have to pay me."

"Damn me the bitch don't even know where she is! We're in Tooley Street, we don't live far." With that the boy moved towards Karen and grabbed her arm. Karen remembered her self-defence training. She grabbed his hand and pulled the thumb back as hard as she could. He screamed in pain and jumped back, while the other boy pulled a long very sharp-looking knife out of his waistband and waved it in front of Karen.

"You gonna get cut for that bitch!" He made to lunge at Karen, who stepped back, and precisely at that moment two police cars, their lights flashing, came roaring down Tooley Street and hemmed the boys' car in. Six officers jumped out of the cars. One of them ordered: "Get on the floor! You—out the car!"

The three boys were spreadeagled on the pavement and cuffs were put on them.

Karen was praying none of the officers recognised her but she was out of luck.

"Jesus Karen is that you?" The officer had been on a course at Hendon with her.

"Hi Robin," she replied. "Thanks, you turned up just at the right time."

"What the hell are you doing here?"

"It's a long story, and I need a ride home."

"No problem. A meat wagon is on the way for these lowlifes I'll take you in a minute, and I'll take a statement off you at home, OK?"

Karen thought quickly. Shit, she was late home and drunk. Chau must be out of her mind with worry.

"I'm not pressing charges. Give them a cell for the night and let them go in the morning."

"There's a weapon involved. You did tell them you were a police officer?"

Karen thought again quickly "No I didn't. I thought it might make things worse. As for the weapon, what weapon?"

"The huge bloody knife that boy had in his hand."

"Didn't see it. Can we go now?"

Robin was shaking his head, thinking how damn peculiar the situation was.

"What's going on here Karen?" Robin persisted. "You know as well as I do, that these boys should be done for attacking a police officer."

"Robin, please, I just want to go home. My partner will be worried sick. Look, pop into Rotherhithe Nick tomorrow, we can discuss it then"

Robin just looked straight at her. "OK, let's go."

Karen got into the back of the car and shut her eyes, thinking what a fucking disaster and Chau, Christ, she would be demented with worry.

"Where we going?" asked Robin.

"Seth Street back of Albion Primary School."

"Yeah I know it."

It was only a ten-minute journey and Karen was relieved to find herself standing outside her gaff.

"Thanks Robin you've been a hero," she said gratefully.

Robin was about to reply when the house door opened and an oriental woman came rushing out, crying and obviously in a state. Karen turned towards her and Robin got out of the car at the same time. Chau flung her arms around

Karen and gabbled: "I been so worried, where you been? I thought you hurt had crash or something…"

Robin was standing to one side as Chau started kissing Karen, who stroked the other woman's hair. "Don't worry. I'm home now, everything is OK."

"Where you been Karen?" Chau demanded.

"I went for a drink with some colleagues, my phone battery was dead and that was why I didn't call you."

"You sure Miss Karen?"

"Of course I'm sure." Karen turned to Robin. "Isn't that true Robin?"

Robin left it for one second. "Yes that is very true. Now I suggest you both go inside as it's very cold and I've got a home to go to as well."

Robin made to get back in the car, saying, "See you tomorrow at work."

"Yeah." Karen and Chau rushed inside as they saw the neighbour's curtains were being pulled apart. They went into their ground floor flat.

"Chau don't worry," Karen reassured her lover. "I am home, let's go to bed and we can talk in the morning, I am very tired."

"OK Miss Karen we talk in the morning. And by way, you stink of drink."

Karen went to the bathroom, brushed her teeth and had a pee. She took off all her clothes except her knickers, she slid into the crisp white sheets, and the last thing she remembered was Chau snuggling up to her and then darkness.

CHAPTER 8

Richard Philips was so excited he couldn't stop smiling. The music from his car radio was blaring the strains of 'Come on Eileen' by Dexy's Midnight Runners and he was singing along. Richard was on his way to see Julie, the most beautiful piece of black arse in the entire world. He hadn't had a woman in months and was licking his lips in anticipation.

Richard had finally given in to lust and called Ted Frost, who used to run the Brothel in Peckham. Ted was back working at another London site, so Richard had asked about Julie and found out she was working at the North London brothel in Holloway, funnily enough not that far from the famous women's prison of that name. Richard had got Ted back on his private payroll, calculating that he could prove useful later.

Philips had booked a room at the Travel Lodge, Chigwell Road, in Woodford Green. He laughed as he thought that this would be the best twenty-nine quid he had ever paid for a hotel room.

Julie had been instructed to book in first and wait for Richard. He pulled into the car park, having checked all was clear with Julie on his mobile. He studied reception and saw Julie enter and start reading some tourist attraction literature. He left his car and made for reception. Richard was wearing a long trench coat, and as it was cold he pulled the collar up around his neck, partly to ward off the chill and partly to cover a bit of his face.

He was just to the side of the reception entrance and waited. The door suddenly opened and Julie motioned him in. The receptionist had gone out the back for something, and Julie and Richard skipped past the desk and headed towards the lifts.

The room was compact, clean and tidy. Richard opened his coat to reveal a bottle of Scotch and plonked it down on the small bedside table. He looked at Julie but couldn't speak. She was wearing a classic short black dress which really showed off her long, sexy, slim legs. Richard was content just to look and not touch. He wanted to imagine what she would be like when the dress came off. It had been such a long time that he wanted to savour every moment.

"Let's have a drink," he said to her.

The Final Act

"Sure." Julie was just as keen to fuck with Richard again as he was. He had looked after her before and maybe he would do the same again.

Richard poured two large whiskies into the glasses he'd found in the bathroom. "Bottoms up," he toasted, and Julie repeated it, leaving Richard in no doubt that she would be happy to stick her bottom in the air for him to enter from behind.

He lay on the bed and sipped his whisky, and he patted the space next to him for Julie to sit with him. She duly obliged and lay down. He was studying the contours of her firm muscular body: she was perhaps even fitter than before, but he was determined to take his time.

"So what you up to?" he asked her.

"This and that you know. Surviving."

"Yeah, it's a tough world eh? Where you living?"

"At the moment I'm in-house," she admitted. Which meant she was sleeping at the brothel. "It's not ideal but a girl has to do—"

"—What a girl has to do," Richard cut in. "Yes I understand."

Richard was already thinking ahead, wondering how he could get Julie to move in with him.

Julie sipped her drink and with her other hand slowly ran her finger down Richard's shirt. She stopped at his belt and slowly undid it and pulled down the zipper. She could see a huge erection tucked away in his pants, and she slowly traced her finger along the cock, noting with satisfaction how hard it was.

She smiled up at Richard and bent her head down at the same time. Then she pulled his pants down and the huge cock leapt out. She grasped it and gently moved it up and down. She then slowly opened her mouth, stuck her tongue out and started licking from the base of the cock to the top. She then slipped her mouth over his cock and took it as far into her mouth as she could. Richard was purring with pleasure and knew that the first time would be over very quickly.

Julie sucked and moved, sucked and moved, up and down, up and down. Richard started to push in unison with Julie's movements, he could feel himself nearly there already, and it had only been a matter of a few minutes. Julie could feel him stiffen and knew that the bucket-load of semen was on its way.

She increased the pressure and speeded up. Richard pushed up to match her actions. It was time.

"I'm coming! I'm coming! Swallow it, swallow it all! Oh God!" He bucked and he could feel the semen pumping into Julie's mouth. She gagged a bit because there was so much, thinking, *hell he must have been storing this up for a long time.* Finally, she felt him go very limp and realised that he was finished. She slowly sucked and made sure that every last drop was drawn from his cock. He lay back exhausted and realised that he actually hadn't done much. It was a good feeling, a very good feeling, and it was only the first of many to come.

"That was fantastic Julie," he panted. "You sure know how to suck a man off."

"Well I do get a lot of practice."

Richard didn't like the thought of Julie being with someone else—it pissed him off no end. He had a vision of her sucking a big cock belonging to some fat, dirty, sweaty punter, and he didn't like that at all.

"Look why don't you come and move in with me?" he asked her. "I'm in a rabbit hutch at the moment but that will change dramatically soon, once I've sorted a few issues."

"Do you really mean it? Oh my God I'd love to! Where are you living then?"

"Essex. It's a small place but we won't be there long."

"So I can give up doing, err you know..." She voiced her concern that Richard's plan might be to pimp her out.

"You will never service another punter as long as you live. I promise."

Julie showered him with kisses. "So what would you like next? Another blow job? Or how about I give your arse a good licking? Orrrrr, how about I give you a good spanking?"

"Spanking," said Richard. "Good idea."

He grabbed Julie and pushed her across his lap with her arse perfectly placed. He then licked his finger and started playing with her back passage, very gently rubbing round the entrance, and he heard Julie sighing with pleasure, saying, "Hmm that's good." Richard then slipped a finger inside her and she momentarily gasped. "Gently yes that's perfect," she commented as Richard pushed deeper and deeper. Then he then took his other hand and slapped

The Final Act

Julie's arse cheek. He did it again a bit harder and again even harder still, so that the cheeks were reddening and Julie could feel the heat. "Harder Richard really make me squeal," she begged. He didn't mind, and he gave her an almighty lash with his hand. She jumped a bit and his finger came out of her arse.

"Please Richard, just fuck me now, please!"

Richard flipped her over onto her back and, lifting her legs up high, he entered her forcefully and heard her moan. He pushed in hard and grabbed the linen sheets for some traction, then he pushed and pushed harder and harder. "I'm coming!" she screamed. "Yes keep going! Keep going!" Julie arched her back and felt a massive orgasm that started somewhere near her pussy and spread across her body in waves of pleasure. She crashed back onto the bed. Richard pulled out and was wanking furiously over Julie's face until he cried out "Yes!" as semen sprayed all over Julie's face and breasts. He lay back panting, realising that he was out of condition and didn't know how much longer he could keep going.

"Wow I have been waiting for this day for such a long time," Richard admitted. "I've loved every second of it."

"We haven't finished yet. I've got lots of other tricks up my sleeve, believe me."

With that, Julie started sucking Richard's balls. He moaned in pleasure…

The sex had been worth the risk, and afterwards they had gone to the brothel and picked up Julie's few belongings and were soon on their way back to Essex.

Richard was driving very carefully because he didn't want to get stopped for some stupid mistake. He was also thinking about Paul Bolton and how he was going to get his money and pay him back for getting him shipped to Long Lartin Prison. He had to admire Paul a bit, for he was a good operator, but once he had got what he wanted that wouldn't stop him killing him.

Richard turned and smiled at Julie. Yeah, things were getting better, a lot better, and now he had some female company he was well pleased.

They arrived at the small one-bedroom flat in Basildon. Julie got to work straight away, cleaning all the rooms and washing the dirty clothes that lay strewn around. She opened the fridge to find mouldy out-of-date cheese and a bottle of milk with a crust on top.

The Final Act

"I need to go to the shops and stock up on food and cleaning materials," she complained. "How you could live like this I don't know."

"Single man, you know what it's like," said Richard in his defence. "So now you're here will the place be pristine and will we be eating five-star meals every day?"

Julie wanted to put down a bit of a marker. "It will be clean and it may not be quite five star, but the food will be good and tasty."

"Fantastic! Whatever it is it will be a vast improvement on what I've been living on."

"So have you got some dosh then?"

"Yeah 'course what do you want? Don't worry—here, take this, and when you need some more, just ask." Richard handed Julie a thick wedge of twenty-quid notes held together with an elastic band: it was five hundred quid.

Julie took the money and judging by its weight she knew straight away it was a few hundred and was very happy there was going to be no shortage of money. In truth Richard was living off savings but he was a wealthy man, with over a million pounds in the bank.

"Don't be long and make sure you get plenty of booze," he told her.

Julie laughed. "You bet I will and I'm going to buy some better wine than my usual five-quid-a-bottle stuff from Asda."

She took the car keys and left the flat.

Richard sat on the sofa and reflected that the meet was set up with Paul. He knew what he was going to ask for, get that sorted, and then fuck him with the tapes. Richard felt like he was in heaven, and he got up, went to the kitchen and took the vodka bottle from the fridge. He didn't bother pouring it in a glass, he simply unscrewed the cap and started drinking. After a few seconds he stopped and he just laughed, he began to laugh insanely and loudly. There was no doubt that if anybody had seen him they would have come to only one conclusion, and that was that there was something wrong with his head!

* * *

The meet with Paul had been agreed and it was to take place in the café at the Imperial War Museum in Lambeth Road. Richard had gone as a kid a couple of

The Final Act

times and loved it. This was a slightly different type of venue than usual, but it was a public place and would be busy, which gave Richard a level of comfort and security.

Richard arrived early and firstly marvelled at the huge ships' guns at the entrance. He then spent an hour wandering around the exhibits, spending a lot of time at the recreated WW1 trenches section, and particularly enjoyed looking at the massive tanks. Paul was due at two p.m. and he turned up dead on time.

Philips had found a table in the corner of the café and was sitting there facing the wall. He kept an eye out for Paul, and when he saw him enter he turned and raised his hand.

Richard wanted it to be friendly, but if it turned out otherwise then he was prepared for that eventuality. Paul had one minder with him: a very tall man whom he later found out was called Duke.

"Paul," Richard said in a friendly tone, holding his hand out to the other man, who shook hands and sat down opposite Richard. Duke sat at a nearby table.

"So Richard. How are you?"

"Great thanks Paul. I've got a nice place in Essex and for one reason and another things have improved tremendously over the past few days, so yeah couldn't be better."

"That's good." Paul noticed Richard's very short hair; there was a pair of glasses on the table which he presumed that Richard wore as some sort of disguise.

A waitress appeared and they ordered two lattes. Paul asked for his to be extra hot, stressing that, "Most of the Lattes you get are lukewarm, and I like mine really piping hot."

After she had gone there was a momentary silence.

Paul spoke first: "So let's get down to business shall we?"

"You have a proposal for me?" asked Richard.

"Yes I do."

The Final Act

Richard was excited but also realistic. Paul was never going to give him what he wanted, but knew that he would be keen to find out exactly what he did have in mind.

"So how much?" Richard asked.

Paul thought for one second and then decided he would go ahead with his plan.

"I'm not giving you a penny, but I'll come to that in a minute," Paul told him.

Richard was shocked. "If you've come here to waste my—"

"—Wait and let me finish." Paul put his arm on the other man's before continuing: "I want you to understand it has only ever been about business. Circumstances threw us together and it could easily have been me in prison and you on the outside." Paul took a sip of the scalding-hot coffee before going on:

"Jack came to me with the deal to become partners. I didn't initiate it and would never have done so. Now I understand you lost out big time—the brothels were bringing in a fortune and I have enjoyed some of that income. The main thing I want you to understand is that this is the end of it. Once we reach agreement today that's it finished. I don't want to be looking over my shoulder all the time you understand."

"I couldn't agree more," Richard replied, "and I understand fully what you're saying but the deal has to be right for me or I won't be happy and then that will lead to friction between us."

"OK. I'm prepared to return to you what in a way is rightly yours, by that I mean the complete brothel business as it is today."

Richard was shocked. This amounted to ten brothels turning over millions.

"Let me understand this," he probed. "You are going to give me the ten brothels back to own myself? Or to run for you?"

"I don't want anything to do with them. They will be legally signed over to you at the earliest opportunity, and, by the way, there are only eight operating at the moment. Peckham and Soho got raided and closed."

"Oh yes I had heard something," Richard answered. "I don't need to think about that offer. I accept—I'd be mad not to, as it's a generous deal."

The Final Act

"As I said they were never mine and I won't miss them. I'll get Roddy to tie up the paperwork and he'll be in touch with you as soon as possible."

"Good," Richard said. "Is there anything else?"

"Not really. Except that the two men who killed Jack and tortured Mary are dead and, believe me, they suffered."

That put a bit of a dampener on things but Paul wanted to make sure Richard aware that he was not a soft touch.

"Good," said Richard. "They overstepped the mark by treating Mary the way they did."

They both sipped their coffees.

"So, Paul, thank you for being so reasonable. I appreciate it."

"I'm just pleased it's all over. We must get together sometime for a meal and drinks."

"Sounds good," Paul agreed. "Let's get all the paperwork done and then we can meet up."

Paul stood up and they shook hands again. "Goodbye Richard. Be seeing you."

Richard nodded his head and smiled as Paul, followed by Duke, made for the exit.

The escaped prisoner sat back down and relaxed. He was more than happy to get the eight trading brothels back; run properly they would generate millions in profits. He also had the sex tapes which was more fun than anything but Paul would have to pay for them: payback for tipping off the prison service about his planned escape from The Scrubs. It had been a good day and now he had to get back to Basildon to fuck that gorgeous pussy Julie. He stood up and almost galloped to the exit.

The Final Act

CHAPTER 9

Tony was as drunk as a lord. He'd been drinking since eleven a.m. and it was now six pm. The only reason he was still compos mentis was that he had eaten a huge lunch which must have helped soak up the alcohol.

He and Sharon were celebrating. It was Tuesday, and early that morning he had received confirmation that ten million pounds had been transferred into his Swiss bank account. Tony immediately decided to paint the town red and headed back into his favourite place: Bermondsey.

The newly rich man decided he wanted something a bit more upmarket than a local boozer and they ended up in the Bermondsey Square Hotel in Tower Bridge Road. On approaching Tower Bridge Road Sharon had commented that she hoped lunch was not going to be pie-and-mash again. In fact, Tony would have loved to visit Manzies again but had thought better of it. Tower Bridge Road also brought memories flooding back to Tony of when he shot the copper in his car, but he quickly forgot about that as he reminded himself that he was celebrating.

The hotel was a modern boutique establishment that offered four-star service in the heart of Bermondsey. On arrival Tony had marched straight into the Grill and Bar and ordered the best champagne available. A chilled bottle of Moet & Chandon duly arrived and was polished off in double-quick time. Tony then reverted to his favourite tipple, which was whisky, while Sharon sipped at her Sauvignon Blanc white wine.

Lunchtime soon arrived and they sat by the window looking out at the busy square. People were sitting at the tables outside even though it was hardly a warm day, but it did make the square come alive, plus people were visiting the Shortwave Cinema and the pubs and restaurants in the square.

They both started lunch with mackerel fillets with horseradish and watercress. Tony then ordered the Angus rib-eye steak with green peppercorn sauce, while Sharon went for the more ladylike grilled salmon with steamed potatoes and spinach. They finished off with a superb selection of British cheeses that gave Tony the excuse to drink half a bottle of Taylor's Vintage Port. The food was delicious and Tony felt as if he was back on top of the world; Sharon was also very happy because now Tony had so much money, she was hoping he would relax about the relationship with his brother Paul and maybe even think seriously about moving abroad.

The afternoon had worn on with Tony getting louder and louder and then he started buying drinks for everybody in the bar. It was turning into a real Bermondsey piss-up and Sharon was worried that Tony would do something stupid or, God forbid, someone would say something and upset him.

Sharon needn't have worried: for a change the booze had mellowed Tony, the world was his friend and nothing was going to ruin his big celebration. It was about six o clock and Sharon whispered to Tony that perhaps they should leave while they were ahead. He surveyed the bar as though he was some sort of Roman emperor and agreed with her. He then announced: "Drinks all round" and ordered his last one of the day, a large whisky.

She had to remind Tony to pay, and nearly fainted when she looked at the lunch and bar bill, and discovered they had spent over seven hundred pounds. Sharon then remembered the ten million and laughed to herself, realising that money was now no object.

They headed to the exit and as they passed reception Tony noticed someone booking in. "Hey Gregg how you doing? Millwall!" he sang at the top of his voice. The receptionist looked shocked but Gregg took it in his stride.

"Hello mate," the other man called back. "How's it going? Been down the Den recently then?"

Tony slurred his words: "Not as much as I want to but you know, busy, you know busy."

"Yeah I know. Anyway nice to see you, have a good one eh?"

Tony stumbled towards the door. "Great bloke that Gregg Wallace, yeah mate of mine you know? Yea a good mate, yeah mascer, marcser, some fucking chef thing. What do you say we go down the Mayflower in Rotherhithe Street for a pint?"

"Don't you think you've had enough?" said Sharon, shaking her head and beginning to get slightly annoyed.

Tony was trying to speak coherently but was having difficulties.

"Never enough Sharon just one, oh go on don't be a fucking mean cow."

The Final Act

Two minutes later they were jumping into a black cab.

"The Mayflower, Marychurch Street!" spluttered Tony.

"Yeah I know it," replied the cabbie. "Be ten minutes."

Tony sat back and made himself comfortable. "Good. I'm looking forward to a nice pint."

The cabbie was looking in his rear-view mirror at Tony and Sharon. Tony looked a bit messy because of the drink, and the driver thought they were a weird couple and something about them was not quite right, but the thing was, he couldn't put his finger on what it was. But he gave up wondering and went back to concentrating on the driving and headed towards the Mayflower.

They soon arrived and Tony positively jumped out the cab.

"Haven't been here for ages," he said, turning to Sharon. "Pay the man darling."

Sharon gave the cabbie a tenner and said keep the change—after all she could afford to be generous. Tony was on his way into the pub already.

She looked up and saw a relatively smallish façade, sandwiched between two large buildings.

There were the remnants of hanging flower baskets, which had seen better days.

There were also two big name signs featuring ships—she decided to ask Tony what their meaning was.

The last thing Sharon noticed was the round sign with the date 1799 on it. Wow she thought, that was old! The pub had black window frames and a white exterior, which enhanced the pub's aura of age.

Sharon hated it when Tony just waltzed off doing his own thing, it was so disrespectful. She walked in and was not surprised to feel that the building's interior reflected the same historic ambience.

Tony was at the small bar ordering a pint of best bitter and a white wine for her. There were wooden tables with seats that were similar in some ways to the 'church-like pews' they'd found in Manzies, where Tony had taken her for the spectacular lunch treat.

The Final Act

There was a beautiful old brick fireplace, which added to the overall lovely ambience of the building.

Although hardly sunny Tony wanted to sit outside on the wooden decking, right beside the famous River Thames. Sharon had to admit even with a fair breeze coming off the river she was moved by the history of the pub. Tony loved it, sipping his pint and watching various barges and boats of all shapes and sizes going up and down the river.

They were quiet for a couple of minutes until Tony piped up:

"Our ancestors, the Pilgrims, sailed from here to America." He was shaking his head as though he couldn't quite grasp the history of it. "And of course the pub is built from timber from the Mayflower ship that took them, 1799 it says on the wall outside."

Even Sharon was impressed, remembering seeing the date earlier, not only with the history but the fact that Tony was interested and knew all about it.

Tony had now drunk so much that he had become inebriated for a second time, but was now sobering up. Sharon could not believe a man could drink so much alcohol and still be standing, let alone be able to hold a conversation.

He had to go for a pee and left Sharon sitting admiring the river traffic.

Sharon was lost in her study of the riverboats and did not notice the two men approach her.

"Hi there. You enjoying the view?" one of them asked.

Sharon looked up and saw two middle-aged overweight executive types standing over her. They had obviously had a few drinks too many.

"Yes it's lovely isn't it?" replied Sharon.

"What's a beautiful young woman drinking on her own for?" one of the newcomers asked. "You're lucky we arrived."

"I'm not on my own. My husband is in the loo and will be back any minute."

"That's what they all say," said the other man, laughing.

"Why don't we sit down and have a nice drink together and see where we go from there?" suggested the first man.

The Final Act

Sharon was now worried sick. The two half-pissed idiots had sat down and Tony would be out any minute. *Fuck, what should I do?* she thought.

She suddenly stood up and turned to go back in the bar.

One of the men grabbed her arm and swung her round.

"Leave me alone!" screamed Sharon.

Tony was in a good mood. He had so enjoyed his food and wine and was looking forward to Sharon sucking his cock when they got home, to be followed by a good kip. He walked out onto the wooden decking just as Sharon screamed.

He moved straight towards the two men, and he hit the first with a clenched fist to the jaw. Tony heard the crack as the man flew through the air and landed on the ground with a crash. The bigger of the two chancers couldn't believe what was happening and held his hands up, shaking them in surrender.

But Tony didn't give a shit about conciliatory gestures. He grabbed his arm, swung him round and threw him into a table, scattering smashed glasses in every direction. The first man was struggling to his feet when Tony saw him, grabbed him by the collar and punched him bang in the middle of his chest. The man went down like a bag of spuds, crashing to the deck. Tony looked at his victim: he didn't seem to be breathing.

The second man stumbled to his feet and had collected his senses. He grabbed a bottle from the table and smashed the end off, then held it in front of him shouting: "Come on you fucking bastard! Come on!"

Tony sobered up even more: broken bottles could be dangerous in the right hands, but unfortunately the man was not used to violence. Tony ducked under the swinging bottle and punched the man in the eye, quickly following that up with a reign of punches to his man's face. The older man collapsed in a heap and Tony kicked him in the head twice for good measure.

Sharon grabbed Tony's arm in a panic, saying, "Let's get out of here, quickly! The police will be here any minute."

Tony collected his thoughts. Police? *Shit*, he thought, and rushed to the exit with Sharon. A big guy in the pub blocked his way and began to speak: "You need to wait for the—"

The Final Act

He didn't finish. Tony kicked him hard in the balls and hit him smack on his nose as he fell to the side, clutching his crotch. The couple made it out into the road, Tony leading, and turning left. "This way quick," he said, hurtling down the road and hoping that Sharon was not too far behind.

They had gone a hundred yards and Tony was beginning to feel exhausted, but he looked round and was pleased to see Sharon had almost kept up with him. "Well done Sharon let's go," he told her, sprinting to the right up Swan Road, just as he heard police car sirens winding down as officers arrived at the pub.

"Keep going Sharon," he shouted. Tony turned right at the Adam and Eve pub and kept pumping his legs. He turned again to see that Sharon was lagging behind. "Push Sharon! Push your legs, come on! Can you see the station?"

Sharon looked up and saw the sign for Rotherhithe Station, and she got a second wind and increased her speed to catch Tony up. "Good girl Sharon, now let's go!"

They made it to the station and rushed onto the platform, deciding to worry about getting tickets later. Thank God there was a train sitting at the platform. Tony prayed that it would leave the second they got on. The doors opened and they got in and sat down gasping for breath. Tony was looking at the entrance to the platform and praying no police turned up, then he stood up and started pacing. "Fuck! Move you bastard!" he shouted, and the train pulled out just as Tony caught sight of a copper coming onto the platform. He turned to Sharon who was in a state of shock, saying, "Great! Don't you just love it when a plan comes together?"

The police sealed off the Mayflower premises, since it was now a murder enquiry. The ambulance crew thought that the victim, Andrew Parr, had probably died of a heart attack. The other drunken guy, Benjamin Ward, had been taken to hospital with severe facial injuries and was destined to stay there for two days before being discharged.

Tony and Sharon made it back to Lewisham, where Tony collapsed onto the sofa and immediately fell asleep for twelve hours.

When he woke up Sharon gave him a real verbal battering, and the only reason Tony took it was because he felt like complete shit and he also knew she was right. He could easily have ended up back inside just because he had once again lost his temper.

The bad news was that police now had a description of the man and woman at the scene. But the good news was that nobody would identify them as Tony Bolton or Sharon Travis.

Sharon explained to Tony that they would have to find different disguises.

CHAPTER 10

The party was in full swing, for Paul had pushed the boat out and everybody was having a top night. Doing the deals with Tony and Richard Philips had lifted the shadow of disaster from Paul, and he was upbeat, cheerful and back to his usual confident positive self. It was a Friday night and the booze was flowing at the private party in the Den Club. A superb buffet had been laid on and drinks were on the house all night.

Lexi had arrived at eight p.m. and all the other wives and girlfriends were present too, it was going to be a night to remember. The music was blaring, the old Abba songs had got everybody up dancing, even Paul was dancing, if his movements could be described as such, with Lexi.

Paul's girlfriend had made a real effort with her appearance: a tight short black dress clung to her curves in all the right places, and especially showcased her long slim legs. Paul hadn't been in such a good mood for weeks and felt as if the weight of the world that had been on his shoulders had been removed.

Roddy was at the bar with Dave.

"Have you seen Paul?" Roddy observed. "He's gone wild."

"I'm not surprised," said Dave. "He's been under a lot of strain recently."

"Well let's be truthful. We're all chuffed that we can relax, the shit with Tony and Philips could have got well nasty."

Dave was nodding. "Yeah I agree and tonight we can celebrate being alive and able to get very sloshed." Dave lifted his pint and sank the remaining half.

"I need a refill what about you?" Roddy asked.

"Jeez no I'll never last the night."

The party went on until late and the slow dance music was being played, so that couples could smooch as they moved around the floor.

Paul and Lexi were dancing and were stuck together like glue, Paul grinding his erection into Lexi's thigh.

"I think I'd better take care of that for you," she muttered with a giggle.

The Final Act

"Good idea Lexi. But is that now or when we get home?" Paul asked with a smile.

She grabbed his hand and strolled out of the room and made for Paul's office.

"We've never done it on your desk."

Lexi pushed open the office door. She stood in front of the desk and stripped off the black dress to reveal a full black complement of sexy black tights, knickers and bra. She quickly removed them and climbed onto the desk, and then lay back with her pussy hanging tantalisingly over the edge.

"I'm hot Paul. Come and get it then," she coaxed. "What you waiting for?"

Paul had not seen this side of Lexi for a long time—usually she was loving and sensual.

He loved this change in her and dropped his dark blue trousers and matching boxers. He was as hard as iron and rammed his erection into Lexi, and she gasped and pushed a bit to make sure she had taken the entire length.

"OK Paul. Now fuck away for all your worth until I tell you to stop!"

Paul started fucking her roughly.

"Yes Paul! Hard! Go on fuck me then! Slap my arse, and put your finger in!"

Paul was loving it. He pulled Lexi close and hooked his right arm under her arse and found the wet hole. He slipped his middle finger in and heard Lexi moan.

He kept going and Lexi was loving it. "Fuck me then! Fuck me Paul! Yes I love it! Harder!"

Paul was getting close to his climax and, thank goodness, he thought she was nearing hers.

"Yes Paul a bit more! Yes harder! Slow slow, push slowly! Ahhhhhhhhhh!"

She came and pulled Paul almost on top of her as spasms of pleasure coursed through her body.

Lexi kissed Paul ten times, saying, "I loved it so much. How was it for you, as they say?"

"Good very good," he replied. "You always surprise me."

"Hmm. We can do that again then?"

The Final Act

"You bet," said Paul as he contemplated the fact that the next time he sat at his desk, it would never seem the same again, and he laughed.

They got dressed and made their way back to the party.

Pauly and Matt looked at the couple as they came back into the room. Matt nudged Pauly. "Wonder what they've been up to then?" he asked.

Paul was sweaty and Lexi was positively glowing as they went to the bar and ordered more drinks. He ordered a large whisky and Lexi had some more champagne. They turned from the bar and Paul saw the room's door open. One of the doormen entered, escorting a young courier. They marched over to Paul.

"Sorry boss," apologised the doorman, "but he has orders to hand you the parcel personally."

The courier held out the parcel and offered it to Paul.

"It's not a bomb is it?" Paul asked with a smile.

Having handed Paul the parcel, the courier turned and walked back towards the door.

Paul looked at the parcel and juggled it with his hands. It was very light, and he ripped the parcel open at its end.

"Perhaps it's a present Paul." Lexi was excited. "Maybe it's really for me," she said wistfully.

Paul turned the box on end and carefully dropped the contents into his other hand.

He looked at it and all the blood drained out of his face, leaving him white. Lexi knew what it was and couldn't speak. Paul looked at Lexi and took her arm. She could feel Paul shaking as he moved towards the door and then into his office.

Paul put the videotape into the machine and pressed 'fast forward' for a few seconds.

The screen came to life to show two naked women sucking and licking a man's penis and that man was Paul.

The tapes had surfaced at last.

The Final Act

Paul picked the phone's receiver up and spoke into it. "Send Dave and Duke in here NOW!"

He clicked the off button and Dave and Duke soon entered the office. Paul looked at them both and held the tape up in the air.

Dave and Duke both knew what it was and felt very deflated after a good night.

Paul then spoke: "This problem is back and if you don't sort it this time, Dave I will fucking bury you, do you understand?"

"Yes boss. This time I'll take care of it."

The Final Act

CHAPTER 11

Jeff and Karen had spent thirty minutes trying to admire the modern art in the gallery in Southwark Park. They both thought it was a load of tosh and couldn't understand how a white canvas with a black dot in the middle was an incredibly inspiring piece of art, worth perhaps a million pounds. The thirty minutes seemed to be everlasting but thankfully at last it was time to pursue the real reason for being in Southwark Park. It was bloody freezing, as Octobers tend to be. Jeff and Karen were both well insulated against the cold, although Jeff's nose was the same colour as Rudolph's.

"Let's see what Micky has to say for himself then," Karen said.

Jeff nodded, they left the gallery and they made their way to a wooden bench fifty yards from the café entrance. There was nobody in the park, the fact that it was freezing cold and eleven in the morning had kept all but diehard dog-walkers away.

They sat down and sipped at their steaming takeaway coffees, holding them with both hands for the warmth.

"He should be here any minute," Karen said hopefully.

"I bloody well hope so otherwise I could get frostbite."

Sure enough a minute later an old boy shuffled around the corner. He must have been wearing ten layers of clothes as he looked abnormally huge.

"Micky how are you?" Karen greeted him.

"Very well Miss, thank you for asking." Micky was very old-school and liked to be polite, especially to ladies.

Jeff rubbed his hands together. "So what have you heard Micky?"

"Was there something in particular you was after Mr Swan?"

"Well seeing as you ask, we hear Tony Bolton and Richard Philips are back in town."

Micky gave a wry grin. "Are you being serious Mr Swan? This is the last place they'd come back to, don't you think?"

"I'm only telling you what I hear and wanted you to confirm it was true."

"I have to be honest with you Mr Swan. I have heard nothing."

Karen wanted to try the sympathetic approach. "Micky it's so cold. Are you coping alright?"

"I am, thanks for asking Miss."

"Micky this is very special to me and Mr Swan. The money we give you, I know it's not a lot but—"

"No Miss it's very much appreciated and comes in very handy thank you."

"Well look we could give you a lot more for some good info on these two men. You know they are both killers and that Bolton shot an unarmed copper in the head last year?"

"Yes I heard about that. Terrible, terrible."

"So you've not heard anything?"

"No but I'll make a few discreet enquiries and if I come up with anything I'll give you a bell. Would this—Err—extra payment, perhaps cover a cheap holiday for me and the missus somewhere warm?"

Karen smiled, for she had a soft spot for dear old Micky.

"Yes it will. Now listen, you be careful. These two are very dangerous individuals."

"Oh no need to worry about me Miss. I do very low-key safe enquiries." And with that he let out a little chuckle.

Jeff and Karen stood up, and Jeff took a brown envelope out of his coat pocket and handed it to Micky.

"Thank you very much Mr Swan, Miss." The envelope seemed to disappear as though he was a magician and Micky shuffled off in the direction of the park exit.

"How much did you give him?" Karen asked.

"Thirty quid out of the slush fund, Michael knows."

"I love that old boy you know." Karen took hold of Jeff's arm. "Let's go before we freeze to death."

They were soon back in their warm office in Rotherhithe.

The Final Act

"Well we've done all the snitches, put the word out more than ever and nothing," Jeff grumbled. "Not a dicky bow."

Karen looked thoughtful. "Yeah I know. Depressing isn't it?"

The phone rang and Jeff grabbed it before Karen did. "Yes DC Swan, CID," Jeff said, then listened for a few seconds.

"OK we're on our way."

"What is it?" Karen asked.

"Looks like a murder and assault down at the Mayflower."

"Bloody hell that's a bit close to home." For some reason Karen wondered briefly if this could be anything to do with Bolton or Philips.

They arrived at the pub fifteen minutes later and immediately had the whole area sealed off. Statements were taken from staff and customers, they had numerous clear identifications of the two perpetrators and a police artist had soon produced a reasonable likeness of both Tony and Sharon. The forensics team arrived and began the painstaking search of the pub for clues.

Karen and Jeff were interested in finding out how the couple had arrived at the pub and where they had been before, so they put a call into a black cab contact and asked for assistance in finding out if anyone had dropped the couple at the pub.

The policeman who had chased the couple to Rotherhithe Station was interviewed and confirmed that the artist's likenesses of the pair were indeed accurate.

Two days later a black cabbie came forward who recognised the couple from the leaflet he had been shown. He confirmed he had picked them up in Tower Bridge Road and taken them to the Mayflower pub. Interestingly, he also commented that he had thought at the time that they were a funny couple, feeling that there was just something 'not quite right' about them. The woman had given him a tenner and said keep the change, he'd said, and no, he did not know where they had come from, but the man had seemed to be pretty drunk.

Karen and Jeff then decided to do some old-style police work and went down to Tower Bridge Road. They found the exact spot where the cabbie picked the couple up and looked around. The obvious place to start was Bermondsey Square, so they walked smartly to the square and stood and took in the scene.

"So where do you want to start Jeff?" Karen asked.

Jeff swivelled round and saw the GB Grill and Bar, the Del'Aziz Restaurant and the Bermondsey Square Hotel.

"I tell you what Jeff," she went on. "Let's start with the hotel."

"OK let's go."

They entered the main entrance and approached the reception desk at the far end of a small corridor. They showed their badges and asked to see the manager, then sat by the window waiting for him to turn up. Five minutes later Bob Newbie arrived and introduced himself. He took them into the bar and sat them down at a table.

"So what can I help you with officers?" Bob asked.

Karen took a poster out and handed it to the manager.

"We want to know if this couple were in the hotel on Tuesday of this week. It would have been around lunchtime."

"Well you're in luck. Tommy the barman works that shift and he happens to be in, let me call him."

Jeff and Karen look at each other as though to say 'a good start'.

Tommy looked like a typical barman: black trousers and white shirt with a black bow tie. He said hello and sat down at the table.

Karen gave him the poster. "Have you seen this couple before?" she asked him. "Maybe last Tuesday lunchtime?"

Tommy looked at the poster. "Ha! Who could forget these two characters? I remember them well, what have they been up to then?"

"We just need them to help us with our enquiries, so please tell us more."

"They came in about eleven and had champagne if I remember correctly," the barman explained, "and then got plastered and had a big lunch. Their final bill was £700 odd quid."

"That's a lot of money for lunch."

"I got the feeling they were celebrating something. They bought drinks for everybody in the bar."

"How did they pay? It's very important."

Tommy spoke the words Karen did not want to hear: "Cash! Can you imagine? All cash."

"Did you by any chance hear their names?"

"No, sorry, no idea on that score."

"Have you ever seen them here before?" Jeff asked.

"No, never."

Jeff and Karen just sat there silently thinking. Finally Karen spoke: "OK thank you for your time. If we need to speak to you again we'll be in touch."

They left the hotel feeling disappointed. Although they had made progress there were no clues as to who this couple were or where they came from.

"Jeff," Karen said thoughtfully. "I've just got a feeling about this. Everything may not be as it seems."

"What do you mean?" Jeff asked, his interest piqued.

"I don't know. Copper's instinct, call it what you like. I've just got a feeling that..." Karen let the thought hang. "OK let's get back and see where we are and plan our next move."

They made quick time and were soon back in the office at Rotherhithe Nick.

They took their coats off and, although it was an old building, the heating worked really well and it was lovely and warm.

"That's better," said Jeff rubbing some colour and warmth back into his face. "So coffee then?"

"Bloody hell Jeff we'll both look like a cup of coffee soon, and I keep having to go to the loo all the time. Oh alright then if you insist," she said with a giggle.

Jeff shot off to the canteen for more piping hot lattes, while Karen sat down and thought about the strange nameless couple.

Her colleague returned from the canteen. "Here you go. That's two pounds twenty please."

"Thanks. I'll give you an IOU later."

"What time are we seeing Paul Bolton?"

The question broke Karen's thoughts. "Err three-thirty wasn't it?"

"Yeah. Look we can chat for a bit, have a bite to eat and then get going over to Soho."

"Sounds good to me."

Karen and Jeff talked for an hour and decided they were at a dead end with the nameless couple. They had the 'Special' in the canteen which was anglicised lasagne, which was more Grimsby than Rome. They then set off to the Den Club to visit Paul Bolton.

Jeff pulled the car into the kerb outside the Den, then he took his seat belt off and stepped out of the police Ford Mondeo car. He glanced over to Karen, who was already opening the passenger door.

They approached the entrance and were met by two doormen blocking the entrance.

Richard was head doorman and had the nickname Tricky, and that was down to the fact that he was extremely tricky to deal with and always had an answer. He was six-foot-three tall, well-built, and had a third Dan judo black belt and didn't take shit from anybody. The second man, Don, was much shorter but was built like a bulldog: five-foot-seven of solid muscle, and the crew cut gave him a very menacing appearance.

Tricky turned to Don and whispered out of the side of his mouth: "Coppers. Let's have some fun."

The former man took the lead, saying, "Yes can we help you?"

Karen was in front so she spoke first: "Yes we have an appointment with Mr Bolton." Karen flashed her badge.

"And what time was that for?"

"Three-thirty."

"You're early. I'm afraid I'll have to ask you to come back at three-twenty-five."

Karen was eyeballing Tricky and looked at her watch: it was three-twenty-one.

"I'm not sure Mr Bolton would be very happy if he found out you were keeping us waiting out here in the cold," she told him.

"I'm paid to look after the door and that's what I'm doing."

The Final Act

Jeff stepped forward. "Look you've had your fun. Now fuck off out the way and let us in. That is unless you would like to be arrested for preventing a police officer from carrying out his duty. What's it to be?"

Tricky didn't even register what Jeff had said, he merely slowly lifted his arm and looked closely at his watch.

"You may go in now. It's three-twenty-four. I'm letting you in early."

Karen strode in and as Jeff passed Tricky he spoke quietly: "I'll remember your ugly fucking face!" Tricky smiled, knowing he had wound the copper right up.

The two officers then approached a further door that was also guarded by two doormen.

"We have an appointment with Mr Bolton," she said again, once more flashing the badge. Jeff and Karen then noticed the tall doorman from outside come and stand to the side, watching the proceedings.

Mick was ex-army intelligence and Little Joe was six-foot-six, lightning quick in his reactions and strong as an ox; the pair were a formidable team.

Mick was in charge of door two. "Can I have both badges please?" Little Joe asked.

Karen was looking daggers at the doorman.

"What for exactly?"

"So we can establish they are genuine and, if necessary, check with the Metropolitan Police that you are who these badges say you are."

Jeff spoke. "Are you having a laugh?"

"Sir I am being very serious. We have procedures to follow and if we don't I could lose my job." And when he said that he looked at Tricky.

Karen turned to Tricky. "He is absolutely right. Procedures are in place and must be followed to the letter."

Jeff and Karen handed over their badges and they were scrutinised by Mick.

"These would appear to be in order. Thank you,.." So saying, he handed them back.

"Could you open your handbag please?"

Jeff began to say something but Karen held his arm.

Karen opened her bag and the giant, Little Joe, had a quick look and confirmed it was clean.

Mick then spoke into his face microphone: "Appointment for Mr Bolton two individuals, escort required please."

Everybody just stood there looking at each other and waiting.

Two minutes later another mean vicious-looking man opened the door from the club side and said, "Follow me please."

Karen gave Tricky one last lingering look and Tricky prayed he didn't meet either of these two under different circumstances.

The pair were led through a maze of corridors and they couldn't help but notice how many heavies were standing at various doors along the journey. The man eventually opened a door marked 'private' and entered a small cubicle. The door was locked behind them and there was a click, and the entrance way in front of them opened and they moved into a small corridor with a desk at the side. There was of course a further guard here, who asked them to stop and wait. The man picked up a phone receiver, saying, "Mr Bolton's two guests have arrived."

Almost immediately a very attractive, sexy looking, well-dressed thirty-something woman came strutting down the corridor and introduced herself as Carla Westburgh, Paul Bolton's Personnel Assistant.

"If you would follow me please, Mr Bolton will see you now."

Karen looked at her watch. It was nearly four o'clock.

Carla opened a door and stepped in, announcing: "Here are the two police officers, Mr Bolton."

Karen and Jeff followed Carla in as Paul Bolton stood up. "Hello," he welcomed them. "Would you like some tea or coffee perhaps?" He looked at Jeff and Karen enquiringly.

The female officer spoke for both of them: "Two lattes would be very nice, thank you."

"Can you arrange that, please Carla?" Bolton ordered.

"Of Course Mr Bolton." And she disappeared out of the door.

"Please have a seat officers," Paul said. "What can I do for you today?"

Karen was not happy. "Well first of all it's taken us half an hour to get through your security. Are you expecting trouble of some sort?"

Paul was as smooth as silk. "Not at all. We reviewed our security recently and just decided to make some improvements. I'm sorry if they were overzealous but really, they are only doing their jobs."

There was a tap on the door and Carla entered with the two coffees, which she placed on a small side table.

"Is there anything else Mr Bolton?" she asked.

"Yes, bring me a bottle of water please. My usual."

Carla left the office.

"I've got a feeling you have reviewed your security because your brother Tony and Richard Philips are on the loose, isn't that the case Mr Bolton?" Karen stated.

"I've already explained that."

"So have you had any contact or spoken with your brother or Richard Philips since they have been on the run?"

"I haven't seen them or spoken to them, and to answer your next question I have no idea where they may be."

Carla returned and placed a bottle of mineral water on Paul's desk.

"I hear that HMRC and the Serious Crime Squad are beginning an investigation into your business very shortly," Karen remarked.

Paul was momentarily shocked and, for a second, it showed on his face.

"I do hope you're not scaremongering Miss Foster," he addressed Karen by name. "I have friends in very high places who would take a very dim view of police officers doing that."

Karen ignored the veiled threat. "We will of course be watching known associates of both these criminals as part of our efforts to apprehend them."

Karen was giving Paul the message that probably him and other associates of Tony and Philips would be under surveillance.

Paul didn't like that but kept quiet. His aim was to get these two officers onside as much as he could.

"Look it's no secret I fell out with Tony and Richard Philips but that's all in the past, we have all moved on. If I was you I would look for Tony in Spain or somewhere hot. Why the hell would he stay around here?"

"Because he's a Bermondsey Boy, it's that simple. He was born and has lived his whole life in Bermondsey, and it's not that easy just to leave it all behind."

"So is there anything else I can help with?"

Karen thought for a second. "Did you hear about the trouble at the Mayflower?"

"No what was that about?"

"A man was murdered and another was severely beaten a couple of days ago."

"Oh I did hear something, but murdered you say? That's shocking," said Paul, shaking his head.

"Well thank you for your time Mr Bolton."

"It's a pleasure. Always happy to help the local constabulary."

Everybody stood up, Jeff opened the door to leave, but Karen had saved the best till last: "Oh Mr Bolton there was one other thing."

"Yes? And what is that?" He smiled.

Karen took a poster out of her inside pocket and unfolded it.

"Do you know who these people are?"

Paul took the poster and looked at it. He tried to remain expressionless but he was shocked. It was Tony, dressed in his disguise, with some woman.

Karen detected his sudden nervousness, and was sure Paul knew something.

"I don't know them," said Paul, handing the poster back to Karen. "Who are they?"

"Well the man is wanted in connection with the murder that took place at the Mayflower. As to the woman, she is obviously a friend or partner of his."

Paul took a deep breath. *That lunatic Tony was killing people already!* He shook his head at no one in particular.

"Are you alright Mr Bolton?"

"Yes. Sorry. If I can be of help in the future at any time please call Carla and make an appointment."

Carla took Karen and Jeff to the security door and said goodbye. They were then escorted out of the club premises by another security guard. They got in the car and Karen turned to Jeff.

"He knows who it is," she said angrily. "The man on the poster. He fucking well knows him, I'm sure of it! Did you see his face?"

"I agree. But what do we do next?"

"Fuck knows. But things are beginning to stir in the pot."

CHAPTER 12

Nothing gave Richard more pleasure in his life than wrapping up and sending one of the tapes to Paul Bolton. It was of course a copy and he still had the three originals.

Before sending it he and Julie had sat and tried to watch all three tapes, but they had only made it halfway through the first one before Richard grabbed her and fucked the living daylights out of her for a measly four minutes, before he shot his load all over her arse.

Richard was happy he had done the brothel deal with Paul and couldn't believe how lucky he had been. Well, he reasoned to himself, it was about time he had some good news.

The follow-up and payoff for the tapes were the difficult and dangerous times, the next phase was to contact Paul and ask for a sum of money, and how much was the big question.

Julie and Richard were living in a small cramped flat in Basildon. It was far from perfect but they were both enjoying it very much. Julie was no longer 'on her back' all day or on her knees doing it 'doggy style', so that alone made her happy beyond belief. She knew that no one could imagine what it is like to earn your living as a prostitute, for it was truly the pits of hell.

Richard had spent six months terrified to leave the flat. He had been doing all his shopping at an out-of-town Asda, always late at night when there were very few customers and staff. Julie now did all the shopping at normal times, Richard felt much more relaxed, and, of course, the sex and companionship they shared was wonderful.

Julie was thirty-one and had grown up the hard way, fostered as a young child in numerous homes. She had never known her parents, and had gone to children's homes where she was sexually abused by the people meant to be helping her, and eventually, when she was eighteen, she started selling her body for a living. She was more than tough, she had been through awful times but had managed to keep body and soul together.

She knew full well that life didn't owe her anything, for thousands of people worldwide were in far worse situations than she was. Julie had a sense of humour and could be more loyal than a dog to its owner, if she was treated

The Final Act

well. She had also kept her slim figure: five-foot-seven tall, a lovely rounded arse that she could shake for Britain, plus a very firm medium-sized pair of breasts that as yet had not drooped too much. Overall she was a very sassy sexy woman. Richard had more than a soft spot for her, he really fancied her big time and intended to keep her with him as long as possible.

Richard was drinking a bottle of San Miguel in the lounge while Julie was cooking dinner. He was mulling over how much to ask from Paul for the tapes.

"You alright Hun?" shouted Julie.

"Yeah fine thanks."

Ten minutes later Julie placed a plate of steaming hot spaghetti bolognese on the small wooden dining table, calling out, "Come and get it."

"Hmm that smells and looks delicious," he said.

"Forget the flattery, get your arse in gear and eat it while it's nice and hot."

Julie sat down and sipped at a glass of wine that Richard had poured for her.

Between mouthfuls of spaghetti Julie asked a question: "So moody chops. What is it?"

Richard smiled at the moody chops quip. "Nothing really. I'm just not sure how much to ask for the sex tapes, that's all."

Julie thought for a moment.

"And this Paul, he is the man who has just given you the brothels back, which are worth millions?"

"Yes, but you don't know the whole story. He stitched me up in prison. I did extra time because of that bastard and remember, he only gave me back what was rightfully mine."

"I'm just saying things are good," Julie reasoned. "You got that bloke Ted running the joints for you, so all you gotta do is count the money."

"You still don't understand. He turned me over, I lost face. I need to see him pay for that or I...I can't be the same man I was."

"Fucking hell what does that mean? You want to pay him back for some shit. OK then, ask for a million."

"That's nowhere near enough babe, he's got to pay. It's got to hurt him. More like three I reckon."

Julie was smiling and let out a short chuckle. "Why the fuck would anyone pay millions for a couple of sex tapes? They're three-a-penny for God's sake!"

"Julie it's his ex-wife and his current partner. Imagine the embarrassment if they ended up all over the internet. We could also threaten to send them to the ex-wife's family, now that would be an eye-opener for them. In fact we could take the money and then still put them on the internet."

Julie could see this was going to be a long drawn out affair and had a bad feeling about the possible outcome.

She moved close to Richard and looked into his eyes. "We have something good here. I like you very much. Please don't ruin it by chasing after more money than we could ever need."

Richard was a stubborn bastard on occasion and was getting slightly annoyed. "Just remember whose side you're on! He's got to pay and he fucking well will!"

With that he slurped at his San Miguel and tucked into his spaghetti bolognese.

Julie had one last thought before resuming her meal, and that was to get as much money in her account as possible in case it all went tits up. She did not want to return to working on her back or on all fours.

They sat in silence for what seemed ages but was actually only a couple of minutes. The silence was broken by Richard: "That was good, so… I've… decided I'm going to ask for three million."

Julie didn't bother saying anything, she just thought there could be a lot of trouble on the way.

"So what do you think?" he asked.

"It's your decision. Seems a lot to me."

"That cunt will pay. I know him. He's weak. He'll pay and then he'll pay again."

Richard went back to the lounge and started planning how he was going to get the money off Paul. The first thing he needed was some help, for he couldn't possibly plan and carry out it out on his own.

"Julie, come here."

Richard was smiling from ear to ear.

"Darling, listen we are going to get that money and when we have it you can have half."

Julie was shocked. One-and-a-half million would be enough to set up for life.

She gave Richard her hardest look. "You promise?"

"I swear it on my mother's life."

"Then what are we waiting for?" Julie was now smiling as well. Richard reached out and pulled her towards him.

As she collapsed onto Richard's lap a thought stopped her laughter. "Is your mother still alive?"

"That's a minor point for God's sake," said Richard, laughing.

"You, you're terrible," replied Julie as she held Richard's neck and pulled his lips towards hers.

CHAPTER 13

"Get your coat. If you spend any more time getting ready I'm going to be late," Tony snapped.

"You want me to look my best don't you?" Sharon said.

"I've already told you you're only coming for the ride. Now get your fucking coat and let's go!"

Tony had been irritable since he got up early at nine o clock. His foul temper could also have had something to do with the bottle of whisky he drank the night before. It was Thursday 12th October and winter had set in, and whatever time of day or night you looked out of the window, the wind was howling, it was raining and it was bloody cold. Tony had told Sharon they were going on a short trip so he could meet up with someone. Sharon was to drop him off, look after the car, and then pick him back up when he called her.

Tony had changed his appearance once again and now looked like a scruffy labourer in dirty overalls and a flat cap. He'd shaved most of the moustache and beard off, leaving a thin tash and a stubble on his chin.

Sharon had changed the colour of her wig from red to blonde, which Tony said suited her.

They made their way out of the back door and locked up. Tony scanned the road left and right as he always did when leaving the house. Nothing looked suspicious and he marched to the blue Ford Mondeo that was sitting in the road.

"You drive," he told her.

"Do I have to?" pleaded Sharon.

"Yes. I've got stuff to think about." He opened the passenger door and sat in. Sharon got behind the wheel and started her up.

"So where to?"

"Stratford, but wait a sec while I put the satnav on." Tony fumbled with the satnav and finally got it plugged into the cigarette holder and started tapping in an address. He finished and stuck it onto the windscreen in front of himself.

The Final Act

"OK let's go," he said. "Head towards the A127 and then follow the instructions."

"Yes boss." Sharon was peeved that he was treating her as if she was a taxi driver.

She scowled at Tony. "You can buy me—"

"Shut the fuck up! I'm thinking and I don't want to hear your moaning voice." He gave her a nasty look, so she turned and concentrated on the road ahead.

Tony looked closely at the satnav: twenty-five miles and it should take fifty-four minutes. He glanced at his watch: it was just gone ten. Good if there were no hold-ups he would arrive on time. He sat back and shut his eyes and thought of the meeting ahead, feeling excited. If the meeting went well then his brother Paul would soon be dead and he would be back in control of the clubs. Sharon looked at Tony and caught him smiling to himself. It sent a little shiver down her spine.

They were soon on the A127 heading east.

Tony was back in the land of the living and was enjoying the views. "Keep to the right!" he suddenly shouted. Sharon bit her lip to stop herself from shouting back at him and moved to the right lane. They hit Gallows Corner and Sharon increased her speed on the approach to the flyover.

Sharon was doing a steady forty miles per hour, they merged onto the A12 and were soon passing places Tony knew well from his past: Collier Row, Romford, Chadwell Heath. He saw Newbury Tube Station and then they were on the Gants Hill roundabout. They came off the A12 at the Green Man interchange and headed towards Leytonstone. It wasn't far now, Tony thought. They crossed over a further couple of roundabouts and then saw the sign to Stratford.

Tony was feeling a few nerves. He had never liked the man he was meeting, but he would sort that out as the first priority. He rubbed his sweaty hands down the sides of his overalls, realising that they were nearly there.

He was looking for the pub he wanted when the satnav blared out *You have reached your destination*, and Tony saw it just down the road.

"The Cart and Horses over there," he pointed it out to Sharon. Tony looked at his watch: five past eleven. Good, he thought, it would have just opened.

"Drop me over there on the corner and I'll call you when I'm ready," he told her. "Don't go too far, park up somewhere sensible, I reckon I'll be an hour at the most."

Sharon dropped Tony off and sped towards the town centre to do a quick bit of shopping.

The Cart and Horses was an old fashioned boozer on the corner of Windmill Lane and Maryland Point. Tony knew the pub from when he was a very young man. He entered the main bar door and looked for his contact, finding that the pub was empty save for an old boy and his dog. Tony went to the bar and ordered a large whisky. The bar lady was old-school: big tits and a tight shirt to show them off. She gave Tony his whisky, he paid and then sat in the corner round from the front door. He had a good view of anyone coming in before they could see him. He took a slug of the whisky and looked at his watch: quarter past eleven. He was late.

It was eleven-twenty-five and Tony was getting pissed off. He went to the bar and ordered another large whisky, he paid and turned round to head back to his seat. As soon as he turned the door opened and a man walked in. Tony's contact had arrived.

"Tony, how are you?" said the man, stretching out his hand.

Tony moved close, took it and shook it warmly.

"Hello Richard, long time."

"Yeah, a lot of water has passed under the bridge, eh?"

"Let me get you a drink. What do you want?"

Richard looked at Tony's glass. "Same as you would be fine."

"Sit over in the corner and I'll get your drink."

Tony went back to the bar and ordered two more large whiskies.

He sat down with the other man. "How was your time?"

"Easy enough, but I have no wish to go back. What about you?"

"Broadmoor's not like a normal prison. It's easy but you are surrounded by a load of nutters."

They both laughed and drank their whisky.

"Look Richard," Tony began, "we were never best buddies but I think we both want the same thing, which is to get even with that cunt brother of mine."

"I couldn't agree more. So what are you saying?"

"Let's have a pact. Be partners, and when it's all over we go our separate ways."

They shook hands again and then laughed as Tony whispered: "It's going to be a fucking bit of fun this, us two against Paul. He hasn't got a fucking prayer!" And with that they knocked back the whiskies and Richard got up.

"My round I think."

The one-hour meeting lasted four and both Tony and Richard were well pissed. Richard left in a cab while Tony rang Sharon and asked her in a slurred voice to pick him up. Sharon was not in the best frame of mind when she got to the pub, and seeing Tony legless made it even worse.

"It's good news darling," belched Tony.

"Wonderful, I'm so happy for you," Sharon spat out sarcastically.

"No need to be like that." Tony then slumped back in his seat closed his eyes and was asleep. Sharon looked across and stuck her tongue out at him, then she flicked 'V' signs in his direction and lastly gave him the finger. She would not have dared to do any of them if he had been awake. She pushed the accelerator down and headed for Lewisham.

CHAPTER 14

Paul had told Lexi all about the deals with Tony and Richard Philips and she was over the moon. The only real problem to sort out was the tapes but they had not received any word from the person who had sent the sample. Paul figured they were being made to sweat, the contact would be made eventually, and all they could do was wait. The thought of the films finding their way onto the internet or, even worse, into the hands of Emma's family brought him out into a cold sweat. He had already decided to pay so he could finally rest with no major issues in his life.

Paul felt that the weight of the world had been removed from his shoulders. He was almost a new man. Lexi certainly thought he was, as he had suddenly taken a great interest in her body again and was giving her lots of his time. The apartment in Kings Quay, Chelsea Harbour had taken on a new life. Paul had filled the flat with flowers which gave off a beautiful scent, especially noticeable when you first entered.

Lexi adored the first-floor apartment with its magnificent terrace that had glorious views of the marina. She also liked the fact that she could drive her Golf GTI into the reserved parking space in the underground car park, following visits to the Kings Road or other nearby fashionable shopping locations. The apartment was ultra-modern and had all the amenities expected of a one-and–a-half million-pound property. They had decided that even if they did buy a place in the country they would keep the apartment, as they both loved it so much. Lexi would have been happy to stay living there, but as soon as she finished her degree she wanted to start a family and Paul was all for that.

The brothels had been signed over to Richard Philips and were no longer a worry for Paul. He heard through the grapevine that Ted Frost was fronting up the business with Philips taking a back seat. He hadn't really had a choice as he was in the top ten 'most wanted' criminals in the UK. Paul was just delighted to be free of the aggravation, because although the money was incredible the hassle was extreme.

Paul had started getting home earlier than usual, and one of the subjects that constantly arose was Christmas. Paul wanted a big bash with lots of people, while Lexi preferred to keep it small with a few very close friends. Paul had even talked about inviting his brother Tony for Christmas lunch. Everything had

The Final Act

been agreed except where to spend Christmas Day. Again there was a difference of opinion. Lexi wanted to stay in Chelsea Harbour while Paul wanted to spend Christmas Day at the Den. Paul's thinking was that it would be great to have waiter service at the club, while Lexi wanted to cook a traditional meal for Paul at Chelsea.

They decided to compromise in the end: Lexi would cook on Christmas Eve and Boxing Day and Christmas Day would be spent at the club. Lexi knew full well that Christmas Day at the club would turn into a marathon drinking session with all Paul's cronies in attendance.

Lexi's parents would be visiting on Christmas Eve and she was only seeing them every four or five months, so she was really looking forward to that.

Paul was at the club when the letter arrived. It was marked 'Private and Confidential', and he immediately wondered if it could be the contact regarding the videotape. He opened it with a knife he kept on his desk and took out a folded piece of paper. He opened it and saw it was handwritten in biro ink. He read from the top:

Paul,

As you know I have the three tapes, they are stored somewhere very safe and only I know where that is. I want £3 million for them, you will get further instructions when you have signified that you are going to pay. I don't have to tell you what will happen if you decide not to, or try any funny business. To let me know you are going to pay move the huge cactus at the front of the club to the other side of the door. It's very simple. As soon as you do that I will tell you where and how to pay the money.

The first thing that struck him was that the use of the name Paul suggested he knew him. So it was almost certainly someone who worked in one of the clubs or knew Paul from somewhere. Perhaps someone from the Starlight Club, where the tapes had been recorded? He just had a feeling that it was a person who knew him quite well. He immediately called Dave on the internal phone and asked to see him.

Dave read the letter.

"So what do you think?" asked Paul.

"Pretty basic isn't it?" Dave said. "I agree it could be someone who knows you."

"Well we don't really know fuck all, do we?"

"We could get a friendly cop to analyse it and see if we could get a DNA match."

"I knew there was a reason I employed you," Paul answered, smiling. "Get on it straight away."

"Are you going to pay it? It's one hell of a lot of money."

"I need to think. It's a lot more than I thought he, she, or they, would ask for. Move the fucking plant and let's see what happens next."

CHAPTER 15

Tony was like a lion in a cage, endlessly walking around the house but all for no real reason. Sharon would watch him. He'd be sitting in the lounge and would suddenly get up and go to the kitchen, he'd come back with a sandwich, sit down and eat it. Ten minutes later he was up again and went for a pee, and after the same period again, he got up and made for upstairs. Goodness knows what he did there, Sharon thought, but he was back down after five minutes and back in his chair again.

"Tony what is wrong?" she asked eventually.

"I'm fucking bored that's what's fucking wrong, stuck in this fucking house day and night, hardly able to go out." Tony was shaking his head. "I swear I'll go fucking loopy with all this sitting about."

Sharon laughed. "Do you want to stick your big throbbing cock into me?"

"No I fucking well do not."

Now Sharon knew something was seriously wrong: Tony not wanting to shag her was astonishing.

"Look we have the money," she reasoned. "Let's get out into the country and enjoy ourselves."

"How many times do I have to tell you? Not until that cunt of a brother of mine pays!"

"He's just given you millions. Can't you just leave it?"

Tony got up from the chair and raised his fist. "I've told you, keep fucking quiet about it! It's fuck all to do with you so keep out of it! If you annoy me anymore I swear…" He held his fist near her face, as if he was about to hit her.

"OK. Sorry Tony I didn't mean anything by it, you know I'm on your side. I promise I won't mention it again."

Tony looked at her, trying to decide whether to smack her or not, and then lowered his arm. "Next time OK, just keep it shut," said Tony, holding his finger to his mouth. "Make yourself useful. Go to the corner shop and get me a bottle of whisky."

The Final Act

Sharon was about to say she had bought him one only yesterday, but decided to keep quiet and just do it. The time she spent away from him would do them both good.

"Anything else you want?"

"Eh yeah, get me some of those Dorito things."

"Sure." Sharon got up and went to get her new blonde wig, cap and coat. "See you in a bit then."

Tony didn't bother replying and heard the back door slam. He instantly took his phone out of his pocket and pressed a few numbers and spoke:

"Yeah it's me. What's happening? OK. So have you been over to Chelsea Harbour yet? Was the bitch in? That's good, I'll let you know when I want it done."

He smiled to himself: at last things were beginning to take shape. Tony went to the fridge and took out a Becks. It was ice cold and burnt his throat as he guzzled it. His mobile rang and he looked at the number.

"Yeah it's me," he answered.

"What, what's his fucking name?"

"An old boy. What the fuck is going on, where? Don't worry I'll sort it."

With that he clicked the mobile off and thought for just two seconds. He then put his thick wool coat and hat on and left through the back door. He jumped into the Mondeo and slammed his foot on the accelerator and roared away. He knew exactly where he was going and took the back streets where he could, and he had to be quick to make sure he got there in time.

It was about six odd miles during which he calmed down, knowing he had plenty of time. He was quickly into Catford and then passing the University Hospital, up past the railway station. He shot over a couple of roundabouts and then saw the sign to Rotherhithe: he was making good time. Southwark Park Road and he was almost there, turn right onto Jamaica Road, second left into Cathay Street one hundred yards and there it was: Samuel Smith's Angel Pub in Bermondsey Wall East. A nice little boozer right on the Thames and a bit secluded—perfect.

Tony parked up in Cathay Street and walked the short distance to the pub. He pulled his collar round tight, adjusted his glasses, and pulled his cap a little over his eyes, then he entered the red-and-brick decorated pub through the front door. He scanned the downstairs room and saw there were only two couples sitting at the bar. Tony made for the stairs and climbed to the upstairs lounge bar. He entered the lounge and glanced around and found what he was looking for. He went to the bar and ordered a pint of Carling lager. The man he was after was sitting on a bar stool with a pint and what looked like a local paper.

Tony turned to the man. "Hello mate. Quiet in here today, isn't it?"

The short fat overdressed man smiled. "Yes but you want to be here in the summer when it's hot. You can't move then."

Tony laughed and stuck his hand out. "I'm Andrew. How are you?"

The man shook hands with Tony. "Micky, yeah I'm good thanks. Now I've retired I lead a quiet life." He had nearly finished his pint.

"Let me get you a refill?" offered Tony.

"That's very kind of you indeed, thank you."

"It's nothing really."

Tony ordered the pint and they talked about how the local area had changed over the years and were soon chatting like old friends. After a short time Tony suddenly leant close to Micky and whispered in his ear:

"I understand you're looking for some information?"

Micky's demeanour changed, and he suddenly had a guarded expression. "And who told you that?"

"Suffice to say I've got friends. Look I may be able to help you, but what's in it for me?"

Micky looked at the man more closely: he looked like a typical Bermondsey Jack-the-lad type, out to make a few quid.

"I promise you if you have what I want, then I will make it very much worth your while," Micky said.

"I want a ton. Then I can give you an address for the person in question."

Micky could suddenly see the sea and the palm trees swaying in the breeze. He also had the money on him, which meant it could be sorted quickly.

"OK, tell me."

"Cash now?"

"Yes."

Tony looked around him. "Not in here, one pair of eyes is too many for me. Let's go outside where nobody can hear us or see you give me the money."

Micky didn't really want to go outside but he was so excited to think that he would soon be calling Jeff Swan and Karen Foster with the good news. He downed the last of his pint and smacked his lips. "Lovely. Let's go then."

Tony led the way, they came out of the pub and turned left. The younger man looked over at the car park, noticing that it was very quiet. They walked past the dead-end bollards and strolled to a couple of trees nearby. Tony went behind the tree and Micky followed.

Micky spoke first: "So what information do you have?"

"The money and I'll give you the address."

Micky looked around and regretted leaving the safety of the pub.

"OK." He took his wallet out of his inside pocket and opened it. He withdrew a wedge of notes and counted five twenty-pound ones and handed them to Tony. Micky smiled at him.

"So the address is?"

Tony smiled back. "Tony Bolton is living at 34, Brockley Road, Lewisham."

"You're sure about that?"

Tony laughed. "Yes I'm sure. But it won't do you any good."

Micky was worried. "What do you mean?"

Suddenly Tony's eyes were shining and Micky understood. He turned to run but was never going to make it. Tony grabbed his collar and held him tight.

"You fat cunt! Who are you snitching for?"

"I don't know what you mean, I—" Tony didn't give him time to finish, just lifted his arm and punched Micky straight on the nose. The crunch of breaking bone was horrible and blood gushed down his face and chin. Micky was in terrible pain and could barely speak, but he also knew he was in extreme danger. Tony was beginning to enjoy himself.

"I asked you a question! Who are you snitching for?"

Micky lifted his face as best he could and spluttered: "CID at Rotherhithe."

"Names?"

"Jeff Swan and Karen Foster."

Tony was thinking for a minute.

Suddenly he smelt urine, and when he looked at the man's crotch he saw the wet patch spread out down his trouser leg.

Tony shook his head. "You fat little cunt pissing yourself. So tell me, what have they got on me?"

"Nothing as far as I know, they just had a hunch you could still be in Bermondsey and asked me to make a few discreet enquiries. I won't tell anyone please I—"

Tony pushed him to the ground and stomped on his face. He repeated the action five or six times, grinding his heel into Micky's eyes, mouth and cheekbones. The informer was soon unrecognisable as a human being, and Tony did not stop there. Micky was whimpering and curling himself into the foetal position to try and protect himself. Tony could hear his sounds through the blood and gore. "Please, please," he begged.

Tony pulled back his leg and kicked Micky's head just as though it was a football. He kicked him and kicked him repeatedly, until he felt the skull break and still he continued to kick. Bits of Micky's face were now flying in all directions: teeth, an eye and pieces of skin.

"This'll teach you to fucking interfere, cunt!" And Tony jumped in the air and landed with both feet on what was left of Micky's face. He looked closely at Micky and decided without question that he was dead. Serve the cunt right, he thought.

Tony pulled Micky's fat little body by the legs and hid it as best he could in the shrubs and trees. He looked again at the car park and back to the pub, seeing that no one was around. He set off briskly back to his car, got in and was soon back on Jamaica Road, heading towards Lewisham. The old adrenalin had been flowing and he had never felt better.

The killer arrived back at Brockley Road where Sharon had been frantic. She had returned from the local shop to find Tony had gone out, leaving no note, so she had phoned him straight away, only to find out he had turned his phone off. She then thought, 'Have the police got him?', but then told herself not to be stupid: there would be coppers all over the house if that was the case. She concluded that he'd probably just gone for a drive or a walk and would be back soon. That had been two hours ago. She then heard the back door open and rushed to make sure it was Tony.

"Tony oh God, I've been worried sick." She flung her arms around him and hugged him tight. She eventually pulled away.

"Where have you been?" she asked him. "Thank God you're back."

"Get me a large whisky."

The peremptory way Tony had said it made Sharon go quickly to the cupboard and bring the bottle out, along with a glass. She began to open the bottle and noticed something red all over her hands, and she couldn't grasp what was happening.

"What's this Tony?" She turned to look at him and noticed blood on his hands, she looked at his clothes and noticed dark bloodstains, then she retched as she saw something that looked like skin and bone stuck to his trousers.

"Oh God what's happened! Are you injured? Jesus, Tony please, why do you have to be like this?" She was crying and then she noticed his shoes covered in more blood and gore. She sank to the floor and covered her face with her hands.

Tony had helped himself to the whisky and drank straight from the bottle; he'd never felt so alive. He stripped off all his clothes and heaped them in a pile on the floor, ready for washing.

"Sharon get me some more clothes," he ordered, then took another pull at the whisky.

"Sharon wait. Come here."

The Final Act

Tony pushed her against the kitchen table so that her arse was in the air, then he lifted her dress and pulled her pink lace knickers down. He entered her hard and heard her gasp as he pushed in as deep as he could.

"No Tony not now, not like this, the blood please," Sharon begged, aware that this was not how it was meant to be.

Tony's eyes were shining and there was no stopping him. He pushed and pushed until he shot his load. Sharon's dress fell back into place and she stumbled onto one of the kitchen chairs.

"I'm going to have a shower, so get something cooking eh? I'm hungry."

Sharon got up and stumbled towards the fridge...

CHAPTER 16

Jeff was in the CID office at Rotherhithe Nick. It was the end of October and the weather had turned really nasty. It was freezing cold but as yet no snow had fallen. A deputation from all officers in the station had requested that the heating be turned up, otherwise they would be unable to work.

The radiators were now so hot you daren't touch them, testament to the wonderful strength of group rebellion. It was ten minutes past eleven and Jeff was on his second latte of the day, and Karen had phoned to say she would be in late, arriving at about eleven fifteen.

Jeff had fallen in and out of love with Karen on too many occasions to count. He loved her sense of humour, her commitment to a cause and her commitment to him as her partner. He had felt this way for a long time and the huge problem now was that she had fallen in love with another woman: Chau. He sat at his desk imagining the sexual shenanigans that the two of them must be getting up to. He pictured them using a huge twelve-inch double-headed dildo and he felt a stirring in his crotch. He moved his hand down to readjust his manhood. He thought for a second and decided he would love to have sex with both of them at the same time.

The door was swept open.

"Jeff good morning how are you?" Karen was wearing one of her sexy short skirts and the kind of far-too-tight white shirts that Jeff loved.

Jeff didn't speak: this was like a different person, and he just gazed at her.

"Latte, very nice too," she said.

"I'll get—"

"No need to worry I'll get my own," said Karen as she waltzed off towards the door and disappeared into the corridor en route to the canteen.

Jeff shook his head, pondering on the mystery. Women? You could never figure them out. If he had known that Karen had had multiple orgasms about an hour ago he might have been able to understand her good mood. Chau was now the sexual master of the relationship and spent hours on the study of her favourite subject: sex.

Karen reappeared with a steaming hot cup of coffee. "I swear they put less and less coffee in these lattes. It's like drinking bloody hot milk," she said as she took a sip.

She sat down in her comfortable high-backed leather chair and put her feet up on the solid wooden desk. "You know what Jeff? Life is good." Karen was thinking she would willingly have another session of orgasms when she got home that night.

Jeff was slightly startled, for Karen hadn't been in such a good humour for a long time.

"So why the good mood today?"

"Oh God if I told you, you would be shocked beyond belief."

"I doubt that very much, but try me."

The phone on Karen's desk rang, and she answered it.

"Yes, Karen speaking."

Karen turned white and her eyes filled with tears. "Yes OK. Thank you. We are on our way now." She hung up and slowly turned to Jeff. "There's a body near the Angel pub. The publican says it's a man called Micky."

All pretence at holding it together disappeared and Karen slumped into her chair, crying.

"That was our fault," she protested. "He didn't deserve to die, oh God, shit, please, fuck! Why can't something go right for a change?"

Jeff came over and put his arm around Karen's shoulders. "I know you liked him."

"Jeff he could never have defended himself. Whoever did this is a monster, I swear I will catch this bastard, I promise that, if not I promise I will kill him."

"Put the face on Karen and let's get going."

Karen pulled herself together and got up from the chair.

"You drive Jeff, let's go."

They were soon on their way and arrived at the Angel pub in five minutes. Crime scene had already arrived and tape surrounded the pub and area where the body had been found.

Jeff and Karen introduced themselves to the crime-scene technicians, who knew of them anyway.

Karen went to see the body and pulled down the zipper on the black body bag. She braced herself for what she would see and it was a good job she had. Micky's face had been smashed to pieces and was like something you would see at a butcher's shop. She turned away and, just for a second, thought she should walk away from it all. *I don't need all this horror* she thought, *I need a sensible job*.

Karen spoke to the crime-scene technician close by: "So anything noteworthy?"

"On first examination he's been beaten to death and probably by someone kicking him. There are clear foot imprints all over the head and upper chest. It was a very nasty person who did this."

Karen looked at Jeff and could have screamed. She turned back to the technician. "Of course he's fucking nasty! Are you living in a dream world? The man has kicked Micky to death do you fucking understand that? Kicked him to fucking death!"

The crime-scene technician walked away from her. He had learned not to bring emotion into the job, knowing that if you did it would destroy you.

Karen had to go. "Jeff take over, I'm going. My head is spinning, I feel sick, I've got to go." Karen was as white as a sheet.

"Go home," he said. "We'll catch up in the morning."

She looked at Jeff with a deadpan expression. "I won't be in tomorrow and I may not come back at all. I can't cope with any more of this. Too many dead bodies. I'm taking the car."

Karen rushed to the car, got in and started it up. She checked her mirrors and pulled out into Cathay Street, straight up to Jamaica Road and knew she would be home in ten minutes.

The Final Act

"Chau it's me." Karen had dialled and was sobbing as she spoke into the hands-free phone. She couldn't put a whole sentence together. "I'm on my way home."

Chau was surprised and concerned. "What's happened? You alright? You not hurt?"

"No not me." She thought of Micky's face and shuddered. "I'll be home in a few minutes." Karen clicked the phone off and sped up, aware that she had to change her clothes and shower, for the metallic smell of blood, the body parts, urine, it was still with her, lingering.

Karen parked up and dragged herself to the front of the house, she turned the key and pushed open the communal door. Chau came out of the flat door and rushed into Karen's arms. "What's wrong? Don't worry let's go."

Chau led her into the flat. Karen was in a daze and could not speak.

"Come sit down."

"Dead body. Face, smashed to pieces." The crying and sobbing started afresh. Karen couldn't control it and she shuddered with terror as she continued to remember the face. Chau led Karen into their bedroom and sat her on the bed. She took off her shoes, then her dark blue jacket and then her matching trousers. She pulled back the duvet and told Karen to get in. Karen crawled into the bed, Chau got in next to her and took her in her arms.

"Don't worry Miss Karen I will look after you, you need to rest, you no go back to work, that place horrible, job horrible, dead people very horrible."

Karen whispered: "I want a shower."

"Don't worry, you sleep. Then I take shower with you and wash all bad away, you know Chau take care of you."

With that Karen managed to fall asleep in Chau's arms.

After five minutes Chau slipped out of the bed and pulled the duvet up to Karen's neck, she then went into the lounge and picked up her phone, and she pressed a fast dial and it rang at the other end.

"CID Rotherhithe," was the answer.

"Is that Jeff speaking?"

"Yes it is."

"You bastard! You fucking bastard! Karen ill, very ill, she in bed, she not coming back to work, you all fuck off, she no coming back, you understand?"

"Chau I don't know what to say. Is Karen OK?" Jeff protested. "You know I care about her, she has been my partner for a long time."

Chau was incensed. "You no see her again Jeff, you no good for Miss Karen you go fuck yourself!" And with that she pressed the 'end call' button.

At Rotherhithe Nick Jeff stood still, phone in hand. Shit, he thought, what a mess. Karen had hit the ropes big time and he wasn't surprised she needed a good rest after all the killings and bloodshed she had dealt with over the past few months. He thought for a couple more minutes and then moved towards Michael's office.

CHAPTER 17

"Don't worry we have plenty of time," Richard said. He was wearing 'smart casual' clothes for travelling and was driving a silver Ford Focus rented from Hertz. Julie was also dressed casually. Sitting in the front passenger seat, she kept looking at her watch and checking with Richard that they would make it in time to catch the flight.

Julie had never been on a plane and was so excited at having a weekend in Belfast that she was almost hyperventilating. The flight was leaving Gatwick at eight-twenty and arriving at Belfast International Airport at nine-forty-five.

It wasn't far. They had already paid their toll and crossed the Dartford Bridge, and were fast approaching the turn-off from the M25 for the M23, which would take them straight down to Gatwick. It was six-fifty-five, they would get to the North Terminal at about seven-fifteen.

"So are you looking forward to the weekend?" he asked.

Julie was all smiles. "Never looked forward to anything so much in all my life."

Richard had been there, done it and got several of the tee shirts. He was surprised that it took so little to get someone so excited, he was also happy about taking Julie away, as it would be a mini break and he was already looking forward to some great sweaty, dirty sex.

They passed the South Terminal on the left as they crossed the last but one roundabout.

"How much further then?" Julie asked.

"In five minutes we will be parked up in the short-stay car park and two minutes after that we will be in the Terminal."

Julie suddenly went all serious. "You think the err, plane will be alright?"

"What do you mean?"

"You know, that it's not going to crash or fall into the sea or anything?"

"Don't worry. You're more likely to be hit by a flying elephant than be in a plane crash." Richard laughed but was also conscious that it was Julie's first flight and she might be very nervous.

Richard took his parking ticket from the machine and ten seconds later pulled into a space on the ground floor, right in front of the Terminal entrance.

"This place is huge," said Julie as she surveyed the Terminal buildings.

Richard grabbed the two small suitcases from the boot, locked the car and they made their way across the road into the North Terminal building.

Julie was taking in all the sights for the first time, since she had never been in an airport before.

"Where are the planes then?" she asked innocently.

"A long way from here believe me. Come on we'll go through security now and find some breakfast. I'm starving."

They found the lifts and took one to 'Departures' on the second floor. They came out of the lift and Richard looked around and saw the sign to Departures. There was no booking in, since Richard had done that online and had two e-tickets.

The couple showed their boarding passes to a man who looked as though he was half asleep and then moved on to the security checks. It was suddenly a lot busier with five baggage queues. Richard headed to what he thought was the smallest. He went first so that Julie could copy his procedure: suitcase onto the conveyor belt, jacket off, belt off, both placed in a plastic tray, followed by his watch, coins and mobile. He then walked through the metal detector, there was no beep, and he was ushered through with no body search. He went to the small conveyor belt to pick up his belongings and glanced back to see how Julie was doing. Julie was also through and, smiling like a Cheshire cat, she snuggled up to Richard.

"Very exciting isn't it?"

"Yeah, let's go—I can smell breakfast from here," said Richard, with raised eyebrows.

They moved through the short corridor and entered what Julie thought was Aladdin's shopping centre.

"Wow look at this!" Julie could not believe what she was seeing: Harrods, Ted Baker, Caviar and Champagne Bar. She looked up and saw the restaurants and shook her head, saying, "Incredible!"

The Final Act

Richard grabbed her arm and headed straight to the escalator to go up to where all the food outlets were. They passed a fantastic looking Mercedes car, which apparently you could win by buying a ticket.

"Let's get a—" shouted Julie, but Richard was already past and nearing the escalator. Julie quickened her pace and caught up.

"Fantastic place," she enthused. "I must buy something."

"After we've eaten, OK?"

They got to the top and looked around. Jamie Oliver's restaurant and the Sushi Bar were both closed, the Pret A Manger was busy on the corner, so Richard went straight in and started looking in the fridges.

"This is no good. I want something hot."

A 'Pret' worker just happened to be passing and heard and directed them to the hot-food display counter. Richard got two bacon rolls while Julie was almost too excited to eat, but in the end chose a sausage roll.

"Hardly a full English but I suppose it will do for now," said Richard with a sneer. They grabbed two high chairs at the counter that overlooked the concourse. Richard wolfed his butties and coffee and wiped down his mouth with a napkin and looked at his watch. It was seven-fifty and they had thirty minutes before take-off.

"Come on, let's go," Richard said as he got up.

"I haven't finished."

"Do you want to miss the flight?"

Julie jumped up, shoving the last of the sausage roll into her mouth. Richard rushed off to view the departure information boards for Belfast flight EZY818 departing at eight-twenty. The board showed it was at Gate 24. Richard had noticed where it was on the way in and headed back to the escalator to go down. They were soon marching along a massive long corridor to Gate 24 prior to boarding the plane. Julie was looking out of the huge windows and saw a real-life plane for the first time.

"Richard there's a plane, it's EasyJet," she said.

"Yes it's a plane," he said, shaking his head.

They arrived at Gate 24 and joined the queue that had formed to board. They showed their boarding passes again and were told to enter the rear of the aircraft, they then went down some stairs out through a double door and onto the tarmac. Julie was once again looking all around and her eyes settled on the motionless EasyJet plane that was a hundred yards away. They followed the people heading towards the rear of the aircraft and climbed up the steep steps into the body of the plane.

"Boarding passes please?" asked the flight attendant.

Richard showed him the tickets.

"16 A and B just up on the left-hand side," said the attendant. "Thank you."

Richard led the way through the cabin and soon saw the seats, he turned to Julie, saying, "Do you want the window seat?"

Julie swallowed and couldn't answer. Richard stared at her for a second.

"You get in first and have the window," he reassured her. "You won't see much but it's good at take-off and landing." Julie did as she was told whilst wondering how this huge metal plane was ever going to get up in the sky.

They made themselves comfortable and put on their seat belts, Richard having to help Julie with hers, as her hands were shaking.

"Are you alright?" he asked.

"'Course I am. It's a big plane isn't it?"

Richard was very relaxed. "Not really there's a lot that are bigger."

Julie couldn't imagine anything bigger than this. She glanced at the three seats on each side of the gangway—it was huge!

The seats filled up, and they sat through the safety demonstration, which left Julie terrified, especially when they brought out the life jacket to use in case they crashed into the sea. The loudspeaker welcomed everybody on board and informed them they would be taking off in about five minutes' time.

Julie learnt over and whispered to Richard: "I can't swim."

Richard just looked at her and then smiled. "Don't worry everything will be fine, I promise."

Suddenly the plane jumped and moved slowly forward. Julie looked out of the window and saw they were moving towards what looked like a huge long runway. She sat back and decided that she would say a prayer: 'Dear lord, please make this thing fly and not crash into the sea, thank you.' The plane had manoeuvred to the main runway and stopped. Julie looked round to see if anyone was concerned but nobody was paying any attention. The plane just remained motionless. The tannoy system crackled: "We are in a queue and should be taking off in hopefully two or three minutes."

Julie swallowed and coughed at the same time. She turned to Richard and linked her arm in his and prayed again. Ten seconds later the engines roared and Julie was so scared she thought she might wet herself. The plane taxied down the runway and stopped again. *Jesus is this never going to end?* Julie thought.

Then it happened: the engines roared and the plane shot off at a pace down the runway, it was getting faster and faster, and then she felt it lift off. She looked out of the window as the plane left the ground and headed up into the sky. She quickly shut her eyes and was praying for the third time when she suddenly heard a rumbling coming from underneath the plane. She squeezed Richard's arm so hard he pushed her away, saying, "Calm down, it will be alright."

"That noise what is it?"

"It's the undercarriage coming back up—that's the wheels to you."

"God I thought something was wrong."

"You can open your eyes now."

Julie did so and looked out of the window, but all she could see was clouds. She looked around and everything seemed alright.

"Do you want some coffee?" Richard asked kindly.

"Coffee? Yes that would be very nice, thank you."

Julie took a deep breath and relaxed, however at that precise time the plane hit some turbulence and dropped suddenly. Julie let out a little scream as she thought the plane could be crashing. It came back up again and then settled. Julie turned to Richard, saying, "I'm not sure I'll get used to this flying."

"Relax, the coffee will chill you. Do you want a muffin to go with it?"

"No thanks."

The plane journey was uneventful and they were in the air for one hour five minutes, when the tannoy again burst into life: "We are beginning our descent to land and should be on the ground at nine-forty-four. The temperature is 16 degrees and the weather is very lovely, we thank you for flying EasyJet and look forward to seeing you again soon. We wish you a safe and pleasant onward journey, good morning."

Julie had ear pain on the landing but she was so happy to still be alive that she forgot about it instantly. They climbed down the steps at the rear of the plane and made their way walking to the Terminal entrance. They passed through the baggage pick-up and walked straight into the Terminal, no passport checks, and no luggage checks, nothing. They walked down the final corridor and through the double doors into vast sunlit car parks.

A uniformed chauffeur was standing next to a beautiful immaculately shining grey Rolls Royce Phantom. Richard strode to the Rolls and spoke to the chauffeur. "I'm assuming you are from the Merchant Hotel?"

The chauffeur straightened himself up. "And I take it you are Mr Philips, sir?"

"Yes I am."

The chauffeur took the two cases and placed them by the boot, then he opened the rear passenger door.

"Would Madam like to enter?"

Julie was still in shock and was staring at the chauffeur, so Richard gently nudged her towards the door. She got in and took in the smell of leather and the feel of a very luxurious car. Richard got in after her and smiled. "Not bad eh?"

"If this is the car, what is the hotel like?"

Richard held up his hand splaying out the five fingers and whispered, "Five star all the way baby."

The chauffeur got behind the wheel. "Are you ready to proceed sir?"

"Yes we are ready thank you, drive on."

The Phantom glided silently away from the Terminal building and headed towards the five-star Merchant hotel in Belfast city centre.

The hotel was in Skipper Street and it took exactly thirty minutes to drive the eighteen miles into Belfast and arrive. The front of the building was absolutely majestic, and apparently the place was originally the headquarters of the Ulster Bank before having a major extension built in 2010. The building, constructed using Giffnock sandstone, was elegant, substantial and had the appearance of being very prosperous, making it perfect for a five-star hotel.

The Phantom's door was opened by a uniformed concierge and Richard and Julie were escorted up the glorious steps to the hotel entrance. They entered and were ushered to the very elegant black sophisticated looking reception desk.

"Good morning sir and welcome to the Merchant," said the receptionist.

"Thank you, it's good to be here," Richard replied.

"This is your key card. Steve will show you to your room, enjoy your stay with us here at the Merchant."

Steve was a very well-dressed and well-groomed concierge, who took their bags and led them to the lifts. Julie was just speechless, awestruck by the fabulous luxury and kept looking at all the stunning décor, furniture and bowl after bowl of beautiful flowers.

"The suite you have booked is lovely and Madam will particularly enjoy the luxurious bathroom," Steve said as he smiled at Julie, who smiled back inanely, unable even to string a few simple words together. The lift was so quiet they did not even realise it was moving until the door opened. They followed Steve down the corridor, enjoying the extra thick carpet which made it feel as if they were walking on air. They reached the room and Steve swiped the card and stood back for Richard and Julie to enter. Richard let Julie go in first and she nearly died on the spot.

She spoke softly to herself: "Oh my God!" as she scanned the suite. There was a huge bed at the end, a lounge, and she almost ran to the bathroom and gasped when she saw the luxurious stand-alone bath. Richard strolled in and said in a matter-of-fact way:

"Nice, very nice."

"I'm glad you like it sir, shall I open the Veuve Cliquot champagne?"

The Final Act

"Yes please." Richard forgot that he had ordered champagne in the suite on arrival.

"Julie, champagne."

Julie skipped over to Richard and planted a big kiss on his cheek, and whispered into his ear: "This is fantastic, I love it!"

Richard was delighted to see Julie looking so happy, and he knew she would repay him later with plenty of great sex. Richard gave Steve a crisp fresh tenner off a huge wedge he had in his inside pocket and the concierge disappeared, telling them to 'Please call for anything you require'. Richard and Julie sat down on the luxurious sofa and looked at each other. They burst out laughing and clinked champagne glasses.

Richard finally stopped laughing. "This is the life and long may it continue."

"Amen to that," said Julie as she went to get the bottle for refills.

They finished the champagne and Julie was a little tipsy, since it was very early in the morning, and she normally didn't drink until later. Julie spent the next half an hour studying the literature on the spa and gym. The gym didn't hold much attraction for her but being pampered in the spa was right up her street. She studied the list.

"Richard, can I book a couple of treatments in the spa?" she asked.

"Of course whatever you want eh? Make it for lunchtime tomorrow, as I have a small bit of business to attend to."

Julie was immediately concerned. "And how long will that take?"

"Couple of hours max, I promise."

"I hope that's all."

Julie didn't hear a response so went back to looking at the list of treatments. She took the Merchant hotel pen that was provided and started to tick off the ones she wanted. The Caviar and Champagne Facial sounded too good to be true so she ticked that, Champagne Nails got another tick, as did a 'full body massage', 'steam room', 'sauna' and 'hydro pools'. She then worried how long all the treatments would take but decided to book them anyway. She rang the spa and told them what she wanted and gave her room number. It would be easy to spend a fortune in a place like this, she thought. It was soon lunchtime, and Richard was starving as usual. He grabbed Julie into his arms.

"So do you want to start with more champagne or shall we visit the cocktail bar?"

"Oh God such tough choices, eh? More champagne please."

"Great it's called the Veuve Cliquot Champagne Lounge, bloody hell it's posh here isn't it?"

They went down to the Champagne Lounge and Julie again was astonished at the opulence and beauty of the décor. There were decadent black velvet sofas sitting on rich thick Veuve Cliquot bespoke carpets. They ordered another bottle of champagne and relaxed into the sumptuous chairs.

"Where are you going tomorrow then?" Julie asked.

Richard shook his head and tapped his nose. The message was clear: don't ask any more questions. Julie knew when to keep quiet or change the subject.

"I'm having a full body massage tomorrow," she told him. "I bet you'd like one of those."

"Well we don't have anything planned for this afternoon so…"

Julie sipped at her Champagne. "Better not drink too much then, had we?"

They finished the bottle of champagne and made their way to the Cloth Ear, which was the public bar of the hotel. They fancied something simple and would have something special in the evening. It was a busy lively bar with lots of laughter and noise. Richard grabbed a menu and checked through what was available.

"I'm starving," Julie told him. "Any fish-and-chips?"

"As it happens yes." He laughed. "Listen to this: beer-battered haddock, porta-something scampi, lemon mayonnaise and a pea salad, now that's what I call fish-and-chips."

"I'll have it," she jumped in.

"For me, yeah a nice chicken curry with mango, coriander, Himalayan aged basmati rice and chapatti bread, sounds fantastic, but what the fuck is Himalayan aged basmati rice?"

The Final Act

They ordered their food, and Richard had a pint of lager while Julie had a large Pinot Grigio. Julie was once again thinking of Richard disappearing at lunchtime on the following day, which was Saturday.

"Where did you say you were going tomorrow?" she asked.

Richard gave her an 'Are you trying to be funny' look. "I never told you where I was going, so I'm only going to say this once more. Keep your fucking nose out of it. Why do you women always want to stick your fucking nose in where it's not wanted?" Richard moved his face close to hers. "Keep the fuck out of it!"

"I get the message. I'm sorry, I was just concerned."

"Well don't fucking bother, just enjoy your fish-and-chips." And with that he tucked into his curry with relish.

They had a couple of further drinks and then went back up to their room. Richard had been admiring Julie's arse when they got in the lift and he was looking forward to getting a hand on each of the cheeks. They entered the room and Julie knew exactly what was coming.

"Just hang on a minute—I've got something special for you," Julie told him.

Richard was all ears.

"Lie on the bed and I'll be back in a minute."

Julie took a small bag from the floor on the side of the bed and made for the bathroom. She entered, removed her shoes and lifted her dress over her head. Next she reached back and undid her bra strap, releasing her large firm breasts. She then pulled down her black lacy knickers and stood in front of the near full-length mirror. She had shaped her pubic hair into a nice Mohican and she loved her nipples as they started to harden at the thought of Richard's huge cock entering her various orifices. Richard had tried to push his huge cock into Julie's anus before but up to now she had resisted. It was not that she didn't like anal but it was the last thing she had to give away and wanted to keep it for a special occasion, and that day had finally come. Julie was going to thank Richard for this luxury by letting him do whatever he wanted to her and in a way she was looking forward to giving her arse to him.

She opened the bag and pulled out a selection of brand new lacy white underwear. She pulled the briefs on first, knickers that looked so sexy they turned *her* on, so God knew what they would do to Richard. Next was the white bra to match the knickers, then the pièce de résistance: the very sexy white stockings and garter belt. She pulled them on slowly, luxuriating in the silk feel that she knew would have Richard dribbling. She buttoned them to the garter and looked in the mirror again, thinking of what she would do as she smiled, contemplating getting Richard's huge cock in her mouth.

She could feel her pussy actually getting wet even now. She dabbed her 'Lovely' perfume on her breasts and round her pussy and behind her ears. It was time. She opened the bathroom door and presented herself for anal fucking. She stepped into the room and walked sexily towards the bed, but when she got close, her mouth fell open. He was asleep, fucking well asleep! Here she was, ready to take it up the arse and he was asleep!

"Fuck, Fuck, Fuck!" she said.

Julie thought for a second and then felt a wave of tiredness envelop her, and she lay down next to Richard and was asleep in seconds; her last thought was that he could have her arse when he woke up.

Much later they were having breakfast in the restaurant. Richard had gone for the Full English, while Julie had a poached egg on toast. They had slept through the night and she had not as yet given her arse to Richard. The couple felt that the tiredness was due to the travelling, and of course the amount of booze they had consumed, which was huge. Julie was looking forward to her spa treatments, and Richard was going to some sort of big secret meeting.

It was eleven o'clock and they were on their third coffee of the morning. The staff were so attentive it was becoming tiresome.

"More coffee for you sir?" asked the waiter.

"No and don't come back here again." Richard gave him a hard stare that almost had him wetting himself.

"Yes sir, of course not."

"Fucking hell can't they leave us alone for a minute?" he snapped to Julie.

"He's only doing his job," she said.

"Well let him fucking well do it somewhere else." Richard glared at the table. "I'm not happy Julie."

"Why's that my darling?"

Richard gave her a bit of a hard look, not linking the soppy sentimental chat. "Because I wanted your arse so much and then I fell asleep."

Julie gave him a huge smile. "Don't worry. You're going to fuck my arse big time tonight."

Richard felt an erection straight away. He was going to have her arse tonight or there would be trouble for someone. They went back to their luxurious suite and chatted for half an hour, Julie then went off for her spa treatments, while Richard ordered a taxi to take him to some pub restaurant called Robbie Calhoun's in Queensway, Lisburn. The taxi arrived at the hotel and they set off for Calhoun's.

Twenty minutes later the taxi pulled into a large car park and Richard saw the pub restaurant, which seemed like a big place. He got out of the taxi, paid the driver, and strode through the main entrance into the pub. The lighting was not very bright and the dark wood furniture made it even more uninviting. There was a huge bar to the side and a barmaid spoke to him in a thick Irish accent:

"Were you looking for lunch?" she asked.

Richard strained his ears trying to understand and thought he caught the gist of what she had said. "Yes, the restaurant please."

The barmaid pointed. "Up the stairs and round the corner."

Richard smiled at the young girl, noticing her ample breasts almost spilling out of a white shirt. "Thank you," he answered as he wondered how big the nipples were and what they would feel like.

He followed the directions and was surprised when he turned the corner to be confronted by a huge restaurant and bar area. There were very few diners and he was sure the man he was looking for was not there yet. A waitress asked him if he wanted a table, he said yes but that he was waiting for someone.

Richard sat by the window which looked out onto another large car park. He had a pint of Guinness while he waited and felt the adrenalin kick in as it always did when things were getting interesting. He kept looking out of the window and at his watch. The meet was due to take place at midday and it was ten to twelve. He sat back and relaxed, watching the restaurant entrance and the car park. He was looking at the entrance when a nondescript young man appeared there and scanned the restaurant. He made eye contact with Richard and then disappeared as quickly as he had appeared. A minute later a middle-aged man strolled into the room and made straight for Richard's table. He held his hand out and spoke:

"Richard? Very pleased to see you. How's it going then?"

"Fine thanks Patrick," he replied. "How did you know it was me?"

"The taxi driver is one of mine, and I know everything that goes on around here believe me."

"Tony sends his regards."

Patrick sat down. "And how is Tony?"

"Very well."

"I heard he's out and about again."

The waitress delivered a whisky for Patrick. "Yeah, that's right," Richard replied.

"Let's order lunch and then get down to the nitty gritty. They do a very nice pork sausages with champ and cabbage—it's really very good."

Richard wasn't bothered what he had to eat. "Great I'll have that."

Patrick ordered the lunch and refill drinks.

"So you and Tony need some help," Patrick began the discussion. "Did he tell you about our last gig?"

"Yeah he did. Fucking bazooka job on the Serco van. Brilliant, fucking brilliant."

"So you need something similar?"

"We need a couple of guys who could come over for a few days and help us out with a small problem."

"And I'm thinking that small problem would be Tony's brother Paul?"

This bloke knows everything thought Richard. "Yes Paul Bolton. He's not just Tony's problem, he's mine as well."

"As I told Tony I'm semi-retired but I have already sorted two great lads who'll come over and give you a hand."

The steaming plates of food arrived and they both tucked in.

Richard didn't want to appear to be stupid but he wasn't sure how it all worked. "So what about equipment?"

"The boys will come over, normally by plane, and the equipment will come by a totally different route that you don't need to worry yourself about."

Richard held up his hands, saying: "I don't need to know."

"To be sure this champ is delicious," said Patrick with a big smile on his face.

They finished lunch and the deal was done.

CHAPTER 18

"The soup is good for you, if you want get well you have to eat your soup," Chau said.

Karen was sitting up in bed surrounded by fruit, flowers get-well cards and her much loved bottles of fresh orange juice. Most of it had arrived from Jeff and colleagues at Rotherhithe Nick. Chau was feeding her which she had done since Karen came back from the murder at the Angel pub. The doctor had said Karen needed total rest for at least a month as she had had some kind of nervous breakdown. Chau refilled the spoon with home-made chicken soup, which was one of Karen's favourites, and positioned it in front of her mouth.

"Chuff chuff here come train, open tunnel please."

Karen laughed at the utterly ridiculous child-like language from Chau.

"See you laughing, you getting much better Miss Karen."

"Why wouldn't I get better with all this fantastic care I'm getting? Chau I really mean it, thank you so much."

"It is nothing, you know I love you, so it is pleasure for me look after you."

The soup was finished.

"Now you try sleep for a bit while I go do some shopping."

Karen lay back and closed her eyes and she was soon asleep.

Chau looked in on her before leaving and pulled the duvet up and tucked her in. She looked down at Karen and reflected on her past year.

Karen's girlfriend had been born in Beijing, the capital city of China. She had worked diligently through school and realised her dream of enrolling at Tsinghua University. She had then worked even harder and left with a first class degree in World Economics. The plan had then been to travel as much as she could on limited resources.

When she had seen the advert for nannies to work in London she thought it was the answer to her problem: work abroad and earn some money at the same time. She contacted the European recruitment company and everything seemed very well organised, her parents were worried but succumbed to their

The Final Act

daughter's charms and perseverance. Finally Chau received an Air China one-way ticket to Heathrow, London. She sat and stared at that ticket for fully an hour: it represented the culmination of childhood dreams, to travel, to see the world and she was starting with one of the most famous cities in the world.

Chau had then had to wait two weeks until her flight and it was the longest two weeks of her life. Finally the day came and her parents took her to the airport to see her off. It was Chau's first flight and was an incredible experience in itself. London was 5,053 miles from Beijing and even with the diversion of all the meals and snacks the flight lasted a long eleven hours. A tired worn out Chau landed at Heathrow in the early evening. She collected her luggage and had been told she would be met by someone outside arrivals with a board with her name on it. She came through onto the concourse and just as they had said, there were two men there, one holding a name board. The men were not quite what she had expected, for they were wearing black leather jackets and scruffy denim jeans. She went across to them immediately and they took her case and escorted her to a silver Range Rover car in the short-stay car park.

They put the cases in the boot and opened the back passenger door, and one of them had to help Chau in as it was a big step up. The man got in with Chau and asked her for her passport, Chau had queried why they wanted it and the man said he needed to check that the visa was in order. She handed it over to him and he put it in his inside pocket. The car pulled out of the car park and they were supposed to be on their way to a hotel, where she would stay until she was be introduced to the family who'd be employing her. Chau asked when she would get her passport back but the man just ignored her. Chau then took more of an interest in the two men and that was when she began to worry. She asked where they were going and the men did not reply. She asked what the hotel was called and the man beside her shouted at her.

"Shut the fuck up Chinkey," he yelled, and pretended to give her a slap with his hand. Chau was now terrified and began to panic.

"Where you taking me? I want know?" she asked him desperately.

He grabbed her arm and squeezed very hard, knowing how painful it would be. "I told you fucking keep it shut!"

Chau was shaking inside and almost peed herself. The car drove on for about an hour and then the driver slowed down, entered through some electric gates and pulled up in front of a large detached house. Chau calmed down slightly as

The Final Act

she assumed it must be the home of the family she was supposed to join, even though they had said she would be in a hotel for a couple of days. The men got out of the car and motioned her to follow. They went to the front door and it opened to reveal a large well-dressed man in his forties, who was obviously in charge.

It was Ted Frost. Chau had arrived at the brothel in Peckham.

Ted looked at Chau and smiled. Chau did not smile back.

After they had talked for a short time one of the men who had brought her to the house took her arm and guided her into the hallway and then up some stairs to the first floor. As they were climbing up, a scantily clad young girl came down the stairs and gave Chau a perfunctory look. Chau may not have been worldly wise but she was beginning to understand: there was no nannie job, she was here for some other reason, and after seeing the young girl with hardly any clothes on, she began to guess what it was.

She pulled away from the man and ran down the stairs towards the front door, grabbed the handle and turned but it would not open. The man sauntered back down the stairs and stood three feet from her. He crocked his finger, gesticulating for her to move towards him, and she had no choice but to do so. And as she got close he lifted his hand and slapped her hard across the face. The force of the blow sent her flying and she landed in a heap on the floor.

"Don't ever fucking do that again, do you understand?"

The man's face was an inch from hers and his breath stank of garlic, tobacco and whisky. Chau nodded—she was terrified beyond belief. They went back up the plush red-carpeted stairs and the man pushed her into a small hotel-like bedroom and shut the door. Chau heard the key turn in the lock so she knew she was trapped. She sat on the bed and the tears flowed, she was worried sick at what she had got herself into and prayed that she could be back in Beijing. Chau didn't sleep well at first but slumber had taken hold finally, when she heard the key in the lock turn. She knew the moment of truth was not far away. A young girl opened the door and spoke to her:

"I'm Tracy," the newcomer said. "Come and have some breakfast luv."

Chau couldn't move. She was surprised and shocked, for she had been expecting to see one of the thuggish men yet here was a young elfin-like girl in stripy pyjamas. She jumped out of bed and ran to the girl and held her hand.

Tracy seemed to understand and squeezed hers tightly in return and gave her a lovely smile.

The girls skipped down the stairs, and Tracy led them to the back of the house where they ended up in a large kitchen/breakfast room. There were several girls sitting at a large table drinking coffee and eating toast and crumpets. Chau took a great interest in them: some were old, some very young, some looked like they had seen better days and some seemed too young to be there. This was the precise moment that Chau knew she was in a brothel. The various women nodded at her or gave a gruff 'Hi' or 'Hello darling'. Tracy got her some coffee and toast and they sat at two spare chairs at the end of the table. Chau found she was hungry and tucked into the toast, adding spoonfuls of Robertson's thick-cut orange marmalade. The girls were chatting away and then it went very quiet. The man who had answered the door the night before had entered the breakfast room.

He exuded confidence and looked at the girls in turn, his eye finally resting on Chau; he pointed at her, leaving her in no doubt as to who he was addressing.

"You come to my office now," he said, and then turned round and strode out. Tracy pushed Chau, pointing for her to follow the man. The Chinese girl refused to move and grabbed Tracy's arm and would not let go. Tracy started to get annoyed.

"You'll get me in trouble. Go to the office," Tracy snapped.

Two seconds later one of the thugs charged into the room and got Chau round the throat, while the other girls moved away as far as they could. The man dragged her out of the room as Chau began to cry and kick her legs. They arrived at Ted Frost's office and the man carried Chau in and dumped her in a chair in front of Ted's huge mahogany desk.

"You let me go, bastard!" screamed Chau.

Ted Frost nodded to the thug.

The man took hold of Chau's hair and twisted it tight, and then he hit her in the mouth with the back of his hand. He repeated the action twice before Ted nodded that it was enough. Chau was groggy and bleeding heavily from her mouth and nose. Ted Frost spoke:

The Final Act

"You will do as you are told without any question. If you do that then you will be alright and we will look after you. If you do not, my friends here will make you suffer until you change your mind."

Ted Frost told the thug to take Chau back to her room.

Once there, Chau was terrified: she was alone with no possible way of escape. The door opened and Tracy slipped in.

"How did you get in?" Chau spluttered.

"We made some keys—it's easy to distract the minders." And she cupped her ample breasts and Chau got the idea.

"Tracy what you do here?"

"Can't hide it darling. This is a brothel. Men come here for pleasure and we provide it."

Chau's worst fears were confirmed. "Me no do it! Me no do it!" she said it for a third time and screamed it out loud at nobody in particular "ME NO DO IT!"

Tracy put her arm round Chau's shoulders. "Listen if you don't do as they say they will…"

Chau looked up. "What will they do?"

"I can't say for certain but they will beat you and … worse."

"You mean they will…?" Chau couldn't say the words but she knew they would very possibly rape her.

Tracy put on her best smile. "It's better to do what they say. Nobody knows you're here, they can do what they want with you—even kill you."

As soon as Chau heard that she started crying even more. "God help me!" she repeated over and over again.

"I've got to go before I get caught." Tracy hugged Chau and whispered in her ear. "You get used to it, it's not that bad, and who knows? At some time you may get out."

"Get out, how get out? Me prisoner, no passport, no money not good at English me stuck! No way out!" Tracy kissed Chau on the cheek and left the room and re-locked the door. Chau curled up on the bed and tried to sleep. She was woken by a man shaking her and telling her to get moving. She got off the bed and stood waiting. Another girl entered the room—she was older and looked like she had been 'working' for some time. The woman nodded at the minder and he left, closing the door behind him.

"My names Sabrina and I'm going to show you the ropes."

Chau did not understand. "What is ropes please?"

Sabrina laughed. "It means I am to show you what we do here and get you ready for work."

"Ready for work no no no, me no working." Chau was shaking her head as if to emphasize her determination.

"Listen honey, tonight you just watch, listen and learn, you don't have to do anything, OK?"

"No point. Me not working. Finished. Not working, you understand?"

"Hun you don't understand. They will beat you and rape you and give you drugs. Please, for your own good, do as they tell you."

Although tiny in stature Chau had a strong and resolute belief in Buddhism which gave her great strength of mind. She got back on the bed, tucked her feet under her thighs and sat with a straight back and began to meditate.

Sabrina knew what would happen the minute she reported that the girl was not getting ready for work.

"Please Chau, please!" Sabrina was getting ready to beg but she could see it would be a waste of time: the girl was in another world. She shook her head, turned, opened the door and left the room.

Chau had gone to another world away from brothels and rape and drugs. She was in a much higher place but it didn't help when she felt her arm pulled and she hit the floor with a crash. She looked up at the two Serbian minders who had brought her to the brothel.

"Last chance, you get ready for work."

Chau didn't answer. She closed her eyes and got ready for the assault that was surely to follow as night follows day. They beat her mercilessly from head to toe, they used their fists and small hard truncheons. When it was over Chau had bruises over the majority of her body. They had been careful not to break any bones, but the swelling and bruising would take days to disappear. Chau had felt some pain but after the initial onslaught was half unconscious as the beating continued. The last feeling she had was of being thrown onto her bed.

She awoke a day later in extreme discomfort and pain, and when she tried to move, her whole body was in rebellion. She opened her eyes and found out that she could only see a little through her left eye. She opened her mouth and the sourness and pain was intense. Then she lay for what seemed an eternity and then was aware of someone else in the room. A hand touched her cheek gently and she felt warm breath on her ear.

"Chau we're here for you," said a woman's voice. "It's Sabrina and Tracy."

Chau felt a touch of juice on her lips—it was delicious.

Tears were rolling down Chau's cheeks. "Thank you so much," she whispered.

She felt a damp cloth being gently rubbed over her face and it made her feel a tiny bit more human. After that her new friends crept in as often as possible to give Chau food and water. She was getting better but it was three weeks before the swelling and the black-yellow colour around her eyes had almost disappeared. Ted Frost had been in to see her and told her again he had paid good money for her and he expected a return on his investment, and when he said work she had to do so, or she would suffer.

The dreaded time had come round again. Chau was eating in the breakfast room when she was called to the office to see Ted Frost. The other girls looked at each other, as if they were imploring God to make Chau change her mind and work like the rest of them. Chau entered the office and immediately saw the two Serbian animals that pretended to be men. Ted Frost was behind his desk and he pointed at a chair in front of it, which Chau sat on.

"So, Chau, I hope you have come to your senses," he began. "Are you ready to work?"

Chau waited two seconds and then said very slowly and deliberately: "Me cook, me clean, me wash clothes. But me no work what you want."

Ted Frost just stared at her and then looked at the Serbs and nodded.

The two men grabbed an arm each and frogmarched Chau back up the stairs to her room. Sabrina and Tracy were peeping round the breakfast room door and knew what was going to happen next.

Chau was thrown onto the bed and one of the two brutes spoke: "You going to work?"

"No."

The Serb moved quickly and grabbed her pyjama trousers and pulled them half down. Chau fought back and kicked out at his face, but he punched her legs and eventually pulled the pyjamas away. The other man had got hold of her top and he ripped it to shreds and threw it on the floor. Chau was cowering on the bed as the two huge men surveyed the tiny, thin, breast-less but cute Chinese girl. Chau shouted loudly. "Me having period! Lot blood, not good!"

The larger of the two thugs laughed. "We don't give a shit," and so saying he looked at his partner and they began to undress. They were soon naked and Chau was again terrified. She looked at the huge hairy men with their massive erect cocks swinging from side to side.

"Are you going to work?"

Chau nearly said yes, as she was scared beyond belief. She was also a virgin.

"No I cannot. Do what you must do."

One of the men got behind her and held her arms in a vice-like grip, while the other got onto the bed and faced her, pulling her legs apart to reveal her vagina. He moved forwards and held his cock at her entrance. She tried to pull away and knew it was useless, then she gave in and mentally removed herself from her body—she was now somewhere else, somewhere warm, comforting and friendly.

Then the pain hit her. It was like a tree trunk was entering her body. She pulled back but the man gripped her and thrust in deeply, and she screamed in agony as he entered fully. The girls downstairs heard the frightening scream and shook their heads. Chau was raped straight away by both men and they did not use condoms.

They asked her again if she was going to work, and she had replied no. They then both penetrated her at the same time, vaginally and anally, and the pain was so intense that she passed out. As soon as she woke they asked her, "Are you ready to work?" They knew the reply before she even said it: "No."

They raped her again and again until she could no longer feel the bottom half of her body, was only aware of the pain. The two rapists eventually left and

The Final Act

Chau spread herself on the bed. When she put her hand down between her legs she felt dampness, and when she lifted her hand she was horrified to see it covered in blood. She had not been having her period so where did the blood come from, she wondered? She could feel terrible soreness between her legs and once again investigated, this time standing in front of the mirror: she appeared to have a rip between her vagina and anus, which was bleeding profusely. She rushed to fetch a loo roll, unrolled several sheets and folded them into layers, and then placed the pad between her legs. Then she found a pair of knickers and slipped then on. Chau felt better but knew that she would need some stiches, just as the women at home did after having a difficult birth.

Tracy was the first to visit her and she hugged her, asking, "Are you OK?"

"Yes OK. But ripped and bleeding. Need stiches." She looked down so that Tracy got the message.

"Those bastards. One day they'll get what's coming to them. I'll tell Frost, he'll get the quack in."

"What is this quack?" asked Chau in her sweet voice.

Tracy laughed. "Oh it means the doctor. He'll come and stitch you."

Chau managed a smile at the mistake of words and then just blurted out. "Quack, Quack, Quack, Quack!" The two girls burst into laughter simultaneously. Tracy rushed off to tell Ted Frost that his thugs had damaged Chau, and that she needed to see a doctor.

The doctor duly turned up and got very well paid for a few minutes' work, but more attractive than money to him, was the opportunity to play with a woman's vagina and anus.

Chau soon recovered, the stitches were eventually removed and she felt a lot better. Life seemed to have gone quiet. She went to breakfast, lunch and dinner with the other girls, but was always aware that things could change in an instant for the worse.

And that was exactly what happened. One day Chau returned to her room after breakfast, and sat on the bed, planning for when she got out of the house—for there was never any doubt in her mind that she would escape. Then two men came in, the same animals who had raped her, and immediately one of them slapped her across the face, stunning her so that she was groggy and could not fight back. They lay her on the bed and one of them removed a small bag from his coat pocket. The bag contained a spoon, alcohol swabs, a syringe, a lighter, a brown material (which was heroine), and some cotton.

One of them took a chunk of the heroine and placed it on the spoon. He then used the syringe to suck up about 60 units of water and squirted it onto the spoon. He then heated its base with the lighter to dissolve the heroine. He then rolled a small piece of cotton and dropped it into the heroine in the spoon: it puffed up like a sponge. He then pushed the syringe into the centre of the sponge and sucked up the heroine, the sponge serving to filter out any harmful additives.

The other man pulled back Chau's sleeve and rubbed her arm with an alcohol swab. He then placed the needle flat on the skin and inserted it into a vein. After taking care to make sure the needle was well into the vein by pushing gently, he drew out some blood to verify he was directly into the vein. Next he pushed the plunger in, forcing the chemical to flow directly into her system.

Chau was away with the fairies. She had plugged into a never-never land and was dreaming of sunshine and flowers; the heroine intensified these feelings and in moments Chau was happy and warm and contented. The bastard Serbians then raped Chau again, aware that she had not fully recovered from their previous attentions, the stitches only having been recently removed.

After two weeks of constant fixes of heroine, Chau was prepared to do whatever they wanted to get her next dose of the drug. She was soon servicing twenty-plus men a day, and they wanted straight sex, blow jobs, sex involving dressing-up, plus every other sexually deviant practice you could imagine. She soon became addicted to the brown, and walked around for most of the time like a zombie.

Then there was a raid on the brothel by DC Karen Foster of the Metropolitan Police from CID Rotherhithe. As a result of that, Chau was treated for heroin addiction at Newham General Hospital, and this was what almost certainly saved her life.

CHAPTER 19

Lexi was so excited she was wandering around the apartment cleaning vases and furniture over and over again. She couldn't think straight and eventually sat down and tried to pull herself together. It was eight p.m. and Paul was on his way home. The beef casserole had been slow cooking in the oven for three hours and the smell coming from the kitchen was lovely. This meal was one of Paul's favourites and serving it with sauté potatoes and broccoli would make him very happy.

Ten minutes before Paul arrived, Lexi was up again and placing crystal champagne glasses on the dining table. She had got out the candles and best cutlery, and she'd also made a real effort with her appearance, putting on a short pink dress she knew Paul loved and applying a bit more slap than usual. She was daydreaming when she heard the key in the door and Paul walked in. She ran to him and gave him a huge hug, followed by a very seductive kiss on the lips.

"Hmm, what did I do to deserve that?" said Paul with a heartfelt smile.

"Nothing at all. Just being you is enough for me and I love you so much."

"Have you dropped one of my very expensive bottles of wine or something?"

Lexi laughed and replied in a loud voice: "No, I'm just happy to see you."

Paul smiled again. "Well in that case perhaps we should go to the bedroom. You look great." Paul turned towards the kitchen. "And something smells absolutely delicious. On second thoughts, let's eat first," he said playfully.

"Go and have a very quick shower," she said, "none of that playing with yourself, and get back here pronto."

With that Paul disappeared into the bedroom and Lexi went back to the kitchen. He returned fifteen minutes later and couldn't wait to eat and then 'eat' Lexi afterwards. Lexi poured the champagne and handed a glass to Paul.

"Champagne eh?" He smiled. "Have we won the lottery?"

"We don't do the lottery but there is a bit of good news." Lexi was smiling too and her eyes were shining bright.

"Come on then, what's the good news?"

Lexi took hold of Paul's hand. "Come and sit down."

They sat at the table and Lexi held her glass up. "Paul my love you are going to be a daddy."

Paul just looked at Lexi as his eyes filled with tears and he started to cry. He stood up and scooped Lexi into his arms and held her tight.

"Thank you for making me the happiest man in the universe, I'm so happy," he whispered, and he continued to blub uncontrollably for a full ten minutes.

Lexi knew that Paul wanted a child but in fact they had been caught out, and she was pregnant by accident, but neither of them cared, they were both ecstatic. They raised their champagne glasses and Paul proposed the first of many toasts: "To our baby boy or girl."

Paul knocked back the champagne. "Where's my dinner? I'm starving, shall I get it out of the oven myself?"

"Don't be silly, I'm just three months for goodness' sakes."

"Maybe but you have to look after yourself: eat plenty of vegetables, fruit, fish for that omega you know, whatever it is."

"Don't worry everything is under control," she told him. "Doc Taylor says I am a very healthy and fit woman."

Paul eyed her up and down. "Well I can't disagree with her prognosis. Let's eat and then we have plenty to talk about."

"Talk? Oh I was thinking you had something else on your mind?"

"Not now, my mind's all over the place. First things first. What about names? Have you thought at all? What if it's a boy?"

Lexi cuddled up to Paul. "Calm down, there's no rush, we have months."

Paul couldn't help it. He was thinking of Emma, his previous girlfriend who had died, and the lost baby, and he started to cry again.

Lexi looked up at him. "What's wrong?"

"I—I can't lose another one. I wouldn't be able to cope. Oh God, please make the baby safe."

The Final Act

Lexi squeezed Paul hard. "Nothing bad is going to happen. This baby will be born, he or she will be healthy and beautiful and live to a ripe old age."

"Yes of course you're right," spluttered Paul. His mind went blank and he sat down on one of the easy chairs. He put his head in his hands and thought about Tony and Richard Philips. He had to make sure the baby was safe, it kept going over and over in his mind: *the baby has to be safe*.

Paul and Lexi eventually ate the delicious beef stew that she had prepared, and Paul drank some more champagne. Lexi was already watching out for the baby by declaring half a glass of wine was all she would ever drink in a day. They talked through the evening and had an early night. Paul slept soundly and woke up refreshed and invigorated ready for the challenges of a new day as a father-in-waiting.

It was early November with Christmas knocking on the door. Paul had confided in Roddy, Dave and Duke that Lexi was pregnant and expecting a boy. He then had to explain they didn't know for sure if it was a boy, but he had a feeling it was. They had all laughed and congratulated Paul ecstatically. Paul had raised the question of Lexi's security and the group all agreed it would be a good idea for her to have some sort of minder. They also knew that she would not be happy with a six-foot-four mountain of muscle following her around in the local supermarket. Paul came up with an idea that everybody thought would work out well.

Charlie had been the lad who had stolen Lexi's purse in the Strand one night. Since then he had been working hard in the bar and kitchens of the club for several months and, although Paul was sceptical of the boy's chances at first, the reports he had received were very positive and he was glad that he had given the youngster a chance. Now was the time for him to repay that favour by staying with Lexi as a minder-come-'gofer'. Charlie wasn't overjoyed at first by the offer of being little more than a bag-carrier, but changed his mind as he understood that doing so would put him on good terms with the power brokers of the business, and was especially pleased that he would be with Paul on a regular basis, which, if he behaved himself, could only be beneficial to his career. What Paul didn't know was that Charlie worshipped him and wanted to follow in his footsteps.

Charlie was twenty-one, and he'd been in and out of trouble during most of those years. Duke had grabbed him in the Strand after he'd picked Lexi's

The Final Act

pocket and that was when he had first met Paul. He had fully expected him to call the police and was overjoyed when he didn't. Then Paul had told him to come and see him in his club and there might be a job going. Although Charlie tried to act cool, underneath he was excited.

So Charlie had gone to the flat in Chelsea Harbour with Paul after work one night to meet Lexi again. It was the first time he had seen her since the incident in the Strand and he was a tiny bit nervous. He shouldn't have been: Lexi was very friendly to him and if Charlie read the signs correctly he felt as if she actually liked him. Charlie loved the flat and moving in was no issue for him. He might be carrying the shopping but he would be living in a millionaires' playground. And things changed dramatically at the flat: every time Paul walked in there would be something new lying about—a pram, baby walkers, a baby bath, boxes of wet wipes and more. One day Paul came home and got the one of the biggest shocks of his life, albeit a pleasant one.

"Hi darling how was your day?" she asked.

Paul took Lexi in his arms and kissed her on the lips. "Great but more importantly how are you?" said Paul as he rubbed Lexi's tummy.

"I'm very well and, before you ask, Charlie is doing a great job."

"Where is he?"

"Gone to the newsagent's to get me some magazines and then he's going to get me a few jars of pickled gherkins." She smiled at Paul.

"Are you serious? Gherkins? I didn't know you even liked them."

"I didn't, but now I can't get enough of them!"

"Any other funny cravings I should know about?"

"Just that my craving for you has not diminished in any way at all." And Lexi gave Paul a passionate kiss. Lexi grabbed Paul's hand and took him towards one of the bedrooms.

"Close your eyes and no peeping," she said.

"Just a small peep?" Paul said playfully.

"No, close them. OK into the room then."

Lexi turned on the light. "OK you can look."

Paul opened his eyes and looked around. "Wow this is just beautiful." Tears filled his eyes—he couldn't seem to stop crying these days. The room was now a beautiful nursery for the baby and, most excitingly, it was done in multi-coloured shades of blue.

"Lexi I love it. But the colour. Isn't it a bit premature to be—"

"I saw the doc today. It's a boy. I want to call him Paul after his dad."

Paul had to wipe the tears from his eyes as he took Lexi and hugged her. "I've never been happier in my life than right now. Are you sure about the name?"

"Yes I am. Are you happy with it?"

"More than happy. I'm—I'm deliriously happy."

"That's settled then. Let's go and have some dinner." And as Lexi made for the kitchen Paul heard her giggle and shout: "And where are my gherkins?"

CHAPTER 20

It was a Saturday in the first week of November. Aedan O'Brien and Carrick Doyle walked out of Heathrow 'arrivals' area, took a taxi and were soon speeding down the M4 into central London. They were both in good humour: to get a job in London for a couple of months was unbelievable and it was their first visit. They had been given an address in Harlesden which was where they would be staying for the duration of their stay. They arrived at number 45, All Souls Avenue, in the early evening. It was getting dark when they knocked at the door, and that suited them. It opened to reveal a good-looking and fit black woman. They both stared at her in awe, and couldn't move.

"Are you standing out there all night gawping or are you coming in?" she demanded.

The two young men moved quickly and entered the house.

"Sorry missus we had a long flight," Aedan told her.

Julie wasn't going to give them her real name. "Call me Kate. Right, here's the keys, fridge is full, your beds made and Richard will be in touch tomorrow, OK?"

Aedan spoke up: "Fine missus—I mean Kate. Is there any booze?"

Julie laughed and did a mock Irish accent. "To be sure you'll be finding it in the kitchen so you will, beer in the fridge and whisky in the cupboard."

The two boys smiled. "OK. So we'll see the man tomorrow?"

"That's what I said," Julie replied as she walked to the front door, opened it and left.

Carrick spoke for the first time. "So have you ever had a black woman?"

"You name it I've had it, a pussy's a pussy, but it's what the woman does with it that counts."

"I'd like to have a go at that, you know," Carrick enthused. "Fit woman and no mistake."

"Maybe we'll both have her one night. What do you say?"

"Sounds good, let's have a drink."

The two boys drank a couple of cans and made an early night of it. They were up at the crack of dawn and Carrick found some sausages and bacon so he made a tasty fry-up with some eggs and a tin of baked beans. The breakfast went down well and they were relaxing in the lounge when Aedan's mobile rang.

"Hello?" he answered.

"It's Richard. Have you settled in alright?"

"We've settled in fine and you've missed out on a huge fry-up, so you have."

Richard laughed. "Good. I'll be over about eleven. See you then."

"Okay." Aedan turned to Carrick. "He's coming at eleven."

Aedan and Carrick were both twenty-four years old and were hired guns; they had no pretence about who they were or what they did. Someone would pay them and then they might disfigure, burn, torture or kill people to order. Neither of them were particularly bright, especially since they had hardly ever bothered going to school. Both were from broken homes that had no parental discipline. They were mates who lived on the same road in Belfast and had been left to run wild on the streets. People sometimes mistook them for brothers because they looked to be of similar build and facial appearance. They were tall, rangy and good looking in a rough way, and had the habit of always wearing clothes that didn't quite go together.

The first person they killed was a police grass in Belfast; it had been simple, which was the way they preferred it. They had walked into a barber shop and each put a bullet into the back of the man's head. For this job they were being extremely well paid at twenty grand each and the boys were happy to do whatever was requested of them.

It was soon eleven and Richard turned up on the dot. They shook hands and then settled down with coffees. Richard explained the situation and gave them an idea of what would be required of them. All they did was nod their heads, for it didn't matter to them who it was or why they had to be killed, their modus operandi was: 'tell us who the target is, where to find them and then leave the rest to us.'

Richard had bought them an old but reliable Ford Focus, and after discussing one or two details he left and went back to Basildon. The boys did nothing for a couple of days until the Tuesday morning, when they got up early and drove up

The Final Act

to Liverpool. It was two hundred odd miles, which translated into about a three-and-a-half hour journey. The two of them shared the driving and they stopped at the Welcome Break Warwick Services for coffee and one of their favourite full-English breakfasts.

They arrived in Liverpool at ten-fifty a.m. and headed towards Wallasey, and arrived at the Riverside Business Centre in Dock Street some thirty minutes later. They drove to the back of the estate and found what they were after, a small unit with a board above the entrance which read 'Star Transport Services'. Aedan went in and ten minutes later returned to the car and placed two large travelling bags in the boot. He got back into the passenger seat, smiled at Carrick and said: "All sorted, let's go." Carrick pulled away. They now had a boot full of various weapons that had been collected from a fishing boat off the north Scottish coast the day before. The drive back was long and boring, they never exceeded the speed limit once, and eventually pulled into All Souls Avenue at six o'clock. The lads unloaded the bags and hid them as best they could in the upstairs airing cupboard.

They were tired and a bit grumpy so decided to cheer themselves up by going to the pub. They left the house and walked twenty yards and turned into Herbert Gardens, they quickened their pace and then turned left into College Road. A short walk and they were outside The Island gastro pub, which they both regarded warily. Carrick was the first to speak: "What sort of fucking pub do you call this?" The walls had been plastered but not painted, which gave a strange 'unfinished' overall feel to it, and there were three huge windows in the front which would have seemed more at home in a church.

Aedan and Carrick eventually went in and found that it was quite busy. There was a decent-sized bar on the ground floor and a sign to a restaurant downstairs. They went to the bar and then stopped and looked at each other, surprised that all the conversations around them were being conducted in Irish accents. Aedan whispered to Carrick: "Jesus it's just like being at fucking home."

The boy's had not been aware that there was a huge Irish community in Harlesden and most of them seemed to be in the Island pub that night. They had a couple of pints of the black stuff and sat well away from anyone else, for the last thing they needed was to get into conversation with people from back home. They finished their pints and wandered back to their flat, agreeing that next time they would find another pub that didn't have the Irish element.

The Final Act

CHAPTER 21

Jeff Swan was lost. Karen had been off sick for two weeks and he was missing her like hell. He couldn't believe that he would miss her so much and was annoyed with himself for being so pathetic. He spent most of his time in the CID office trying to find something to do, not being able to and constantly wandering down to the canteen for yet another latte. Jeff had friends at the Nick but losing your partner was like having one of your arms chopped off. He had been shocked by the call from Chau, who basically had told him to stay away.

The Nick had arranged a whip-round, after which a forty-quid bouquet of flowers were sent, and a 'thank you' card came back two days later. Jeff was praying Karen would return, but from the way Chau screamed at him on the phone he knew she would try to get Karen to leave, possibly on sick grounds, with a substantial payoff. Not much was happening locally, and the Angel and Mayflower pub murder investigations had both hit brick walls. They were no nearer identifying the man they wanted to talk to and Jeff needed Karen's sharp mind to help track him down.

Richard Philips had been taking risks and he knew it. It wasn't so bad in Basildon but he had come into London on a couple of occasions and hadn't bothered with any disguise at all. It was another one of those 'undisguised' times as he parked up at a friend's house in Argyle Way, just off the Old Kent Road. He stayed at the house till lunchtime and left at midday, and on his way home he decided to quickly stop at the McDonald's, which was two minutes from Argyle Way, on the Old Kent Road.

Jeff Swan drove away from Rotherhithe Nick at eleven-fifty. He went a short distance down Lower Road, he indicated right as he saw the Surrey Quays underground station ahead, he turned onto the A228, hit the small roundabout, and shot up Rotherhithe New Road towards the Old Kent Road. He was hungry and before heading on to the B & Q DIY superstore he decided to stop for a burger-and-chips at McDonald's.

Philips crossed over the Old Kent Road and pulled into the McDonald's car park, right in front of the main entrance. He opened and rummaged around in his car's ash tray, taking out a collection of coins which included several two-pound ones. He got out of the Audi, opened the rear passenger door and took

The Final Act

out his coat, then he put it on, clicked the central locking button on his key fob and walked to the nearby main entrance.

Jeff swung his old Ford Mondeo into the McDonald's car park and pulled up alongside a very nice silver Audi, a car he had coveted for years. He looked in his mirror and saw the back of the man who had got out a second before. 'Bastard!' he said to himself. Jeff opened his driver's door and stepped out into the cold, pulling up the collar of his short jacket to try and keep the cold out, and he didn't bother locking the car as he made for the door into McDonald's.

Philips entered the restaurant and made straight for the counter. There were a few people sitting eating and he was thankful that he was just ahead of the big lunch rush. He was second in the queue and was studying the menu, even though he knew what he was going to have before he even entered. He felt someone join the queue behind him and casually turned and looked briefly at Jeff Swan before turning back.

Jeff joined one of the queues behind the Audi driver. He had his hands in his jacket pockets trying to keep them warm. The man in front of him turned and Jeff caught a side view, but he thought nothing of it and continued to shuffle his feet and look at the menu.

"Quarter-pound meal with white coffee," Philips asked the girl behind the counter, looking forward to getting his hot food.

"Large chips?" she queried.

"If I'd wanted large chips I would have asked for them."

The girl smiled: she was used to it. Philips paid with his coins, she trayed up the meal and he took it and sat down by the window.

Jeff had got himself a Big Mac meal with a diet coke. He took his tray, fetched some ketchup and sat down at a table by the window. He was two tables away from Philips, and facing him directly.

The criminal was enjoying his burger-and-chips washed down with the hot coffee.

Jeff tucked into his Big Mac and soon it was all over his chin and he was having difficulty holding the large bun together. He glanced up and looked at the Audi driver.

The Final Act

Philips took another bite of his burger and met the gaze of the man sitting two tables away. The guy was looking at him, so Philips stared at him for a second to scare him off.

Jeff felt the stare from the Audi driver and just for a second he thought he knew him from somewhere. He went back to his food and started chomping on the chips. He glanced at the man, and again he thought his face was familiar.

Philips saw the man look at him again before quickly turning away. He angled his head slightly so the man could not see his full profile, and continued to eat.

The policeman noticed the man's quick movement and got the feeling that he was trying to hide his face. The Audi driver then pulled up his coat collar as high as he could, and also started to eat very quickly.

Philips was getting slightly worried that this stranger was looking at him, almost as if he was taking a little more interest than he should be. He began to sweat and he felt his hands become clammy.

Jeff took one more look and suddenly it hit him like a sledgehammer: *it was Richard Philips!*

As Philips made eye contact with Jeff he knew that he had been recognised.

They both stood up at the same time, not taking their eyes from one another.

"Stand still! I am a police officer!" shouted Jeff as he moved towards Philips.

Police. That was all Philips heard, his head was swimming, he was thinking, 'you stop for a burger and a fucking police ...' And then realising, '*shit* the officer is so close!'

Philips reached into his right coat pocket and gripped his gun. He had no choice but to draw it and aim directly at Jeff's head.

Jeff stood up and shouted again: "Stand still I am a police officer!" and moved towards Philips. Too late, he saw the criminal reach into his pocket and bring out a black deadly-looking firearm.

Still aiming at Jeff's head, Philips pulled the trigger, and there was a huge bang as the gun went off.

Jeff threw himself to the left as he was fired at, he felt something and then there was nothing but silence and darkness.

Philips saw the officer go down. He didn't know whether he was dead or not, and he heard people screaming. He turned and walked calmly to the entrance. In five seconds he was screeching out of the car park onto the Old Kent Road.

Aabharan, the manager of the restaurant, had dialled 999 and asked for an ambulance and the police, explaining that a police officer had been shot. He was now leaning over Jeff, trying to see if he was alive or not. It looked as if the bullet had entered his head and Aabharan could see the hole with blood trickling out.

Two marked police cars and an armed response unit arrived within two minutes, and quickly the entire area was sealed off and all the roads blocked. The ambulance took a full ten minutes to arrive, precious minutes if Jeff was to have any chance of survival.

One of the women sitting by the window swore that the man who shot the officer escaped in a silver BMW, that was just like her cousin's car. The police put out an alert to that effect, so any hope of catching him diminished even further with the realisation of how many silver BMWs there were around.

Rotherhithe Nick went into meltdown. Karen was off sick and now Jeff, who was a very popular officer, had been gunned down in broad daylight in a local McDonald's restaurant. Michael, the head of CID, was in shock and couldn't believe what was happening.

Jeff arrived at St Thomas' Hospital and was rushed straight into the operating theatre for emergency surgery to remove the bullet. He was then placed on a life-support machine and was, to all intents and purposes, brain-dead and in a coma.

CHAPTER 22

Later that day Richard Philips got a call.

"The boys arrived then?" asked the caller.

"Yeah," Richard replied. "Nice couple of lads, and looking forward to earning their money."

"That's what I like to hear. People who care about their work."

Richard laughed. "So are you ready?"

"I'm more than ready. That cunt is going to be shocked. It's very important we keep to the plan and the timings, you understand?"

"Don't worry Tony. I'm on the case. Everything is taken care of."

"Good. You know I don't like cock-ups at the best of times, let alone during something like this." He paused. "Did you hear about the copper getting shot?"

Richard wanted to brag saying, 'yeah it was me', but for some unknown reason he kept it low-key. "So I heard. One less to worry about then."

Tony laughed. "Best news I heard all day."

Richard changed the subject. "Anything else I need to know?"

"No, we move on the first of December, and a happy fucking Christmas to my dear brother Paul."

Richard could hear Tony laughing hysterically as he pushed the 'end call' button on his mobile.

Tony was in an incredibly good mood. He had been watching the BBC News when the newsreader announced that a police officer had been gunned down in London. That was good news in itself as far as Tony was concerned, but when he heard the name Jeff Swan he was almost dancing round the room. Swan had been the officer that fat little shit at the Angel had been snitching to. Life couldn't get much better, thought Tony, as he sat watching an afternoon gangster film with a large whisky in his hand.

The Final Act

Sharon had not reacted to the news as well as Tony had. She wanted the violence to end, it seemed it would go on forever, she felt that she had to get Tony to leave the country, but that would not be easy.

All the staff at Rotherhithe Nick were depressed and sick that Jeff Swan had been gunned down locally in broad daylight. Michael was wondering if Karen had heard the news and decided he needed to do something before she found out by reading the papers or watching TV.

Karen had made good progress. She was getting up in the mornings and had started helping Chau with the chores and cooking. She was nowhere near to getting back to work, but was definitely making progress. She was not going out and was not watching TV, so the day after the shooting she still did not know about Jeff. Michael telephoned her late in the afternoon. Karen saw that it was Michael calling and thought for a second before she answered it.

"Hello Michael."

"Karen you sound better, much better."

"Yes I am feeling better, thank you."

There was a silence as Michael tried to think of the right words.

"Michael, are you still there?" she asked.

"Yes I am, I—eh—have some terrible news and I wanted you to hear it from me."

Karen gripped the arm of the chair she was sitting in. "What's happened?"

Michael again couldn't speak.

"Michael *what the fuck has happened?*"

"It's Jeff."

Karen's eyes filled with tears as she waited for the news. "Yes, go on."

"He's been shot..."

The tears rolled down Karen's cheeks as she feared the worst.

"And..." Silence

She screamed down the phone: *"For fuck's sake tell me Michael!"*

"He's in a coma. Shot in the head at lunchtime yesterday in the McDonald's in the Old Kent Road."

Coma!

Karen was shaking, the tears flowed and she spluttered. "McDonald's? How can you get shot in fucking McDonald's?"

"We don't know exactly what happened but it seems he recognised a man and challenged him, then the man just shot him in the head."

Karen was already thinking hard. "It was one of them. I know it was."

"Who?"

"Tony Bolton or Richard Philips. I know it was one of those bastards. How is Jeff's wife and family?"

"They're just about holding things together, and as you can imagine the whole station's devastated."

Karen was surprised how well she was handling the call.

"Michael thanks for calling," she said. "I'll be in touch soon."

"OK Karen. We're all thinking of you."

"Thanks." And Karen hung up. She went to the bathroom and washed her face. As she looked in the mirror she saw a drawn, haggard bloodshot-eyed visage and shook her head. She sat on the side of the bath and a steely determination enveloped her. It was at that exact second she promised herself that she would find whoever shot Jeff and bring him to justice. She would also find those bastards Bolton and Philips, who she still had a feeling were involved. Karen then heard the front door open and knew the next challenge was persuading Chau she was ready to return to work. She stood up and called Chau's name.

* * *

Three days later the desk sergeant nearly fell off his stool when Karen Foster strode into reception and smiled at him with a loud "Good Morning Steve."

She was looking fantastic, she'd had her hair cut short which really suited her, she wore her best dark blue two-piece suit, and she looked very healthy. Word spread round the Nick that Karen was back and once she was sitting in the CID

The Final Act

office there was a procession of 'Good to see you back' shouts all through the morning.

Karen had a meeting with Michael and told him she was back on the case and needed some backup until Jeff was well again. Michael assigned a young career-obsessed rookie to join Karen temporarily. Her name was Penny Tuesday, a name Karen found highly amusing. Penny was twenty-six, petite and very butch, something which Karen thought was going to take a bit of getting used to.

DS Karen Foster went out at lunchtime to St Thomas' Hospital. She already knew there was no change in Jeff's condition but she had to see him. She arrived at the place and was feeling nervous, not really wanting to see Jeff like that, but knew she had to speak to him whether he could hear her or not. She went to the reception desk and explained that she was visiting Jeff Swan, a fellow police officer. The receptionist was obviously aware that Jeff had been shot and she whispered to Karen: "We're all praying for him."

Karen left reception and headed towards the Neurological Department. It was a long walk and Karen felt she was almost in a dream and that any second Jeff would appear and ask her if she wanted a latte. She saw the last sign and pushed the door, she approached the reception desk and for a second had to hold back the tears.

"Hello," she said. "I'm here to see Jeff Swan."

Karen showed her police badge and the lady receptionist smiled warmly at her. "Come with me I'll take you to his room." Karen couldn't move and the lady took her arm. "This way then."

"How is he?"

"When you have such a traumatic brain injury it is difficult to tell but he is comfortable and getting the best care possible."

They walked down a long corridor and Karen could feel the tension growing, she then saw a uniformed police officer and knew they were nearly there. The noise of their steps were resounding through her head as she neared the door. She didn't recognise the police officer who was on guard, so she took her badge out and showed him. He nodded and smiled.

The receptionist opened the door and held it for Karen to enter. Karen stepped in and was conscious of the quietness and then she saw Jeff, lying on the bed.

The Final Act

Everything seemed to be white: white sheets, white walls, and Karen wondered if this was what heaven was like. She walked to the bed to find that Jeff was still, very still. She took his hand and fought back the tears. She gently squeezed his fingers, hoping that he might return the squeeze but there was nothing. He seemed like a shell, a living shell that would never recover and never speak again. The receptionist brought a chair and Karen sat close to Jeff and continued to hold his hand. She heard the door and turned to see the lady leave the room. She turned back to Jeff.

"A right fucking mess you've got yourself in now, eh Jeff?" The tears flooded down her cheeks.

"I'm going to get him, the man who did this to you," she muttered, leaning close and whispering in his ear. "I'm going to find the man and then I'm going to kill him very slowly. He will understand what pain is, Jeff."

She blew her nose and wiped her face with tissues.

"Jeff you must fight. Don't give in, you can recover, you must please. Who am I going to drink coffee with in the office? So you'd better hurry up and get well."

She hoped Jeff had heard her or at least knew she had been there. She pushed his hair back off his forehead and kissed him gently as she stood to leave. She squeezed his hand again.

"See you soon then, bye bye." Tears flowed again as she opened the door and went back out into the corridor and the real world. She stopped to compose herself and spoke to the officer: "Look out for him."

"I will, don't worry."

Karen walked back down towards the hospital entrance, hoping but not really confident, that Jeff would wake up and recover. Karen drove back to Rotherhithe Nick and started work.

Karen always did the same when she had been away from a case for a period of time, and that was to go back to the beginning. This served two main purposes: it got her back up to speed, and hopefully ensured nothing was missed. Karen took the files and started to go through them. First there was the killing of the man in the Mayflower pub. Reading the details she still thought it was a random killing that happened on the spur of the moment. They had eye witnesses but had hit a brick wall. Next was the Angel pub killing of Micky the Snitch. It was almost certain that he had been killed because he

The Final Act

had been asking the wrong questions. Karen was sure that Tony Bolton was responsible but there were no witnesses and no progress was being made.

The last case was Jeff being shot at the McDonald's restaurant, which was still very early days. The witness descriptions pointed at Richard Philips being a suspect, but were certainly not definite. That case too had not progressed far, and the only way forward seemed to be to find Bolton or Philips or, even better, both of them. Karen sat back and played with her biro. What could we do to flush those bastards out where we can see them, she wondered?

"Penny I want you to look at the files," she told her young colleague. "Start at the beginning, go through them thoroughly and see if you can pick up on anything I've missed."

Penny grabbed the files and took them back to her desk and started the laborious job of going through them in detail.

Karen was back to thinking. It seemed that the only lead was the fact that she got the feeling Paul Bolton knew who was in the photo she had shown him. She opened her diary, located the number, and pressed the numbers on her desk phone. It rang three times and then was answered.

"Yes hello. I would like to speak to Paul Bolton please. It's Detective Sergeant Karen Foster."

"Miss Foster, good morning it's Carla Westburgh, Mr Bolton's PA. What can I do for you?"

"I'd like to speak to Mr Bolton please."

"I'll see if he's in."

Karen was pissed off at the 'see if he's in'. She knows if he's fucking well in or not, she thought.

"I'm putting you through."

"Thanks Carla." *Fucking cow*, thought Karen.

"Ms Foster what can I do for you?"

Karen liked that. None of the 'how are you' shit.

"I'm just calling to remind you that if you have seen or know the whereabouts of your brother Tony or of one Richard Philips and do not disclose that

The Final Act

information, then you will be arrested for perverting the course of justice. This carries a very long prison sentence. Let's cut the crap Paul. You know who that was in the photo I showed you."

Paul was thinking hard. "I wish I could help you I really do but—"

"Yeah I know he's your brother, but he's also a maniac who kills people for fun. You saw the news about my partner Jeff Swan?"

"Yes I'm sorry. I hope he makes a speedy recovery. I also hope you're not suggesting Tony had anything to do with that?"

"No. I'm almost certain it was Richard Philips."

Paul couldn't believe his ears. Philips and Tony were nothing short of animals who needed to be shot or caged for life.

"Listen Paul. You don't owe Philips anything. I need help on this one. If needs be I could, well, I'm not going to spell it out for you ... Needless to say I want the man that shot Jeff in the head at point-blank range and left him in a coma. I want him very very badly."

Paul chose his words carefully: "Karen If I can help with your problem then I will. That's all I can say, especially as you may be taping this conversation."

"Think about it. I couldn't be taping this, Paul, because of what I just said."

"Karen, I have your number."

The chat was over.

"OK thanks Paul. I'm sure we will speak again."

"Yes I expect we will." And Paul ended the call.

He sat still for a moment. Had he understood correctly what the police officer had said? She would help with the Tony situation if he helped her with Philips. She had said that in not so many words. Paul smiled. Nothing was easy and probably the best help she could give would be to escort Tony to Heathrow and stick him on a plane out of the country, never to return. The truth was that Paul didn't know where Tony or Philips were holed up. He could certainly get messages to them via their solicitors, so first-things first, he thought.

The sex-tape letter arrived the next morning, posted from Birmingham in the midlands. That location didn't ring true and Paul had a gut feeling that the

The Final Act

person behind the blackmail was in London. The letter was short and straight to the point. The sum to be paid to get back the three tapes was three million pounds.

Paul called in at Dave's place and they discussed what they were going to do. The old days of bags full of used notes were well and truly over: the money was to be transferred into an account in Switzerland within seven days. Once the money had been paid the three tapes would be sent to Paul. The two men came to the same conclusion, namely that once the money was transferred it was lost and the blackmailers could keep the tapes and ask for more money later. They could also of course make copies, so that Paul could never be sure that once he destroyed the three originals there were no more in circulation.

It was a situation that Paul could not agree to. The money was not transferred and Richard was well cheesed off. He went online and purchased a telephone voice modifier which arrived the very next day. He had already set his mobile phone up so that his number could not be traced, and he attached the small piece of kit to it and called the Den Club.

"Yes I want to speak to Paul Bolton," he said when they replied. "Mention 'tapes' and he will speak to me."

He was put through.

"Carla Westburgh PA to Mr Bolton. Can I help you?"

"Mention 'tapes' and get him on the fucking phone."

"There's no need to use bad language madam. I'll see if he's available."

The voice-changer was working perfectly, thought Richard.

"Yes, what can I do for you?" Paul's voice came on the line.

"You didn't pay the money. You have three days to change your mind."

"Look whoever you are. I want to pay and get the tapes back but I could pay you and still never see the tapes. There has to be another way."

There was silence on the phone.

"OK we will use a solicitor. I will give him the tapes and when you have paid he will hand over the tapes to you."

"How will I know there are no copies?"

The Final Act

"There is no way for me to prove to you that there are no copies but for that sort of money I assure you it will all be kosher."

Paul was thinking hard. "OK. But it will have to be a very high-profile London firm of solicitors that I can trust implicitly."

"Agreed. I'll let you know later through your PA woman."

"Fine." And Paul heard the phone click off. It was a bloody woman, although the voice sounded slightly weird, so perhaps it had been disguised in some way, he thought.

Carla later informed Paul that the solicitors would be Shuster and McLaren, a well-known firm of solicitors in the City, and that the tapes would be there the next day, Wednesday, early in the morning. A man called Ian Trent was the facilitator.

Paul immediately called Dave into his office and told him what he wanted him to do.

It was the next morning at eight a.m., a cold, grey-skied day with a slight drizzle. Dave and Pauly were waiting outside the back entrance where all deliveries to the building were made. They knew the package would be delivered by a courier and that it would be one box. They watched as FedEx delivered multiple boxes and packages of all shapes and sizes. Then a UPS van drew up and again had a large delivery that had to go in on a trolley. Dave was beginning to lose heart when fifteen minutes later a DHL van pulled up and a short fat man in uniform jumped out. He took one parcel from the side door and walked towards the entrance. Dave froze, unable to move. Pauly grabbed his arm and he reacted. They moved quickly towards the delivery man and took an arm each.

"What do you want?" he yelled. "Hey leave me—"

"Shut the fuck up and you won't get hurt."

Dave took the box and they marched the driver to the back of the van and opened the doors; this gave them an element of privacy from prying eyes. Dave ripped open the DHL bag. "You can't do that!" the delivery man started protesting but didn't finish, as Pauly slapped him hard across his face, saying, "Shut the fuck up." Dave was happy, as he could see three videotapes.

"Where did you pick this package up from?" Dave was praying that whoever sent it had made the biggest mistake of their lives.

"I don't know. I pick up—" He didn't finish that sentence either, as Dave grabbed him round the throat.

"I asked you where the fuck you picked up this package from?" Dave repeated.

The driver spluttered and looked at the ripped bag. "Err I think it was, yeah it was definitely Staples in Great Oaks, Basildon."

Dave put his face close to that of the driver "What time did you pick it up?"

The driver was terrified. "Mid-afternoon, about three." He wiped spittle off his mouth and pushed his hair back from his forehead.

Dave patted the driver's shoulder and smiled at him. "Now the last thing. This parcel has got lost in the system, do you understand?"

The driver opened his mouth and was about to explain why that couldn't happen, looked at Dave, and changed his mind.

"Of course. It happens all the time," he agreed. "Parcels go missing and nobody knows what happens to them."

"Good man. Now get on with your deliveries and forget this ever happened."

And with that Dave and Pauly walked off back to their car.

They reported the good news to Paul. Their boss was ecstatic and now all they had to do was wait and see if the bastards who had them had made any copies.

On Wednesday afternoon there was another phone call: it was the 'tape woman' again. She was agitated and asking for Paul.

"You cunt Bolton! You'll pay for that believe me you'll fucking pay! I've got copies, you don't seriously think I would just give you the tapes do you?"

"I don't know what you're talking about," Paul replied calmly. "I contacted the solicitors as agreed and the Trent guy told me the package had not arrived. I wasn't going to give him three million quid then, was I?"

"You lying bastard, do you think I'm fucking stupid? The price has gone up to four million."

The Final Act

"I don't believe you made copies. You screwed up, so now you can fuck off." And so saying, Paul put the phone down.

Richard Philips was almost foaming at the mouth. He had listened to that slag Julie. A clean break, she'd said. Return the tapes, get paid and it's all over. They'd turned him over. Three fucking million pounds up the swanny! He was in a terrifying rage and he kept telling himself it was all her fault. She had gone out and he was pacing the lounge working himself up even more. He started throwing plants and pots, he kicked over a small table, he was in a really crazy mood. The back door opened and she had returned.

"Hi darling," she called out. "I'm back."

Richard grabbed the shoulder of her coat and threw her on the hall floor.

"You and your fucking advice!" he yelled at her. "I've lost the tapes and not got paid! I've been fucked by you and Bolton!"

He lifted his arms and started punching Julie all over her body. She scrambled across the floor and made it to the back door and managed to open it. But Richard was on her, trying to drag her back. She turned and kicked, her toe connecting with his balls, so that he screamed and buckled up on the floor. Julie ran down the path, got in the car and sped away with her foot hard down on the pedal.

Half an hour later Richard was still fuming but had calmed down sufficiently to act rationally. It was his fault not Julie's, he knew that and would make it up to her in some way. Paul Bolton didn't know whether he had copies or not so he was going to pay for tapes: whether they had any content was neither here or there. He phoned Julie and told her it was all his fault and that she should come back. She said she would come back the next day, so that he could calm down.

The issue for Julie was where to stay. She didn't have loads of money for a hotel and then she had a brainwave. Yes, she would go and stay one night at the flat in Harlesden with the two Irish boys. She thought for a second about the two fit-looking young men and images of huge cocks appeared in her mind. She shook her head and concentrated on the driving.

It took her an hour to get to Harlesden and she had no change of clothes, and not even a toothbrush. She parked up near the flat and nipped round the corner to the local Spar and bought some essentials.

137

The Final Act

Aedan and Carrick were surprised when they opened the door to find Julie standing there. They may have been surprised but were happy to see her. They were even more surprised but incredibly happy when she told them she was staying in the spare room for the night. It was early evening, and Carrick had returned from the local shops with some Chinese takeaway food and a couple of bottles of wine and some beers. Julie had taken a shower and had found a dressing gown, which she promptly claimed as hers. The boys laid the table, found some wine glasses and called Julie, telling her that dinner was ready.

Julie entered the small dining area in her blue dressing gown with her hair swept back, looking very sexy. The boys could not fail to notice that when she sat down the dressing gown parted to show fabulous long legs, without, they thought, any indication that she was wearing knickers.

She was feeling good. A hot shower followed by a tasty Chinese, washed down with some cheap but acceptable white wine and she was relaxing nicely. The boys had already decided it was too good an opportunity to miss and if they got turned down, so be it.

Aedan was the first to speak: "Julie, you're looking very sexy and we haven't seen a woman in weeks. Are you not worried we might try and take advantage of you?"

Julie looked at the two boys and thought they were sweet, and she wondered how sexually experienced they were. She laughed. "Maybe it's you two boys who should be worried I am a mature woman and know what I am doing." With that she uncrossed and re-crossed her legs, taking her time and showing a good bit of thigh. She saw both boys' eyes staring as they looked at her legs; they were almost dribbling.

The sexy woman had another glass of wine and decided she was up for some fun.

"Why don't you boys take your clothes off so I can see what you've got?"

They didn't need asking twice, and they quickly removed their clothes and both stood there naked as the day they were born. The big difference was that now both boys had erections, and Julie was licking her lips.

"Come here."

She took one cock in each hand and started slowly masturbating them. She soon heard them moaning, so she let go and stood up. The dressing gown fell from her body, revealing her beautiful firm breasts and smooth pussy. The boys were in heaven. Aedan started licking her nipples and squeezing her breasts while Carrick sat on the chair and stuck his tongue up her pussy and started licking that.

Julie was getting very turned on and suggested they go to the bedroom. She lay on the bed. Carrick pulled her to the edge so he could enter her while standing up, while Aedan climbed onto the bed and pushed his huge hard cock into her mouth. Carrick was pushing and so was Aedan, meanwhile Julie was sucking cock like her life depended on it, while thoroughly enjoying Carrick fucking her pussy.

She suddenly turned over and stuck her arse in the air. "I want both of you—pussy and arse." Carrick decided he would like her arse while Aedan moved underneath Julie so that he could enter her pussy. It took a bit of time, as Carrick couldn't enter her without using some lubrication, and they had to use a little olive oil from the kitchen. Soon enough they were pumping for all they were worth and Julie was loving it. Carrick soon shouted: "I'm coming oh God!" Julie quickly turned and took his cock in her mouth as the semen poured. Aedan was not long behind him and they spent the next two hours enjoying each other's bodies. The two boys had got their wish: a threesome with the delectable black Julie.

* * *

Dave and Pauly arrived in Basildon at lunchtime. They soon located Great Oaks, drove past the Fire Station and pulled up in the Imperial Chinese Restaurant car park. They decided to quickly eat and both had chicken curry, washed down with a Becks. They left the car park and walked the one hundred yards to the Staples office equipment store. They went through the automatic doors and headed straight for the reception desk. Dave looked at a pretty young girl behind the counter and smiled at her. She walked over, said good afternoon, and asked if she could help them.

"Yes I'd like to see the manager please," Dave began. "Err what is his name please?"

The young girl smiled. "Andrew Smith. What is it in connection with?"

"A complaint which I would like to discuss in private."

The Final Act

"OK I won't be a moment." The girl disappeared through the back door marked 'staff only'. She came back two minutes later, saying, "Please follow me this way."

She took them through the back door and down a short corridor, the door had 'manager' on it, and she knocked and opened it. Andrew Smith stood up and invited Dave and Pauly to sit down, which they did.

"So I'm sorry to hear you have a complaint," said Andrew.

Dave scratched the stubble on his chin. "Yes a sort of complaint. The truth is, we need your help with something."

"If I can help I certainly will."

"Good." Dave looked at Pauly and he took the ripped DHL bag out of his coat pocket and gave it to Andrew.

Andrew looked at the bag and was slightly confused. Before he could speak Dave continued: "I'm assuming that when someone comes in and uses the DHL courier service they have to give you their address, is that correct?"

Andrew was still confused. "Yes of course that would be normal procedure, amongst other administration."

"Great. So we would like the name and address given by the person who booked that item for delivery. It was picked up from here yesterday at about three p.m."

Andrew was looking at the ripped bag and began to feel slightly uneasy. "And what connection do you have with the DHL bag? Because I can't give out names and addresses to just anyone who comes in and asks for them, as I'm sure you understand."

"But you do have that information available?"

Andrew looked at Dave eyeball to eyeball. "Well yes but—"

Dave turned away and nodded at Pauly.

Pauly got up and went round the desk. Andrew was now really worried. "What is—"

He couldn't finish. Pauly grabbed a handful of his hair and smashed his face onto the hard wooden desk. His nose was broken and blood splattered all over

The Final Act

the desk, as Andrew gasped and let out a muffled scream of pain. He spat out a mouthful of blood and looked up. Pauly lifted his face and held his hair tightly, not letting him move.

Dave leaned over the desk and stared straight into Andrew's face.

"Now what I want you to do is get on your computer and find out the details I want, do you understand?" Dave said quietly.

Andrew nodded. Pauly let go of his hair and he reached for his mouse. He brought up the DHL service and took the ripped bag. He copied the reference number into the system and waited. Three seconds later the full details of the transaction came onto the screen. He pushed his chair to the side and turned the screen towards Pauly. Dave was out of his chair and quickly round the other side of the desk to study the information.

"Print it," Dave commanded.

Andrew returned to the mouse and clicked 'print'. There was a short wait and then a whirring noise from the corner of the office where the printer was, and a single sheet of white paper slipped out of the machine, which Pauly took. He studied the text and looked at Dave, saying, "It's good."

Dave smiled at Andrew. "If I was you I would get to A & E and have that looked at, doors can hurt when you walk into them, can't they? Also if I was you I would forget we were ever here. I wouldn't want to have to come back. You do understand, I hope?"

Andrew understood fully and just nodded.

Dave and Pauly left Staples and rushed back to their car at the Chinese Restaurant. Dave got in, grabbed his satnav and punched in the address, which was one-point-six miles away. He looked at Pauly and said: "Pray this bastard has made a big mistake, he's down the fucking road." And he laughed as he started the engine and pulled out of the car park.

Dave pulled onto Great Oaks and turned right. "Call Paul and tell him what's happening."

They drove down to the roundabout and took the first exit onto Long Riding. Five minutes down Long Riding and Dave took a left into Hockley Road. "What number?" he snapped at Pauly.

"Forty."

Dave clocked the first house on each side, noticing that even numbers were on the right. He drove slowly and stopped at number thirty-six. The two of them sat in the car for a minute without speaking. This was a ritual that they observed to get their head into focus, prior to violence.

They got out of the car and walked slowly towards number forty. The house was a typical small terraced Basildon house, it was in poor condition and desperate for a lick of paint and some new windows. Dave and Pauly looked at each other as though to say 'This doesn't look too promising'. Dave knocked on the door. They heard a noise so someone was in, but it was taking them a long time to get to the door. Finally it opened to reveal an elderly man holding onto a walking stick.

"Yes? Can I help you?" he asked.

"We're looking for a Mr Adam Green," Dave said.

"I'm afraid I can't help you then. Are you sure you have the correct address? This is 40 Hockley Road."

Pauly looked at the printout. Sure enough it said 40 Hockley Road, Basildon.

"That's what it says here."

"Oh what is that?" the old man enquired.

"It's a DHL courier bag. Apparently the man who sent it lives here."

"Never used DHL in my life and haven't been out the house for three weeks."

Dave was sure this man had no idea what they were talking about. "Sorry to bother you. I'm sure we have the wrong address."

"Well I hope you find who you're looking for."

Dave was pissed off. "Yes so do we, thanks."

They turned away from the door walked down the small path and stood on the pavement, looking around.

* * *

Richard Philips was sitting on the sofa having a cup of tea. He was thinking long and hard about the situation with Paul Bolton, and the best way to get the money off him for the supposed 'copy' tapes.

The Final Act

Suddenly he was agitated and stood up and went to the big lounge window and looked out. He scanned the immediate vicinity and then jumped to the side, as he dropped the mug of hot tea on the carpet; the liquid splashed all over his trouser leg, while the mug bounced along the carpet. He was shaking and in a state of panic, because he had looked out of the window and seen the two men across the road at number 40 Hockley Road, the address he had used to send the DHL parcel.

He was sure that they were, without question, two of Paul Bolton's thugs. Richard was in a panic. Had they seen him? Of course they hadn't, *calm down* he told himself. He moved to the side of the window and peeked out through the curtain. The two men were standing on the pavement, just looking around them. Richard relaxed, because it was clear that they had no more information—it was a dead-end for them. He almost laughed.

Even so, they were far too close for comfort. He continued to watch until they strolled back down to a car, got in and drove off. Richard sat down. He was sweating. It was a good job he had given the fake address, but it had been too close to home, a mistake he would not make again.

Paul was disappointed that it was a false address but had expected it to be. Dave and Pauly made their way back to London to report in person to Paul.

CHAPTER 23

Jeff Swan was one of those coppers that old ladies loved. He always had time to stop and have a few words with the elderly and found them to be very thankful to have policemen like himself around to keep them safe. He was also popular amongst his colleagues and had been in the Met for twenty-two years, and it felt like a lifetime. Jeff was married to Mary, who had been his childhood sweetheart from the age of sixteen when they'd met at secondary school. They had had their ups and downs but it was a good marriage, and Mary was devastated when the police car pulled up outside her house and two sober-faced officers had walked to the front door; she had known immediately that something terrible had happened.

DC Swan had seen huge changes over the years from the time when he walked the beat at the age of nineteen as a fresh-faced probationary officer, and he was still only forty-one: a relatively young man. Everybody always said the best thing about being a copper was doing twenty-five years, getting a good pension and then working part-time to keep the brain ticking over. Jeff had never fired a shot in anger before he had killed Bujar Dushka, the people trafficker, with a single bullet to the head. Yes he had arrested many criminals, burglars, violent thugs, rapists and bank robbers, so he had made a positive contribution to law enforcement on his patch. He'd become a bit stale prior to partnering Karen Foster, but she had reinvigorated him, and they had had a good couple of years together. He had fancied her for a long time and regretted that he had never slept with her, but that was all water under the bridge and now they were more like brother and sister.

Jeff arrived at St Thomas' Hospital exactly twenty-one minutes after being shot in the head in McDonald's on the Old Kent Road. He was immediately rushed into surgery where a team of highly trained doctors and nurses had been nervously waiting for his arrival.

It was evident straight away that Jeff had suffered a penetrating head injury, meaning a wound where an object breaches the cranium but does not exit. This was normally a high-velocity projectile or, in simple terms, a bullet fired from a gun.

The team went to work like a well-oiled machine, the wound was inspected and found to be less traumatic than expected. The doctors were unaware at this stage that the weapon used was an old .22 calibre star-Bonifacio Echever Pistol. The weapon had seen better days and in fact did not even fire in a straight line, which may well have helped Jeff survive. The bullet hit Jeff on the side of the head as he was diving to the side, it then penetrated and hit a glancing blow to the skull and breaking it; because of the trajectory it then embedded itself in the skull and stopped. The problem was that a piece of bone had been broken and pushed a tiny fraction of it into the brain. This had resulted in some tissue damage and, following that, swelling and bleeding.

The doctors removed the bullet very quickly and sealed the wound, and the only thing everybody could do after that was to wait and see what happened. Jeff was transferred to Intensive Care and then later to a private room. The head doctor was heard to comment that it was in the lap of the gods whether Jeff came round or not. Jeff had a stream of visitors daily and his bed was surrounded by 'get-well' cards and flowers. Strangely enough, people had brought grapes and an assortment of fresh juices, and since Jeff obviously couldn't make use of them, these were distributed to other patients who weren't fortunate enough to have visitors. Karen didn't take anything when she visited, as she thought the best thing she could give Jeff were some words of encouragement and love.

CHAPTER 24

"Yeah we're off to the sun, sea, sand and yes plenty of that as well," Tony explained. He was in his element sitting round the table with Sharon, Paul and Lexi, eating, drinking and cracking jokes.

Sharon grinned but didn't find the joke that funny. Sharon had been introduced as Tony's latest bit of skirt that he had only recently met.

They had arrived in disguise and been ushered through the back entrance of the club into a private dining room at the Den Club. It was Sunday 30th November and Paul had asked Tony to Sunday lunch. Paul had hoped that they could part maybe not as best friends, but certainly as brothers that would still look out for each other. It had been a good lunch, best rib of beef with all the trimmings, followed by a delicious apple pie with cream. Paul knew Tony loved his basic food and beef was his favourite.

"So when are you going Tony?" Paul asked.

"I'll enjoy Christmas and then, whoosh, I'm flying away to Espana."

"Well I hope you're getting a big place because we'll want to come out and stay."

Lexi was smiling but underneath the mask she was hating every second of sharing the table with Tony and his woman. The man repulsed her and the thought of going to Spain for a holiday with him filled her with dread and horror. She knew Paul felt the same, so it was all an act.

"You'll be very welcome of course. There'll be a swimming pool, sangria, and cold beers, it's going to be a ball." Tony was being incredibly friendly with Paul, but in truth he loathed him, and half the smiles were because he knew what the very next day would bring.

"What exactly are you going to do all the time?" Paul asked. "You can't spend the rest of your life sitting in the sun drinking cold beer."

"Who says I can't? But seriously, I'm thinking of travelling the world so the place in Spain will just be a base."

Paul was laughing inside. *Travel the world?* If he's more than a mile from Bermondsey he gets homesick for God's sake, he thought.

The Final Act

"Where will you go first then?" Paul asked.

Tony had to think quickly and gave the first country he could think of. "India."

Paul couldn't believe his ears. "India? What the hell do you want to go there for?"

Tony thought quickly. "It's a country of great history and culture. And of course, curry."

Paul couldn't speak. *History? Culture?* Tony was even madder than he thought he was.

"Well don't forget to get your jabs. There's all sorts of diseases you can catch out there."

It was Tony's turn to be speechless. Jabs? He immediately forgot about India and changed the subject. "Been to see the boys recently?" Paul asked.

"No, don't have time."

"You?"

"No but I'll go before I disappear," Tony said.

Paul wanted to know if Tony had heard anything about Richard Philips. "You hear any gossip about where Richard Philips might be?"

Tony didn't blink. "Not a dickybird, I reckon he's abroad." He then burst out laughing. "Wouldn't be surprised if I bumped into him on the beach one day." Everybody chuckled and Paul looked at Tony and felt that he was telling the truth.

"Did you hear about the murder at the Angel?" Paul asked.

That caught Tony off guard for one second, something which Paul picked up on instantly.

Tony then put on a very serious face. "Terrible. It's not safe to go for a pint nowadays."

Paul, Lexi and Sharon knew he was the killer, so Paul thought he would push a bit. "Apparently he was a copper's snitch, so I heard."

Tony's face changed to a hard leering sneer. "Well he got what he fucking deserved then, the cunt."

Lexi looked at him and knew why she hated him so much. He had killed that old man in cold blood, inflicting horrible injuries to his face before he died. And here he was sitting eating Sunday lunch, using language that belonged in the gutter.

"Have you been in the Angel recently Tony?"

"You are joking. Hardly ever go out for God's sake." He turned to Sharon. "Isn't that right luv?"

"Yeah we never ever go out, boring life innit?"

Paul just smiled the smile of the knowing.

"Great lunch Paul, I really enjoyed it." Having said that Tony got up. "Lexi it was lovely to see you, and I wish you both all the best for the future."

Thank God, thought Lexi, they're leaving.

"Thanks for coming Tony. Let us know when you're leaving and we'll see you in the summer in Espana," Paul added with a flourish as they walked out of the room.

"Will do." Tony knew the way to the back door. "Lots of new security everywhere I see?"

"Can't take any risks nowadays Tony. So have a good journey home."

Paul went back to see how Lexi was.

"You alright?" he asked.

Lexi was agitated. "No I've got to go and have a shower. That animal makes me feel dirty."

Paul took her in his arms. "I'm sorry darling. But remember, we won't see him now for months if ever again."

"I pray you're right." And off she went to Paul's private rooms.

CHAPTER 25

Aedan and Carrick were in Bermondsey at seven a.m. They were sitting quietly in their Ford Focus, watching. Pauly came out of his flat and turned left up Drummond Road. He quickly took a left into Tranton Road and walked at a fast pace as usual on his way to Bermondsey Tube Station. The Irish thugs were out of the car and followed slowly at a discreet distance, making sure not to arouse suspicion. Pauly came to the junction of Keeton's Road and turned right: he liked to walk because he could feel the community, savour the smells of local life, and say good morning to people he regularly saw on the route.

Pauly strode up the road and looked at his watch: he was on schedule as always. He glanced around as he walked, taking in the local views. Pauly was also alert as to change, and on this particular morning for some reason he felt a slight uneasiness. He glanced round and noticed the two young men in black leather jackets twenty yards behind him, then he saw them turn right into Chalfont House and he relaxed and strode on.

Aedan and Carrick didn't open the door to Chalfont House. They stopped and waited for a minute and then ran across the road and, using the trees as cover, they moved quickly after Pauly. They had two hundred yards to go before they hit Jamaica Road, so there was still time. They had chosen knives, because they were quiet weapons, meaning with a bit of luck they'd have more time to get away. They drew their knives and quickened the pace. It was down to a hundred yards now, and they were almost running, closer and closer and they were almost on him. Then the unbelievable happened: they heard the siren first and then saw the police car turn at the corner of Jamaica Road and head straight towards them. They dropped the knives and slowed down to a walk as the police car screamed past them, heading down the road.

The opportunity had been missed but they kept following their prey. Pauly glanced back, saw them, and in an instant knew they were after him. He suddenly sprinted like hell for the Tube station and safety. The boys snatched up their weapons and followed at a run: they didn't like messing up jobs and were determined to see this one through to the end. Pauly got to the station, ran down the wide stairs and jumped over the barrier, as the guy manning the station concourse shouted, "Hey you! Stop!" Pauly was stopping for no one. He sprinted to the platform and jumped on a waiting train, which happened to be

The Final Act

on the Jubilee Line, travelling towards London Bridge. He had got into the first carriage and immediately marched up the train, heading towards the front. He was exhausted and gasping for breath.

Aedan and Carrick were also shattered but they made it to the first carriage of the train just as it pulled away. Pauly was sick with worry. He had made it to the front of the train but was effectively at a dead-end with nowhere to go. He didn't know whether the two thugs were on the train or not, but knew that he would soon find out. The carriage was empty apart from an elderly couple sitting in the middle section. He thought about his mum and dad, whom he was very close to, and his eyes filled with tears, then he hit himself on the head, telling himself to snap out of it.

Pauly was especially annoyed that he was not carrying a weapon. He tried to phone Paul but could not get a signal. He was watching the door like a hawk, praying he could get to London Bridge. Meanwhile the two hit-men were striding purposefully up the train towards the front. Paul was sweating and worried as he looked around for anything he could use as a weapon, but found nothing.

They were nearly there. 'The next station is London Bridge' came over the tannoy. The carriage door opened and the two boys came in. Pauly put his right hand inside his jacket, pretending that he had a weapon. He looked hard at the boys, giving them the unspoken message that he had a gun and if needs be would use it. His attackers stopped, not sure if he was bluffing. They couldn't take the risk and stood still. The train pulled into London Bridge, and Pauly slammed the 'open' button and rushed out of the opening door. He ran for the exit escalator and took the steps two at a time, then he glanced back looking for the black jackets. There was no sign of the two thugs. Thank God, he thought.

He reached the top of the escalator and looked back again: there was no one— he was safe. He took a long deep breath and let it out slowly, knowing he could relax. He went through the barrier and joined the mass of rush-hour commuters heading for the main station. He noticed the Crème Donut stall, passed the Chocolate Shop, the South African Shop, shirts for sale and the free Barclays Bank cash points. He bounded up the last small escalator and he was in the main station concourse.

The Final Act

The hunted man kept looking back but could see nothing. He slowed, wondering what he should do. Then he made a decision and went towards the main exit, and passed through the wide glass doors. He noticed the entrance to the Shard building and kept left past the small café on the corner and kept going down the road. He passed a couple of bars and saw a sign over a smart looking building saying 'London Bridge Hotel'. Pauly went straight in through the hotel's front door, finding himself in a lounge area. There were two uniformed staff at a concierge desk straight ahead. He approached them.

"Can I get some coffee?" he asked.

"Yes sir. Over to the right you'll find the coffee lounge."

Pauly followed the directions and walked into the coffee lounge. There were tables scattered round the room and on the right-hand side some booths against the wall, which could accommodate six people in each of them. He went to the end booth and sat down, still keeping an eye on the door. A waitress came over and Pauly ordered a latte and a toasted bacon sandwich.

He relaxed and took his phone out, noticing a man wearing a bright red jacket enter the lounge; he was certainly not one of the thugs who had been following him. Pauly keyed the numbers into his phone, taking his eye off the man for a second. The dialling tone sounded in his ear as he felt a pain in his neck. He put his hand up and grasped the handle of a knife, but the pain got worse as the knife's blade was pulled against his throat. He could see blood fountaining away from his face and it was covering his hands, then his mouth filled with blood and he spat.

Then a man appeared in front of him and he saw something green. There was a pain in his stomach which then got worse as a knife was ripped up to his chest. He died as blood and intestines poured out of the huge gash in his torso.

The two killers walked slowly out of the lounge door directly onto the road, turned right and headed back to London Bridge Station with the intention of getting straight back on the Tube. After five yards they heard a loud scream from the hotel. They were soon back on a Northern Line train heading towards Bank Station, from where they would change onto the Central Line for Shepherds Bush, the place they'd planned to go for a drink and a meal. Once they were comfortably seated, both young men took off their jackets, turned them inside out, and then put them back on, so that they were once again wearing black jackets.

The Final Act

* * *

Roddy, Paul Bolton's accountant, had moved out of Bermondsey years ago and lived in a huge old Victorian house overlooking Clapham Common. He caught the same Northern Line Tube train every day at Clapham Common Station, which took him the seven stops to Leicester Square and then, after a five-minute walk, he was sitting in his office at eight-thirty on the dot every morning.

He came out of his front door and descended the steps. He was wearing his brand new Crombie thick wool coat that he'd bought at the weekend, and as he glanced around he noticed the brickwork on the side of the house needed repointing and made a mental note to get someone in. Roddy got to the bottom of the steps and turned left. He was in a good mood and was swinging his briefcase to the tune 'My Way' by Frank Sinatra, that he was singing in his head. He felt a car slow down alongside and someone called out his name. When he stopped and turned to the car he was shocked to see Richard Philips in the front passenger seat.

"Roddy how are you?" Richard called out.

Roddy was terrified. "Fancy seeing you here Richard."

A huge man who appeared to be a bodyguard got out of the back of the car and took a step towards him. Roddy considered running but knew he would not get away.

Richard could see he was a worried man. "Don't worry. If I'd wanted you dead, you'd be lying on the pavement already."

"What do you want?"

"Get in and I'll tell you."

The accountant had no choice and Richard's assistant took his arm and guided him into the back of the Jaguar. Roddy found himself sitting between two big men, aware that there was no escape. The driver put his foot down and the Jaguar pulled out and joined the traffic.

* * *

It was a typical Monday morning for the Bolton household in Chelsea Harbour. Lexi and Paul had got up as usual at seven-thirty. Charlie never showed his face until nine unless Lexi had specifically asked him to get up early because she wanted to go somewhere. Lexi made Paul's usual breakfast, which was coffee and toast with lime marmalade. Duke was usually knocking on the door at eight-fifteen exactly. Lexi would let him in, ask if he wanted a coffee, and he would say, "Not this morning thank you."

It was a ritual that they followed every single day and Duke had never ever had a coffee. Duke and Paul left at precisely eight twenty-five and would arrive at the Den just before nine o'clock. This particular morning was no different to any other. Paul said his goodbyes to Lexi, and Paul and Duke disappeared down to the underground car park. Lexi busied herself with a few chores and then went back into her room to shower and dress. She was due at the doctor's surgery for a standard examination at eleven, so was not rushing. Charlie surfaced at ten past nine and cooked himself some sausages and eggs. Lexi could smell them and decided she too could eat something cooked, and she ambled into the kitchen.

"Charlie they smell delicious," she told her friend and minder. "Any spare sausages?"

"'Course! I always do one or two extra."

Lexi grabbed a sausage off the grill and started to eat it with her fingers. "Hmm lovely, you know we're due at the doc's at eleven?"

"Yeah, no problem, we've got plenty of time."

Lexi went back to her room to finish doing her make-up and reflected on how fond she had grown of Charlie. He was young, brash and excitable but coupled with that he was thoughtful and kind and would do anything she asked without hesitation. She was applying her lipstick when the doorbell rang. Who could that be so early she thought? She listened as Charlie went to the door. Charlie had been told to always check through the spyhole, which was exactly what he did on this occasion. He saw a man in a courier uniform holding a huge bouquet of flowers. He relaxed and assumed that the bouquet was from Paul. The minder opened the door and smiled at the courier. He then very nearly had a heart attack as the courier took his hand away from the flowers and put the gun he'd been concealing against Charlie's forehead.

The man whispered: "Move back and keep quiet or else."

The Final Act

Charlie was terrified. Was he a burglar, he wondered? Another man appeared and followed them into the hallway. Charlie he prayed that Lexi would keep quiet but his prayers were not answered.

"Charlie? Who is it?"

Charlie opened his mouth and was about to speak but the man pushed the gun's muzzle hard into his head whilst holding his finger to his mouth to signify silence. Charlie's heart was thumping and his brain had stopped working. *What to do? What to do?* he was thinking. He finally spoke quietly:

"What do you want?"

The man with the gun at his head again held his finger to his lips. The second intruder now had a gun in his hand.

"Charlie who was it at the door?" came the shout again.

The three of them inched into the lounge and the man pushed Charlie onto a chair. Charlie heard the bedroom door shut and knew Lexi was coming, and he began to panic. It was his job to look after her, he had let her and Paul down, and he had to do something.

Lexi sauntered down the small corridor and pushed the lounge door. And at that precise second Charlie dropped his head and went for the man's gun hand. He managed to grab it and twist it away from him. The gun went off and the shot struck and smashed the mirror hanging on the wall.

It was bedlam: Lexi screamed and turned to run back to the bedroom, knowing that there was a fully-loaded gun hidden in a secret wall safe in the ensuite bathroom. The second man went after her and caught her as she had her hand on the bathroom door. He punched the side of her face and she was instantly groggy, and he then dragged her back to the lounge by her feet.

Seeing the struggle going on, he dropped Lexi, and attacked Charlie from behind, smashing his gun onto the back of his head; he felt the impact of the shattering skull reverberating right up his arm. Charlie went down, apparently dead. Lexi woke up to see Charlie lying on the floor motionless and she feared the worst. What did these animals want, she wondered? She felt powerful arms lift her up and she staggered, eventually standing upright, and this was the second she thought of her unborn baby. *Please let him be alright* she thought.

"You bastards," she snarled. "What do you want?"

"Shut it bitch," one of the men replied. The attackers had a quick look around, and one of them went to the bedroom and came back with some jewellery and cash, saying, "Little bonus for us," as the other man smiled.

The thugs then turned their attention back to Lexi. They taped her mouth and tied her arms behind her back, they then marched her to the front door and opened it. One of them looked around, to check it was quiet, then they pushed and pulled as they manoeuvred Lexi's body, and went straight down to the car park. It had seemed like a lifetime but had all been over in three minutes: poor Charlie was dead and Lexi had been abducted.

Paul was in his office when Duke knocked and entered.

"Something's up and I don't like it," Duke announced. Paul was immediately concerned and stopped what he was doing.

"What's the problem?"

"Neither Roddy nor Pauly have come in. Have you heard anything?"

"No. You've obviously tried calling them?"

"No answer from either," said Duke with a puzzled look.

Paul just sat for a second thinking. "Well maybe they're just late. Pauly may well have been on the piss last night."

That second the phone rang and Paul picked up the receiver: it was Carla and she sounded worried.

"Mr Bolton there's a man on the phone who says he knows where Pauly is."

"What?" Paul was confused. "Put him through."

What Paul didn't know was that Carla had been shagging Pauly senseless for weeks and they were very close.

"Hello?" Paul spoke into the phone.

"Young Pauly's had an accident," was the terse statement. "You won't be seeing him again." And the phone went dead.

Paul looked at Duke as he hung up. "Someone says Pauly's had an accident. I don't get it."

The phone rang again and he answered it.

"It's the detective from Rotherhithe," Carla told him.

"Paul it's Karen," the detective sergeant's voice came on the line. "Listen, there's been a shooting at Chelsea Harbour." As soon as Paul heard the words 'Chelsea Harbour' he knew the war had started.

"Wait Karen," Paul said, calling out to his friend: "Duke get hold of Lexi for me now."

He was back on the line, listening to Karen's words. "There's also been a murder at the London Bridge Hotel. I'm sure I've seen the victim at the club with you."

Now Paul knew what had happened to Pauly.

Duke looked at Paul with a very worried expression, saying anxiously, "No answer from Lexi or Charlie."

"Karen what's happened at Chelsea Harbour?" Paul begged her. "It could be Lexi."

"Give me a minute. I'll call back."

The seconds ticked away. "Keep trying the numbers," he instructed Duke. "Call Roddy again as well."

The phone rang—it was Karen: "A young man's been killed, sorry Paul it happened at your flat. Lexi's gone."

Paul couldn't think or move.

"Paul, you need to get a grip," Duke shook his arm. "We have things to do."

Paul looked at him in total confusion. He shut his eyes and then, with a huge effort, took control of himself. "Yes, Duke, we have things to do. I'm not losing anyone else."

A phone call came in later that morning telling Paul that 'they' had Roddy and Lexi, but who 'they' were was still unclear. Paul drafted in extra muscle and all staff were sent home and the club closed until further notice. Paul vowed that everyone involved in the killing of Pauly and Charlie would pay with their lives. Those involved with taking Lexi would also die but their end would be very slow and very painful.

The Final Act

* * *

The car door opened and Lexi was dragged out. All she knew was that the journey seemed to have taken about an hour. They had blindfolded her securely so she had seen nothing. She could hear voices and could swear she recognised one but wasn't sure who it was. She was taken into a building and suddenly was pushed onto a tall hard-backed chair, her blindfold was ripped off and she opened her eyes, first having to adjust them to the light. Then she saw him.

"You fucking bastard Tony," she said in disbelief. "You were eating lunch with me yesterday and now this. You are a disgusting animal and I hate you so much you couldn't even imagine it."

Tony was about to speak but his mobile rang and he answered it and began a conversation with someone.

Lexi looked round and was shocked to see Roddy tied to another chair close by. "Roddy are you alright?" she asked.

"As well as can be expected. You?"

She looked at the two guys who had taken her from the flat and then turned back to Roddy. "These two thugs like hitting women. Real men wouldn't do that. Scum, that's what they are."

One of the thugs spoke up: "This one's got a very big mouth."

Lexi surveyed her surroundings. It seemed to be a small warehouse of some sort, used for storing junk by the looks of the rubbish at the far end. There was one main door and a few barred windows, while to the side there looked to be a couple of offices. She couldn't hear any noise from outside so assumed they were not on an industrial estate, so it had to a single unit somewhere. The door to the offices opened and she was again in shock, but it didn't stop her speaking:

"My God! So much scum in the same room at one time. I think I'm going to throw up."

Behind Richard were two women, one was the one that Tony had brought to lunch the previous day and the other a strikingly attractive black woman. Lexi was on a roll and spoke directly to the women:

157

"My God what are you two doing with these apologies for men? They killed my friend, a young man in his twenties, this morning. They smashed his skull into pieces, did you know that?"

Julie and Sharon looked slightly shocked and obviously had not been aware of it. Tony was fed up with this and clicked his phone off.

"Lexi," he snapped. "If you open your mouth again you will be gagged."

Lexi framed an answer in her mind but thought better of it and kept quiet.

Tony looked at the two women, telling them: "Go back in the office. We'll join you in a minute."

He thought for a moment and then nodded at Richard, and the two of them followed the women into the office.

One of the thugs eyed Lexi, saying, "You might provide some good fun for us later," he sneered. "Once we're left alone with you, believe me you'll regret all that gobbing off." He looked her up and down, leaving her in no doubt as to what he had in mind.

Roddy had been watching all the talk and various interactions and had kept quiet. He was not a man of violence but he swore to himself that if anybody touched Lexi he would do everything he could to stop them. Nobody realised Lexi was pregnant, and Roddy prayed she would be able to hold onto the baby.

"You alright Lexi?" he asked.

She nodded.

"Don't worry. Everything will work out. It's all about money."

Lexi was pleased to hear him say that, but the possibility of being left alone with the thugs worried her beyond belief.

* * *

Paul was in control and refused to let it all get on top of him. He had broken down when Emma died but he was not going to let that happen again. He now knew the situation: Pauly and Charlie were dead, giving out a clear message that if needs be they would kill again. They had Roddy and Lexi and he was now waiting for some sort of contact. It was not long in coming. The phone rang and Paul snatched it up:

The Final Act

"Paul it's Tony. I—"

"It's not a good time Tony," Paul interrupted him. "Can I call you back?"

"You fucking idiot," Tony jeered at him. "You don't get it do you? Wait a second and listen."

Tony went back out of the office and stood next to Lexi. He held the phone to her mouth and told her to speak.

Lexi didn't know who was on the line, and said, "Hello it's Lexi. I'm fine."

Paul nearly fell off his chair. "Lexi? It's Paul. What's happening? Are you OK?"

Before she could reply Tony grabbed the phone back and resumed the conversation:

"I hold all the cards Paul and I have Roddy as well. If you want to see them alive again you'd better do as I say."

Paul was incensed. "Tony you will regret this. I promise that as long as I live I'll—"

"For God's sake shut up Paul! You're like an old record. You'll do as you're fucking well told or Roddy will be the first and then it'll be Lexi's turn."

"You hurt her Tony and my God you'll regret it—"

"I said shut the fuck up! I want what's mine and that is the clubs."

"You're on the run. How the hell can you run the clubs? You're not capable of running them anyway."

"You clever cunt," Tony snarled. "Always the fucking clever one, aren't you? I'll have the clubs or I'll deliver two dead bodies. It's your choice."

"I need to think. I'm in shock."

"'Course you are. Because I've beaten you. Yes *me* Paul, *me the nutter*." Tony was laughing hysterically. "You have till tomorrow morning. Meanwhile I'll arrange some entertainment for Roddy and Lexi. I'll call you at ten."

"Don't hurt her Tony! I mean it! Tony, *Tony—*" But Tony had gone.

Paul was devastated, Tony had shown his true colours again and it did indeed look like he held all the cards.

Tony and Richard were knocking back whiskies in the warehouse offices.

"What did he say?" Richard asked.

Tony smiled. "We hold all the aces and he's in the shit and he knows it. Don't worry we'll own the clubs and Paul is fucked."

They carried on drinking and Tony was admiring Julie's body. He liked what he saw and wondered if they could try a session of swapping sex partners.

"Richard everything's looking good and we need to celebrate," Tony said. "What about a bit of fun?"

"You know me mate. I'm up for anything."

Tony looked at Sharon and Julie. "What about you girls? Are you up for a night of fun?"

Julie had the experience and knew straight away what Tony was contemplating, but she wasn't sure whether Sharon knew what was going on or if she would be up for a sex session or not. Julie looked at the two men.

"I'm up for anything," she announced boldly. "And I'm looking forward to it." With that she lifted her skirt and the men gasped: she wasn't wearing knickers, and her smooth pussy was looking glorious. Tony was transfixed: he wanted her, he desperately wanted her, and then he looked at Sharon.

Sharon was a sex maniac but hadn't thought about the four of them having a session, however she decided it could be fun. She took a step towards Julie and went down on her knees. Julie's skirt had fallen slightly, so she lifted it back up and grabbed the black girl's arse cheeks with her two hands, and she then buried her mouth between Julie's legs. The ex-prostitute was pleasantly surprised and held the back of Sharon's head and pulled it in tight onto her pussy. Tony and Richard were in heaven.

Julie spoke: "Let's move this to a hotel shall we?"

"Let's go then before I get carried away right now, Richard you ready?" Tony asked.

"Yes let's get going," Richard replied eagerly. "Come on girls."

They left the office and went into the warehouse. "We'll see you two tomorrow," sneered Tony to Lexi and Roddy. "Have a pleasant night."

Roddy raised his voice: "What about some food and a hot drink?"

"Do you good to go without, you fat bastard!" And with that they left. Lexi was concerned. She looked at the two thugs, who were smoking and chatting. They seemed disinterested in her, which pleased her a great deal.

"Excuse me guys, I need the loo," she called out.

The two men turned to her and smiled.

The biggest thug pulled her up and took her through the office to the toilet. He undid her hands and she entered the loo and went to close the door, but he jammed his foot in the door to held it open. She just looked for a second and then pulled her trousers and knickers down and sat on the seat, then she peed, acting as though he wasn't even there. He got a thrill watching her and would love to have fucked her, but Tony had said no touching. He took her back to the warehouse and retied her hands and sat her down. One of the men left and returned thirty minutes later laden with numerous silver foils of gorgeous smelling Chinese takeaway food. Lexi wasn't bothered but she could see Roddy was suffering.

"Why don't you be nice and give Roddy a bit?" she asked them.

"Shut the fuck up!" And with that they went into the office and shut the door. Lexi looked around again for any sign of a weapon or a way to get out. The place was nearly empty but she could see some sort of metal tubes at the other end, about twenty yards away. Even if she got there what good would they be against guns, she thought?

The warehouse was in Tony's back yard: Bermondsey. Specifically it was between Bolina Road and Ilderton Road, close to South Bermondsey railway Station and Millwall Football Club. There was a large tract of wasteland in that area with one or two small dilapidated warehouses which were originally used for storing railway gear.

Tony, Richard and the two girls piled into the Jag and left the warehouse. Richard was soon on Rotherhithe New Road, he got to the junction with the Old Kent Road and saw the McDonald's, and the memories of shooting the copper flooded back. He could feel sweat trickling down his neck and he wiped it off with his hand. Tony turned to him.

"Isn't that the McDonald's where the copper Swan got done?" he asked.

The Final Act

"I reckon so." Richard was desperate to get away, so he put his foot down and they roared up the Old Kent Road towards central London. They passed Walworth Academy, Argos and very soon Richard turned left into the Eurotraveller Premier Hotel car park. He parked up and the four of them made for the reception. As was usual for that hotel, the reception was manned by a lady from Poland, which was fortuitous because it meant that she was very unlikely to recognise them. They booked a double room on the pretence that only one couple was staying, but the receptionist took no interest anyway. Tony was so excited he had a massive hard-on just thinking about what was coming. He hurried the booking process on and playfully slapped Julie's arse as they moved towards the room. Halfway to their destination, Tony stopped.

"Shit, we haven't got any booze and I'm getting hungry," he said. "What about you guys?"

Richard spoke first: "Yeah we need some food and some whisky, I'll go and get some from the bar, I'll be a few minutes, so you start without me." He turned back and set off.

Tony and the girls arrived at room forty and Tony opened the door. It was a budget room but had a good-sized double bed, which the two girls jumped on to and started bouncing up and down. After a minute they calmed down and looked at each other and smiled. Both of them could see the huge bulge in Tony's trousers. They jumped off the bed and fell at Tony's feet. Sharon undid his belt while Julie was quickly pulling the zip down, then Sharon tugged at the trousers and they came down, revealing a huge hard cock.

Julie licked her lips and started paying attention to his balls, while Sharon took him full in her mouth and started sucking. Within seconds Tony was groaning and could feel that he wouldn't last long. He groped at Julie's breasts, and she stopped licking his balls and started peeling off her clothes. Soon she was naked and Tony fondled her full delicious breasts. He then reached down and felt the smooth wet pussy that he was longing to enter.

Then Sharon undressed to reveal a full set of matching black sexy underwear. She took the knickers and bra off but left the stocking tights. Julie liked what she saw and grabbed for Sharon's pussy and inserted two fingers; Sharon was groaning now, as was Tony. He knew he couldn't last much longer now that both the girls were sucking and licking and slobbering all over his cock and balls, and then it happened: Julie reached behind his arse and started rubbing

The Final Act

his arse hole, his cock got even harder and he was out of control, and he thrust into Sharon's mouth faster and faster. Julie moved behind Tony and started licking his arse. It was time. Tony gave one last huge thrust, saying "Ahhhhhhhhh", and semen poured into Sharon's mouth. Julie rushed round and took the cock into her mouth and collected the remains, as she drained every last drop of cum out of his flagging cock.

Tony slumped onto the bed, saying, "God I needed that. You two are the best."

There was a knock on the door and Tony jumped. He then remembered that Richard was coming back and relaxed. Julie opened the door and stepped back as Richard entered the room with two bags and laughed, saying, "You did start without me. I can smell it."

Sharon sidled up to Richard and held his balls through his clothing. "Don't worry we're ready for you next while Tony has a rest."

"Well let's eat first," said Richard, opening the first bag to reveal takeaway trays of curry and rice. The girls took over and passed the trays and plastic cutlery around. Richard opened the second bag and took out a bottle of whisky and four plastic cups. Soon they were all eating curry and knocking back whiskies.

The girls finished eating first and decided to start on Richard. He hadn't finished his food but soon lost interest in his stomach. The girls stripped him naked and made him lie on the bed. Sharon started sucking his cock so that it was soon huge and swollen, and Julie sat on his mouth so that Richard could eat dessert.

Tony was watching and could feel his cock coming back to life. Tony got behind Sharon's arse and entered her pussy with a deep thrust. Sharon was sucking Richard's cock and Tony was slamming into her pussy from behind. Julie then climbed off Richard's face and joined Tony behind Richard. She took his cock in her hand and sucked it and then fed it back into Sharon's pussy; she did this several times and Tony was loving it.

Richard was close to coming and Julie joined Sharon in licking and sucking him off to finish. Richard was gasping "Yes! Yes! Now!" He arched his back and pushed his cock into Sharon's mouth and shot his load, but Sharon swiftly whipped his cock back out and masturbated him so that cum flew all over the two girls. The pair of women were loving it as much as the men were and the

The Final Act

afternoon was a glorious orgy of unbridled sex, which was finished off with Tony and Richard both double penetrating the girls one after the other. They finished the whisky, all had hot showers and then they made their way back to check on Lexi and Roddy.

CHAPTER 26

The phone on Jeff's desk rang. No one had yet been assigned to the sick officer's work station, they were all hoping he'd soon be back.

"Penny can you get that please?" Karen asked the junior officer.

"Sure," Penny agreed, and picked up the receiver. "Hello CID."

Penny listened for a few seconds. "OK." she turned to Karen, raising her eyebrows. "It's Paul Bolton."

Karen was not surprised. "Transfer it over here," she told her.

"Hello Paul how are you?" Karen said into the phone. Penny could hear Paul talking but could not distinguish his words. Karen just sat with the phone at her ear saying the occasional 'yes' or 'no', it seemed to go on for ever and then she said, "OK." and put the phone down.

Penny was waiting and waiting till she couldn't wait any longer.

"Well what was that all about?" she finally asked.

"Nothing." And so saying, Karen got up and strode out the office.

Penny went to the door and saw Karen calling to Michael in the corridor that she must speak with him urgently, then her boss disappeared into Michael's office and began an animated conversation with him.

The younger woman was nonplussed. She had been through the files on the Angel and Mayflower killings and couldn't see a way forward. She had been taught there was always something to work on, but that you had to know every detail of an investigation to be able to find it. Karen had told her she was sure Richard Philips or Tony Bolton were involved in one, or even possibly both, murders but there was no supporting evidence, nothing.

Karen came back into the office with a spring in her step: she had got whatever it was she had wanted. She then rummaged around her desk and found what she was after, and she held out a piece of paper towards Penny. The paper had an image on it.

"Penny this is the killer of Micky at the Angel pub," Karen told her. "Get it out to all officers urgently. It's an image of Tony Bolton in disguise, and the other piece of news is that Richard Philips is holed up somewhere in Essex."

Chelsea Harbour was out of Karen's field of jurisdiction but as a courtesy she had spoken to the detective in charge of the case and filled him in on the Bolton connection. She decided to call him again and see what progress had been made. But that turned out to be a waste of time as there was no progress: no prints, no blood, no semen, no nothing. There was also no DNA present apart from what matched Lexi, Paul and Charlie.

Every police officer in south-east London was looking for Philips and Bolton, prison mug shots had been sent out and Tony's image would now be replaced by the new one of him in disguise. Finding the two criminals was listed as being of the highest priority. Neither sight nor sound had been forthcoming, the men seemed to have just disappeared into the ether.

* * *

Tony and Richard and their partners arrived back at the warehouse to find Roddy and Lexi sleeping. The two guards were drinking beer, smoking and playing cards. The two girls disappeared into the office and sat discussing the merits of vaginal and anal sex.

Tony and Richard had achieved what they had set out to do: they had killed Pauly purely so that Paul would know that they meant business. The boy dying at the flat in Chelsea was just one of those unfortunate things that happened. The two of them agreed that Paul would have no choice other than to agree to their demands, for they knew that he worshipped Lexi and would not let anything happen to her. They spoke with the guards and reiterated the 'no touch' policy with Lexi. Since they had nothing else to do they decided to go home and reconvene in the morning.

Richard and Julie got back to Basildon at seven p.m. It had been a long day and both of them were tired. Richard suggested a takeaway meal, which they bought at a local Indian restaurant and took back to the house to eat. They drank some wine and curled up on the sofa watching the *Braveheart* film on TV. Richard was still thinking about the tapes. Why on earth he had sent the three original tapes he couldn't work out, but in the end he thought it was because Paul had given him the brothels and he was thankful for that and had consequently lowered his guard. Well he wasn't about to give up, and if Paul didn't pay then someone would suffer.

CHAPTER 27

It was still freezing so Tony and Sharon dressed up in coats, scarves and gloves—they were more concerned with keeping warm than how they looked. They got to the warehouse first at ten a.m, while Richard and Julie turned up at ten thirty-five. The two girls were now part of the team and even if they didn't realise it the reality was that they could get a long prison term for the crimes committed by their men because of their association. The two women were sent into the office to make coffee while Tony and Richard discussed their next move at one end of the room, well away from Roddy and Lexi.

Roddy and Lexi had suffered during the night. It was freezing cold and they had been made to sleep on the floor with no covering at all. Roddy had been wearing a suit when he had been picked up, while Lexi had been fortunate that she had dressed warmly, but even so she was still cold. Lexi was becoming more and more concerned about the baby and could easily have broken down in tears and asked Tony to take pity on her. But she refused to do that and remained strong—she kept telling herself she could always have more babies. Roddy was weak and did not have Lexi's mental strength. He was just praying that soon he would be back at home with his family in Clapham.

Sharon came out of the office to see Tony.

"Shall I make some for them," she asked, looking at Roddy and Lexi.

God, please say yes thought Roddy, while Lexi knew that a hot drink would be a life saver.

"Fuck off," Tony snapped. "When I want you to start looking after those two I'll let you know."

Sharon scuttled back into the office. "No drink for the two of them," she said to Julie.

"Jesus they must have been freezing last night," Julie was on Sharon's side. "Surely it wouldn't hurt to give them a hot drink?"

"Do you want to argue with Tony?"

"Last person in the world I'd argue with! Forget it."

Sharon and Julie took coffees out to Tony, Richard and the two guards. Lexi was boiling over with hatred for Tony.

"Tony you are such a shit aren't you?" Lexi called out. "A real moron. Can you even read or write?"

The criminals' girlfriends looked at each other. They were both thinking the same: that this woman is either very brave or very stupid, or probably both.

Tony broke off from talking with Richard.

"This is the last time I warn you Lexi," he said in a low voice. "Keep your mouth shut. One more speech from you and I swear I'll give you to these two as a present. You do understand me, don't you?"

Lexi knew exactly what he meant. The two guards had been eyeing her up at every opportunity. Each time she went to the loo she thought they might attack her.

"Leave her alone you bastard!" Roddy shouted.

Everybody turned to look at the portly accountant. Tony took three deliberate steps and was standing right in front of him.

"What did you fucking well say?"

"I—I said leave her alone!"

Tony pulled back his arm and hit Roddy on the side of his head just above the ear. Roddy and the chair fell over and he did not move. Lexi was terrified, thinking he could be dead. But surely he couldn't be dead from one punch, could he, she hoped?

"You bastard Tony," Lexis said. "Is he alive?"

Sharon and Julie were also staring at Roddy, hoping he would open his eyes or something. Tony was also concerned, as he hadn't wanted to kill him yet.

He looked at the two guards and said, "Who cares if he's dead or not? Pick him up."

They heaved the chair up and Roddy shook his head from side to side and opened his eyes; he was alive.

Lexi was worried. She suddenly had the realisation that Tony was going to kill them both anyway. He was a maniac and of course killing her would be the ultimate way to get back at Paul.

She spoke quickly to Sharon and Julie: "You know he's going to kill us both don't you? Has he told you that? You both will be wanted by the police as accessories to murder." She spoke slowly and deliberately. "When you are caught you will get life in prison. Is that how you want to spend the rest of your days?"

Tony leapt at Lexi and slapped her face, the loud noise echoing around the room. Lexi reeled from the pain.

"You see?" she yelled at the two women. "I told you he's going to kill us."

Richard had been watching all this and felt it was time to intervene. "Nobody's going to be killed," he reassured them. "When we get what we want you'll be set free." He paused, then looked at his colleague. "Let's go in the office Tony."

Once they were alone, Richard let rip: "Tony you better keep your cool or your temper will get the better of you! We need these two alive, so don't do anything stupid."

"Listen to me Richard. They can live for the time being but when we do have what we want they are mine, and what I do with them is my business. Are you alright with that?"

Richard instantly regretted getting involved with Tony, for he was going to kill their hostages. It was clear that he had been planning it all along.

"When we have what we want they are yours," he agreed and went out of the office to get away from the maniac, who he thought was without question the devil incarnate.

Ten minutes later Sharon and Julie were outside getting some fresh air. They were both terrified by what Lexi had said about Tony killing them. Julie had said she couldn't believe Tony could possibly do it just like that in cold blood. Sharon put her straight, telling her that Tony was more than capable of killing them. The two of them stood in silence for a minute reflecting on what they had got themselves involved in.

"Why don't we do a runner?" Julie suggested.

"Listen Julie," Sharon said patiently. "I don't think you understand. Both these men, they are killers. If we ran they would come after us and we would be dead meat. Do you understand?"

Julie was more scared than ever: there seemed no way out.

It was midday and Tony put the call in to Paul.

Carla put the call through.

"I hope you have some good news for me Paul?" Tony began.

"How are Roddy and Lexi?"

"Don't worry about them, they are fine."

"I do worry about them. Tony, let me speak to Lexi."

"No. So do we have a deal?"

"I want to speak to Lexi." Paul had decided he would do nothing until he spoke to her.

"OK." Tony went back into the warehouse. "Say hello to lover boy," he said to Lexi, sticking the phone next to her face.

Tony relaxed for one second. It was enough for Lexi.

She shouted so Paul would hear it clearly:

"He's going to kill us anyway! Give him nothing! Give him nothing, hear me? NOTHING!" She was screaming. Tony pulled the phone away and clicked it off.

"You fucking bitch!" He lifted his arm and punched Lexi hard in the eye. The chair flew back and landed on the floor with a crash.

Before Tony knew what happening Roddy had lifted himself and his chair and flew at him, screaming loudly. Tony couldn't get out the way quickly enough and Roddy struck his body with his head, and Tony went flying. Roddy landed with a bang and couldn't get back up again.

Lexi had managed to turn the chair and could see the whole room. The two guards grabbed Roddy and picked him back up as Tony scrambled to his feet. Tony screamed at the guards: "Give me the knife." One of the guards took a six-inch flick knife out of a leather holder strapped to his arm and he gave it to Tony.

"Now you're going to find out what happens when you really piss me off."

Tony walked around Roddy, slashing at his body with the knife. It was so sharp it went through his white shirt like a knife through butter. He cut Roddy on the arms, blood was pouring from the wounds, and then he started on his legs, swishing the knife backwards and forwards across his thighs and calves. Roddy was screaming, and a huge pool of blood was forming on the floor.

"You cunt! You fuck with me this is what you get!" He slashed Roddy across his face twice, cutting deep wounds from ear to chin on both sides.

Lexi was shouting: "Stop! For God's sake stop it!"

Richard and the guards kept out of the way while the two girls were in the office watching through the window, terrified but unable to look away.

Tony was uncontrollable: nothing could have stopped him. He struck twice more to both shoulders and then stopped. He was gasping for breath and was foaming at the mouth. He threw the knife down and stumbled into the office. He collapsed in a chair and sat there, taking in massive lungfuls of air, but he eventually calmed down and his breathing returned to near normal.

Lexi was looking at Roddy. He had cuts all over his body and face and was obviously bleeding to death. He couldn't speak but was mumbling incoherently and Lexi couldn't make out the words.

"God somebody help him please!" Lexi begged. "Take him to a hospital, please! He's dying! Please!"

Nobody moved. Tony came out of the office looking almost sane. He looked at the mumbling Roddy, picked up the knife, took two steps, lifted his head by the hair and cut his throat from ear to ear. Blood squirted into the air, Roddy made a gurgling noise and died. Lexi was in shock but she thanked God it was over for Roddy. She told him she would probably be seeing him soon.

Sharon and Julie were so terrified that at the moment Tony cut Roddy's throat Sharon wet herself. Even the two guards had been shocked at the level of violence. Tony wiped the knife clean with a rag and slipped it into his pocket.

"It's done, finished," Tony snapped. "He won't bother us again." Nobody could speak and then the smell hit them: Roddy had shitted himself and the smell was spreading out across the room.

"Jesus!" shouted Tony. He collected his thoughts. "You two drag the body to the end over there and cover it."

Neither of the guards moved.

"Well get on with it!" Tony looked at them and they decided to move a bit quicker. Just as they grabbed an arm each Roddy's left leg jumped up. The two men dropped the body and rushed away. "He's still alive," one yelled out in terror.

Lexi shouted: "Oh my God! Jesus help him!"

Tony laughed. "He's not alive it's just his muscles twitching. Fucking hell get on with it."

They dragged Roddy to the far end of the room, found some sacking cloth and used it to cover the body as best they could.

A feeling of depression hung over the room. Lexi was in shock at the death of Roddy while also being terrified for the safety of her baby. Sharon and Julie were sitting in the office unable to even speak. The two guards were back playing cards, seemingly without a care in the world. On top of everything was the horrible smell of blood and shit permeating throughout the warehouse.

"What's wrong with you all? Come on, cheer up, it's not as though we lost a dear friend." Tony was laughing as he said it. "Lexi, are you alright love?"

Once again everybody else in the room concluded that Tony was completely insane.

* * *

Paul was sitting at the boardroom table in his office with Duke and Dave.

"Well you've heard it all what do you think?" Paul asked.

Duke was first to speak: "There was never any doubt that Tony was crazy but in fact he's a very clever scheming bastard who, if he said it was daylight, I would look out the window to check."

Paul smiled. "Well firstly don't worry about me. I have taken all the emotion out of this and am fully focussed on finding Tony and Philips and killing them. We have tried to sort this without violence but it's not going to work. I am not going to be happy until they are both six feet under. We know Philips lives in Essex somewhere but that's all. Tony, God knows where he's holed up and it's quite likely that they would have taken Roddy and Lexi somewhere else anyway, so what do we do next?"

"What about the tapes? Have we heard anything?" Duke asked.

"No and even if I hear I'll tell them to fuck off and do their worst. Lexi and Roddy are far more important."

"I agree. The word's out, we have every area covered, but it's like looking for a needle in a haystack."

"What about building sites in Bermondsey? We all know how Tony likes to bury people in cement."

"I'll get people on that idea right away," Duke answered.

Paul's desk phone rang.

"Yes, sorry Carla what is it?"

"It's your brother on the phone."

The murderer's words were in Paul's ear: "Paul I just wanted to let you know Roddy's no longer with us. I had to teach him a few things and unfortunately he shit himself and died. Mind, that was after I'd cut him into a lot of pieces."

"You are beyond help Tony. You are the sickest person in the world."

"I'll take that as a compliment, thanks. Now are you ready to sign the deal or not?"

"If you can persuade me that Lexi will be safe and unharmed I will do the deal. But I'm not sure you can do that."

"Don't be ridiculous Paul. My word is my bond."

"I want to speak to her again."

"Not this time Paul. I am in charge here not you. Look I have no interest in harming Lexi. What sort of monster do you think I am?"

Paul knew exactly what sort of monster he was: the worst type.

"OK I'll get the papers drawn up for the transfer of all the clubs into your name. But I warn you: harm a hair on her head and I'll hunt you down—"

"For God's sake don't be so dramatic. Nobody will touch her."

Paul knew full well that Lexi was in mortal danger and unless they could find her the chances of her returning alive were slim.

"Dave get more help out on the streets," Paul told his other man. "Offer half a mill to anyone who can help us find them. They'll be in or near Bermondsey I'm sure of it."

* * *

"I don't think I can take any more of this," Sharon was whispering to Julie in the office. "He's killed three people in a matter of weeks. I can't handle it. That man, he was just an accountant for Christ's sake." Sharon shook her head at the memory of all the blood and the smell as he emptied his bowels.

"Don't say or do anything," Julie told her. "You know what will happen if you do."

Julie knew the type of evil creature he was, and Tony was the worst of that kind she had ever seen: one hint that Sharon had had enough and he would without question silence her.

Sharon looked Julie in the face. "Aren't you scared?"

"I made my bed and I'll lie in it. Richard's nowhere near as bad as Tony, believe me."

There was suddenly a commotion at the door. Aedan and Carrick had arrived at the warehouse. The two boys had driven over from Harlesden and were chatting with Richard and Tony. Carrick remarked on the foul stink and Tony told him there was a dead body at the end of the room and 'not to worry as you get used to the smell'.

Tony was hungry and he called Sharon, who smiled at the two boys who, not that long ago, had been fucking Julie up the arse. Tony took out a wedge of notes and peeled of three twenties.

"Get some bacon sandwiches and a bottle of decent whisky," Tony told Sharon.

"It's a bit early for whisky isn't it?"

"Did I ask you to fucking comment? Just do what you're fucking told!"

Tony noticed Sharon didn't seem to be her usual self.

"You alright?"

Sharon managed a weak smile. "Just tired."

"Don't be long."

Sharon got her coat from the office and said goodbye to Julie with a "See you in a bit".

She got in Tony's car and made for the local shops in Rotherhithe New Road. Five minutes later she parked outside a local convenience store. She went in and bought a bottle of Johnnie Walker and one of white Cabernet Sauvignon, then she left the store, put them on the back seat of the car and walked two shops along to the Ace Café. There she ordered ten bacon rolls, five with ketchup and five with brown sauce, and sat down to wait for them. The bacon rolls were soon ready and she collected them, got in the car and headed straight back to the warehouse.

CHAPTER 28

There was pandemonium at Rotherhithe Nick. Officers were rushing through the corridors to collect weapons, body armour, shields and anything else they could lay their hands on. Karen and Penny had drawn Glock pistols and bulletproof vests and were talking to Michael in his office. The phone call had come in at exactly midday and it was now twelve-forty-five. Time was critical and they were fast running out of it.

"Be careful Karen," Michael told her. "You know what these people are like—they'll shoot first and don't care who gets killed."

"I know what they're like," she agreed. "I've seen enough of their handiwork over the past few months. If we can we'll bring them in alive. If not..."

"Keep me informed."

"OK." Karen turned to Penny. "Let's go."

Penny was scared, excited and more than anything wanted to make a name for herself: a dangerous trait when you are possibly going into a gun battle with hardened criminals.

Firearm officers had been pulled in from all the local stations and more were on the way, and it was turning into a huge operation. Karen knew they only had a certain amount of time before their targets became suspicious and ran. The cars were ready. There were twenty armed officers and an ambulance had been ordered to meet them at the rendezvous.

A police car with three armed officers on board pulled into Ryder Drive, Bermondsey. They drove to the end of the cul–de-sac and immediately saw the package. It was all done in a minute, and the package was in the car and they were roaring off to a secret location.

* * *

Tony looked again at his watch. It was twenty-past-twelve, and he was getting concerned. Where the hell was Sharon? He took his mobile out and pressed her contact number. It rang but there was no answer.

"Tony I've given the two boys their instructions just as we agreed," Richard explained. Tony was sidetracked and forgot about Sharon.

"You sure they understand?" he queried.

Aedan butted in: "Don't worry we know exactly what we have to do and we're looking forward to it, and then we can be on our way home."

Tony patted them on their backs. "Give my regards to Patrick."

"We surely will." Aedan and Carrick left the warehouse and within a minute were heading back to Harlesden.

Tony looked at his watch: twelve-thirty. What the fuck was going on with that woman, he wondered?

"Julie?" he called.

Julie stuck her head out of the doorway.

"Has Sharon said anything to you? She's been gone one hell of a time."

"No nothing," Julie reassured him. "Don't worry, she'll be back any minute." Richard's girlfriend tried to be confident, but she had a terrible feeling that maybe her new friend wasn't coming back.

Richard was confused. "So where is Sharon?"

"She's out getting food and drink," replied Tony.

* * *

Karen Foster and the police convoy were speeding down Lower Road, and the four people carriers turned right into Rotherhithe New Road. Karen looked at her watch: it was twelve-fifty-five. She prayed that it would all work out.

Tony was agitated and getting really worried. It was twelve-forty and he could feel that something was wrong. He said to everyone:

"I'm getting some fresh air," and so saying he walked slowly to the door and left. He went to Richard's Jag and stuck a knife into all the tyres and then did the same to the guards' car, so that both vehicles were un-drivable. He got behind the wheel of his Mondeo and started it as quietly as he could, and then moved off slowly, checking his mirrors to make sure nobody saw him.

The four police cars were speeding up Rotherhithe New Road. They went past the railway lines and one of the cars turned immediately into Jarrow Road and drove right to the end of the cul-de-sac. Another car shortly took a left into the Terminal Recording Studios. Twenty seconds later the other two cars pulled into Ilderton Road. One of them stopped after two hundred yards and the other drove to the junction with Verney Road, took a left and parked in Bolina Road, very close to the Millwall Football Stadium. Karen looked at her watch: it was one o'clock.

* * *

Richard was talking to the two guards when he was interrupted by Julie putting a hand on his arm.

"Sharon's not back yet and now Tony's gone walkabout," the black girl said. "Something's not right."

Richard strode to the main door, opened it and went out. He looked left and right. Tony was nowhere to be seen, and where the fuck was his car, he wondered? Panic overcame him, and he rushed to the door, saying, "Julie get in the car. Everybody get moving."

Julie ran out of the door and got to the Jag first, and then she saw the slashed tyres. "Richard—the tyres," she told him.

Richard ran over to the car. When he saw what had happened he looked down and closed his eyes. "We're fucked."

"What do you mean?" Julie demanded. "Talk to me Richard!"

"We've been set up. Tony and Sharon have gone and we are the patsies. Fuck, let's get moving quickly—there might still be time."

Lexi was exhausted, starving and incredibly thirsty, but when she saw the panic on the faces of Richard and the guards she was ecstatic. She almost screamed out: *Fuck off, Fuck off you wimps!* but in the end thought better of it. They were gone and hopefully someone would come. She rubbed her tummy gently, saying, "Don't worry little one, help is on the way."

* * *

Karen was happy. The warehouse was surrounded. She had radioed all units to close in slowly and had repeated the warning that the men they were after were highly dangerous.

Richard, Julie and the two guards were rushing across the shrub land towards Ilderton Road. Richard suddenly stopped and said, "Let's split up." He looked at

The Final Act

the two guards. "You two go towards the bottom of Bolina Road and I'll speak to you tomorrow."

Richard grabbed Julie's hand and they ran on.

"STOP WHERE YOU ARE. LIE ON THE GROUND AND DO NOT MOVE. IF YOU DO MOVE YOU WILL BE SHOT." The police warning from the megaphone rang out.

Richard ducked down, dragging Julie with him.

"I can't see anything—they must be some distance off." Richard glanced around for cover. He saw a pile of disused railway sleepers. "Right, this way and keep low." They reached the sleepers and ducked behind them—they were both breathing heavily.

"What are we going to do?" Julie asked him.

"I don't know. But I'm not going back inside."

Richard took his handgun out of his pocket and checked it had ammunition. He then grabbed Julie's arm.

"I put some money into your account: two-hundred-and-fifty thou to be precise. It'll help."

"Thank you Richard, but I don't think it's going to be of much use to me."

"It is Julie," he said quietly. "I want you to go. Don't worry, you've done nothing. Put your hands in the air and walk slowly towards them. Tell them you are a woman and unarmed, OK?"

Richard suddenly heard shooting in the area where the two guards had gone, but he ignored it.

"I don't know what to say," Julie hesitated. "I should stay with—"

"Go now." Richard pushed her and she got to her feet.

"Goodbye Richard." Tears rolled down her cheeks as she slowly raised her arms and walked slowly towards the police.

"I am a woman and unarmed," she called out. "I am a woman and unarmed."

"Keep walking towards us," came the reply from the megaphone. "*Do not*, I repeat, *do not* make any sudden movements and keep your hands in the air where we can see them."

Julie kept walking saying, "I am a woman and unarmed." Then she saw ahead two police officers with rifles aiming straight at her.

"I am a woman and unarmed." She got closer and closer.

"Stand still and keep your hands up!"

She stopped. One of the officers approached and cuffed her and led her back to the other one.

"Who is the man?" they asked.

"That's Richard Philips. He has a gun and is not going to surrender."

The officers radioed through to Karen and she was there two minutes later.

"So he's holed up by the railway sleepers," she surmised. "Give me the megaphone."

"Philips it's useless," she said into the speaker, hearing her words amplified. "You are surrounded. Come out with your hands up."

"Go fuck yourself you slag!"

Karen was about to speak but was distracted by a blur to her right. She looked across and was shocked to see Penny sprinting away to the right-hand side of the sleepers.

Karen shouted loudly: "Penny stop where you are!"

Penny was so high on adrenalin she didn't even hear Karen. She was very close to the sleepers but could not see Philips. She crept forward and was at the end of the sleepers, she extended her gun with both hands and turned.

"Stand where you—" she yelled and looked but there was nobody there. She heard a noise near the ground, looked down and saw amongst the pile of sleepers a man with a gun aiming at her head. There was a flash and a bang. The bullet entered through her right eye, it penetrated the skull and ricocheted inside the brain causing incredible damage. Penny never stood a chance.

Karen heard the shot and saw Penny collapse with a wound that ripped away some of her face. Karen crumpled into a ball, muttering, "Fucking idiot! I told her! Fucking idiot!"

Karen beckoned one of the officers to come across to her. "I still want him alive if possible," she told him. "Lob some tear gas over."

"There's a danger it could blow back this way," the officer warned.

"Just get the fuck on with it and when he appears Taser him. If he's shooting, kill him."

The officer fired a tear-gas grenade onto the area of the sleepers. The problem was that Richard was already running at full pelt away from them and they couldn't see because the sleepers were in the way and now the tear gas was giving him even more cover. He was gasping for breath as he ran for his life towards South Bermondsey Station. Karen was waiting for him to show himself and nothing was happening; she was getting more and more worried.

She shouted, "He could be running."

Then she spoke into her mouth-piece: "All units. Philips is running. Keep alert—we do not have sight of him."

"Let's go."

Karen leapt up and ran for the sleepers, but she knew he wouldn't be there even before she arrived. She stopped and checked Penny, and didn't even blink when she confirmed the junior officer was dead.

"Come on," she shouted as she ran forward, scanning ahead, ready for any surprises.

Philips was hiding in a shallow trench next to the railway lines. He could see Karen and two police officers running towards the station, and he had also caught sight of two more officers coming down from Ilderton Road. He knew he had one chance and that was to follow the railway line back towards Rotherhithe New Road, hopefully missing the police from Ilderton Road and still keeping ahead of Karen. He set off, hugging the ground as low as he could, sprinting for his life. He got his second wind and kept up a ferocious pace as he ran and ran. Karen and her men met with the two policemen from Ilderton Road.

"He's still ahead of us unless he's found somewhere to hide," she said, then told one of the officers to check behind them. However her instincts were telling her he was running and already ahead of them. She didn't need to speak. She just started running and the others followed.

Two officers found Lexi and released her. She was weak but unharmed and so happy to be free. "Please call my partner Paul he'll be so worried," she urged. "Please call him, I want to speak to him."

"Don't worry we'll do that shortly," reassured the policeman. "You're safe now but we need to get you to hospital."

"I'm pregnant. I hope everything's OK."

The officers called the ambulance forward, telling the crew she appeared unharmed and was pregnant. The ambulance sped off towards St Thomas' Hospital.

Richard was near exhaustion. He thought his pounding heart was going to explode any second, and running on railway tracks was not easy. He was looking left and right to see if there was an escape route, but all he could see was industrial units. The desperate man knew he could not keep going much longer and would have to move off the lines very soon.

Meanwhile Karen and the two officers were finding it hard to keep up; they were struggling but managed to stumble on. Karen had called for more backup, and then some officers from Jarrow Road were running towards Rotherhithe New Road and another car was almost at the point where the road met with the railway lines.

Philips could hear police sirens and felt the net closing, he ducked left off the railway line and ran into the Rotherhithe Business Estate. There were several units and a fair number of cars. People were about and looked at him as he stopped, gasping for breath. Twenty yards away a man was getting into his BMW car. Richard pushed himself as hard as he could, and as the BMW driver started his engine, at that instant his driver's door opened and Philips smashed him in the face with his fist and dragged him out of the car.

Richard saw two men running towards him. He shut the door, crashed the car into gear and pressed the accelerator, and the car leapt forward. A nearby man stupidly jumped in front of the car, thinking the driver would stop, and Philips didn't hit the man full on, but the car's bonnet swept him up and he flew over the top of the vehicle and crashed in a pile on the hard road: he would later die of his numerous injuries.

The Final Act

Philips was away and screeched left at high speed onto Rotherhithe New Road. He was unlucky to find that a police car coming up the road, saw him and immediately gave chase.

Karen and other officers had reached the Rotherhithe Business Estate and saw the injured man, they checked that an ambulance had been called and Karen radioed out that they were looking for a grey BMW with the first part of the registration OTO. She was told straight away that a car was in pursuit of the BMW going west up Rotherhithe New Road. A pursuit car was at the business estate two minutes later, picking Karen up and they set off to join the chase.

At first Philips didn't think and didn't care where he was heading. His immediate idea was simply to get away, and he was driving like a madman up Rotherhithe New Road, causing absolute chaos as he went. He could see the police car two hundred yards behind him and knew that more would be on the way to cut him off. He hit the Old Kent Road and turned with no regard for the traffic. As he swung right two cars trying to avoid him crashed into each other, causing even more problems.

Richard was now in an area he knew very well. He bombed down the Old Kent Road towards the Elephant and Castle, and his mind was computing where to go next. Already, police cars were heading out of central London down Borough High Street and from Westminster to cut him off. He was screaming down the Old Kent Road at over a hundred miles per hour. He came to the first huge roundabout and turned right against the traffic—cars careered out of his way, some crashing into each other. He shot down Tower Bridge Road and took the second right down Abbey Street. Richard could still hear the police car behind him but could not see it. He got to the end of Abbey Street and turned right into Jamaica Road, then roared down Jamaica Road past Bermondsey Tube Station, and he now had a clear plan of where he was heading.

He came to the Canada Water roundabout and went straight ahead down Brunel Road. He couldn't hear the police siren and smiled to himself, but it was at that instant he heard the helicopter. Richard couldn't see it but knew it was there. He swung left and made for the Rotherhithe Tunnel, and entered the tunnel under the River Thames.

Now was the most dangerous part of his bid for freedom. He slowed down and was doing thirty miles per hour, when he suddenly slammed on his brakes and the car behind smashed into the back of him. There was a chain reaction as car after car slammed into the back of the car in front. Drivers appeared, shouting at the driver in front, and the scene soon descended into complete chaos. The drivers on the other side of the tunnel slowed down to a crawl to see what was happening: the plan was working.

Richard got out of the car and edged into the other lane. Cars had slowed down even more here and were soon travelling at a snail's pace. Philips stepped in front of a dark green Jeep and put his hand up to tell the vehicle's driver to stop. The man was unsure what to do but he stopped and stuck his head out of the window. "What's up mate?" he asked. Philips held up his opened wallet.

"I'm a police officer," Richard told him. "And I need your help."

The jeep driver looked perplexed "Eh? What can I do?"

Philips opened the driver's door, grabbed the man's collar, dragged him out of the jeep and threw him to the ground, yelling, "Stay there!" The man could see that Philips meant business and stayed exactly where he was.

Richard was so happy he could have cried. He leapt into the jeep and released the handbrake and pulled away. He made it back out of the tunnel just as the police car entered. The fugitive could also hear the helicopter overhead, but knew that they would be looking for a grey BMW. He was sweating and his heart was still pounding, but he felt happier.

Karen was in an unmarked police car and they were speeding down Brunel Road heading towards the Rotherhithe Tunnel. Karen was sitting in the back and was absent mindedly glancing at cars going in the opposite direction. She couldn't believe her eyes when she looked at the driver of a jeep and saw Philips in the driver's seat. She shouted at the driver: "He's going the other way in the jeep! Turn round quickly!"

Fortunately the officer was an advanced Met police driver, and managed to swing the vehicle around in a tight turn, scaring all the other motorists around. They were three cars behind the killer, and were not sure whether he had witnessed their sudden turn or not. However it appeared that Philips had not seen them and was content to crawl along at a snail's pace, believing he was free and out of danger.

The tension in Karen's unmarked police car was palpable: they were pretty sure he was unaware that they were so close behind him. The traffic flow sped

The Final Act

up and Philips was glad to be moving at a higher speed: he wanted to cross the river and get on to the A13 as soon as possible.

"Where's he heading?" asked the police driver.

Karen was thinking hard. "He's going to cross the river. Get SCO19 blockades on all the bridges. My bet is he'll go across London Bridge. I think we've got the bastard!"

Philips sped up Jamaica Road towards central London. He passed London Bridge Station on the left and took the sharp right to head over the bridge. He was halfway across when he saw the two police cars on the other side of the bridge, so he slowed right down and saw that they were letting all the cars go past them. But then they pulled their car across the road, effectively blocking it for him, and he was stuck with nowhere to go.

He quickly looked in his rear-view mirror: there was a car stopped across the road with police officers getting out, meaning there was no escape. He stopped the jeep, sat back and relaxed. He picked up his gun and checked the ammunition. Then he looked around. It was so peaceful. He loved the river and thought that if he got out of this mess he would buy one of those posh flats by the water.

His peace was shattered by a loud woman's voice yelling: "Philips you cannot escape. Get out of the vehicle with your hands in the air where we can see them."

Richard didn't move. Karen waited for two minutes before shouting again: "Philips, get out of the car now! Lie on the road with your hands stretched out in front of you."

The hunted man sat and decided what he was going to do. There was just one escape from the prospect of the rest of his life in a prison cell and he took it. He opened the door slowly, taking hold of his pistol. Then he jumped out of the jeep and sprinted towards Karen and her team. After covering five yards he opened fire. Bullets crashed into the police car windows smashing them, and the officers instinctively ducked for cover.

Karen lifted her Glock 17 pistol but then decided to change it. She grabbed instead a MP5SFA3 semi-automatic carbine from the officer next to her. She thought of Jeff for one second, then stood and fired a burst in one action.

The Final Act

Philips got hit three times in the leg and body but he kept coming. He was getting closer and closer.

She took careful aim and fired a single shot. It took him between the eyes and he flew into the air and crashed onto the road. Karen just stood there and actually savoured the moment, reflecting that it was one animal that was off the streets permanently. There were two other things Karen had to do, one of which she did straight away. She got back in the car and tried to compose herself.

"Paul it's Karen," she said into the phone after dialling. "Good news for you. Lexi is safe and she is fine, she's at St Thomas' being checked over." She heard Paul sobbing on the phone.

"Thank God, thank God," he kept repeating it more than five times. "I owe you Karen. Anything you want, anytime, just call me."

"Philips is dead," she replied. "And I want your brother."

"I've got to get to the hospital. I'll speak to you soon."

Within five minutes Paul, Duke and Dave were on their way to the hospital. They arrived twenty minutes later and found out where Lexi was. It was a joyous reunion for Paul and Lexi. He vowed then that she would never suffer again and told Dave to organise two bodyguards to be with her at all times. Lexi had been examined and the baby was fine. As soon as she told Paul the good news, he couldn't stop himself crying and they couldn't and wouldn't let go of each other.

Karen had done everything she needed to at London Bridge and was being driven to the Old Brompton Road. They parked in Queensgate and Karen got out of the car alone. She walked round the corner and looked for 121 Roland House Apartments, soon found the place, walked up rang the bell at number two. A plain-clothes police officer answered the door and Karen went through into the lounge.

"Hello Sharon how are you?" Karen asked the woman. "We all thought you were dead. You've had a lucky escape."

Sharon had been brought to the safe-house for her own protection. She was dreading the answer to her question but she had to ask it: "What happened to the others?"

Karen took a deep breath and answered: "Tony Bolton got away, Julie is in custody, Richard Philips and the two guards are dead."

Her heart leapt when she heard that Tony had got away.

She half laughed. "That Tony's got more lives that a cat."

Karen was deadly serious in her reply: "He's an animal and we will get him soon, believe me."

"Oh God. What about Lexi?"

"She's fine and so is the baby."

"She was pregnant? I didn't know. Thank the Lord she's alright."

"So we need to debrief you, but before we do anything, even though it's an unlikely possibility, where have you and Tony Bolton been hiding?"

"14, Brockley Road, Lewisham."

Karen immediately organised a firearms unit to get to the house as soon as possible.

"OK Sharon," she said firmly. "Let's get some coffee on and then you'd better start at the beginning."

CHAPTER 29

Tony had nowhere to go. Sharon would have told them about Lewisham, he was sure she had grassed them up to the Old Bill, and he had managed to get out in the nick of time. He'd taken the Old Kent Road up to the Elephant and Castle, hung a left down Kennington Park Avenue and then taken a right up past the Kia Oval Cricket Ground. He was heading towards Harlesden to hook up with Aedan and Carrick.

The vicious murderer crossed the river using Vauxhall Bridge. Tony took it nice and slowly, feeling relatively safe because no one knew his car, but he wouldn't be happy until he was behind closed doors in the house. He ate the miles up on the Westway and was soon in White City, home of the BBC. He saw the sign for Wormwood Scrubs Prison and wondered what had happened to Richard and Julie. Thinking about the couple reminded him of Sharon. She would get it, he vowed. He was working himself up into a frenzy just thinking about that bitch. Perhaps the Irish boys had heard from Richard, he wondered?

He made his way up Scrubs Lane and five minutes later was in All Souls Avenue, Harlesden. He rang the boys and asked them if they had heard from Richard at all, but they said no and he had no reason to disbelieve them. Tony told Aedan and Carrick that there had been a slight change of plan and that he would be popping in soon for a chat.

Tony Bolton was soon in the house, knocking back a very large whisky and telling the boys a cock and bull story about how there had been a gunfight and he had just managed to get away. The BBC News was all about the shootings in Bermondsey and it was confirmed that the gangster and prison escapee Richard Philips and his two accomplices had been shot and killed by police at the scene.

Although Tony had the constitution of a horse he was drained mentally and physically. The constant stress of the past months had caught up with him and he felt like he needed a good break to recharge his batteries. He thought of that prospect as he filled his glass with another very large whisky and swore vengeance on his brother Paul. He finished the bottle that night and eventually fell asleep on the sofa, which was where he woke up the next morning with the hangover from hell.

Tony decided to stay there for a while, but he felt like a caged rat. He could go out but it was dangerous to do so, therefore all he did was drink whisky and eat takeaway food that he got Aedan and Carrick to buy for him. He had thought about just getting on a plane and leaving it all behind but he couldn't leave Paul laughing at him, it would have to be sorted one way or the other. Carrick had suggested he go back to Ireland with them—after all, he had plenty of money and could set up a club or two in Belfast, where he would be very welcome. The idea appealed but first the boys would have to go through with their plan to sort Paul, then he would decide what to do.

It was now mid-December and Christmas was fast approaching, Christmas lights were blinking on and off on houses and the shops as usual were having pre-Christmas sales to sell off over-stocked lines. It was a time of happiness and festive spirit. Aedan and Carrick had done all the preparations they could and were ready to go. The day had been agreed: Friday December 20th.

* * *

Karen had been to Penny's funeral and met the dead officer's parents. They had said that Penny had wanted to join the police from the age of ten, and were happy that she had achieved her dream but obviously devastated at her death. Karen told them that Penny had died in a very heroic way. She could have added that Penny had been completely stupid and had gone against her express orders, but of course she didn't.

The detective sergeant had been to see Jeff once more and there was no change: he just lay there motionless staring into space, and she wondered how long they would keep the life-saving machines switched on.

Rotherhithe Nick was also in Christmas mood, with the traditional Christmas tree in place in the front reception, the lights were flashing and the angel on top smiling. The Christmas dinner took place on the Wednesday and it was a lively do, but the shadow of Jeff hung over the evening. Partners had been welcome too, but Karen had not taken Chau. Home life for Karen was good: Chau had become less demanding sexually and they had relaxed into a contented domestic situation that suited both of them. Karen wanted to leave the flat in Rotherhithe and move somewhere a little more upmarket, but Chau was settled and she decided to leave it till the new year before bringing the subject up again.

* * *

The Final Act

Sharon had been fully debriefed and Karen was now aware of the involvement of the two Irish boys, Carrick and Aedan. The only annoying thing was that Sharon knew they were in London but had no idea where exactly. Karen had rung Paul and informed him about the two Irish heavies, and told him that they knew they were in London and should be considered a personal threat to Paul and Lexi.

Lexi had gone home to Chelsea with two armed bodyguards, which Paul immediately increased to three. The Crown Prosecution Service had been sent the files and were considering whether to charge Sharon with aiding and abetting a criminal, and also with helping an inmate to escape from Broadmoor. Balanced against her crimes was the fact that Sharon was prepared to go into the 'witness protection scheme' and be the prosecution's star witness when Tony Bolton was finally brought to justice.

The CPS were also deliberating as to what charges, if any, could be brought against Julie. The ex-prostitute had gone to stay with a friend and was determined not to go back to earning her living on her back. The two hundred-and–fifty-thousand pounds that Richard had given her was a godsend which she would use to buy herself a small flat in London. She was relieved to be back looking after herself and making her own decisions. Julie was determined about one thing: she was finished with bad boys for good.

Karen was working on her own now with some administrative support from Tom Fox, a new member of the CID team. Karen's intake of coffee had diminished by at least fifty per cent since Jeff was in the hospital, and because of police humour this was a constant source of jokes and amusement around the Nick. Another result of Jeff being in hospital was that he got blamed for everything. "Who nicked my coffee mug?" asked someone. "Jeff's got it!" some bright spark would reply. "Why hasn't such-and-such been done?" would be another query. "Oh Jeff was going to do that!" was the jokey reply. It was a way for the station to keep in touch with him and not forget him, and everybody understood that, even dull old Michael, the head of CID.

DS Foster was looking forward to Christmas but was worried that Tony Bolton and the two Irish killers may well strike at Paul before Christmas Day. There was nothing else she could do. The whole of the Met was searching for Bolton and the two Irish toughs, but nothing was forthcoming.

She went back over and over the case to see if she had missed anything. She interviewed Sharon endlessly, trying to get something, *anything* that could help them to locate the bastard, but it was all in vain. He had no friends as such and the fact he had so much money meant he could bribe and pay people to keep quiet. Karen thought he wouldn't be far from Bermondsey, but his whereabouts also depended on where the two Irish lads had been staying. The waiting game was a hard one to play.

CHAPTER 30

Carrick and Aedan had driven past the Den Club in Kingly Street, Soho both ways a dozen times. They had also walked past twice and had been around the back. It was a fortress of a place and had so many doormen/guards it would be impossible to get inside unless there was some sort of diversion. They knew the offices were at the back of the club, so to get to Paul Bolton from the front would be tough. Equally, the back was defended just as well so it would need a master plan to get the job done. Carrick watched the front of the building for three days continuously, and Aedan did the same at the back. They came up with a plan and 'Go day' was planned for Friday 20th December.

Tony had decided to keep out of the action that was proposed for the twentieth. He and Richard had paid a lot of money for the two boys to come over from Ireland and he wanted them to earn it. He hoped it would be successful but if it failed he would still have the opportunity to deal with Paul later, on his own.

Carrick and Aedan spent the evening of the nineteenth stripping and cleaning weapons and getting prepared for the next day. Tony was watching and was impressed by their dedication and commitment, making a mental note to tell Patrick later. Tony was continuing his loyalty and commitment to Johnny Walker, who was now his best friend and confidante. Tony was becoming more and more reliant on booze, in fact he had such bad shakes in the mornings when he woke up that he now started the day with a whisky before he even got out of bed.

The day started out normally for Paul. Duke and Dave picked him up from home at eight-twenty and drove to the club in Soho, but there was heavy traffic so they didn't arrive till nine-fifteen. They always parked right outside the main door and Dave got out of the car first and checked the pavement and across the road; he would then signal the all-clear to Paul, who would get out of the back and march into the open door, which took all of two seconds. Duke would then drive the car round to the side of the building and park in Paul's reserved space and then make his way back to the main entrance. Paul was once again hoping that things could quieten down and that they could all have a good Christmas. He was in his office doing some paperwork when the call came through from Carla:

"Good morning Mr Bolton. The detective Karen Foster is asking for you."

"Put her through please Carla."

"Paul good morning. How are you? And more importantly, how is Lexi and the baby?"

Paul laughed "Well I'm fine, and, as you say, more importantly Lexi and the baby are a picture of health."

"Oh I'm so pleased. Give Lexi my love, please."

Paul's relationship with Karen Foster had become close—probably too close, but it had happened and was potentially useful as well as being enjoyable for both of them.

"So what's happening in the Met that I ought to know about?" Paul asked her.

"Nothing at all. We're pulling out all the stops looking for Tony and the Irish boys but no joy yet I'm afraid."

"If they're professional hard-men from Ireland you won't find them. And Tony's a clever bastard, so it was never going to be easy."

"You can say that again. I hope you're taking extra precautions."

"I can't even move around in my own club without a trail of bodyguards, so yes, Karen, precautions are in place."

"Great. Well I only rang to see if there was any news."

"Hold on Karen. Look why don't you come down and have Christmas lunch with me today? Say one o'clock? Come on, it'll be fun."

Karen wasn't sure what Michael would say if he found out but was tempted. "Are you sure?"

"Please come. The champagne's on ice."

"Oh well in that case I'll be there. But one thing Paul."

"What's that?"

"Have a word with your door team so that they actually let me in when I arrive."

"Consider it done," he said, laughing.

"OK. See you about one."

Paul was pleased. You never knew where friendly police officers could end up. Maybe one day Karen would be Commissioner of the Met. Paul called catering and told them he had a very special guest for lunch and that they should make sure everything was perfect. He glanced at his watch: it was eleven a.m.—plenty of time to get some work done.

* * *

Aedan and Carrick loaded the two large holdalls into the boot of the Focus. Tony wished them luck and shook hands with the pair of them as though he was their dad. They left Harlesden at eleven-thirty and made their way, driving carefully, to Soho. They arrived at just gone twelve and pulled into the NCP car park in Brewer Street. They had cleaned the car thoroughly the day before and were wearing gloves so as not to leave prints. It was cold and they both wore short coats over their shirts and jeans.

They had no more use for the car and did not intend to return. Each of them carried one of the holdalls, they came out of the car park and walked down Brewer Street and took a right into Warwick Street, then walked past the Italian Bookshop and the So Restaurant and came to the end of the street, turned right into Beak Street and then immediately left into Kingly Street: they had arrived.

Carrick walked towards the club on the other side of the road, while Aedan stayed on the club side and when he got near the club he ducked down an alleyway and walked towards the back. Carrick came on the opposite side of the club and went to an old door that led up to a flat above a Thai Restaurant. He took a file from his pocket and slipped it between the door and the wall. He pulled down sharply and the old rusty lock snapped and the door opened, so he strolled in as though he owned the flat and went up the stairs. Carrick knew that the owner would not be back until about six-thirty, so had no hesitation in kicking open the door to the small flat.

It was a tiny living space but it had exactly what he wanted: this was a window that overlooked the main entrance to the Den Club. He looked through the window and noted the three guards in charge of the door. He closed his eyes and pictured the layout of the club from the Saturday night when he had visited. Hopefully Aedan was in place, as timing was critical. He looked at his watch: it was twelve-fifty—nearly time.

The Final Act

He opened the holdall and began taking out a selection of weapons. First there was a rocket grenade launcher, then an AK-47 rifle and lastly a 9mm pistol and a couple of ex-army knives. All the arms were ex-IRA, armaments which had been smuggled into Ireland from Libya. He glanced out of the window to check what was happening and was shocked to see that a police car had pulled up outside the entrance and a woman got out and walked into the club. "Shit!" he said out loud—now a copper would be involved as well!

Carrick walked back to the grenade launcher and checked it over. He took his mobile phone out and pressed a speed dial and held it to his ear. "Everything alright?" he asked.

"Fine," was the reply.

"OK we go as planned at one o'clock."

* * *

Tricky let Karen straight into the club, there was no hanging about. She smiled at him and said, "Thank you so much."

Karen was taken straight to the private dining room, which was situated on the first floor and was not widely advertised. It was a beautifully decorated room with furnishings in rich reds and cream, the table could sit ten but the settings had been reduced to accommodate just Paul and Karen. The woman detective was given a glass of champagne and told that Paul would join her in a minute. It was only a minute before Paul walked in.

"My apologies Karen," he began. "I wanted to meet you but an important phone call came and—"

"Don't worry Paul," she reassured him. "I know exactly what it's like."

"So how's the champagne?"

"Delicious. I love champagne—could drink it all day."

"Well you can stay as long as you want," said Paul, laughing.

Paul took a sip of his champagne.

And suddenly there was a massive explosion coming from somewhere near the front of the club.

"Jesus!" cried Paul. "What the hell was that?"

Karen answered quickly: "That, Paul, was a bomb."

They moved to put their drinks on the table and turned as Duke rushed in the door.

"We're under attack!" Duke yelled.

BOOM! There was another massive explosion at the rear of the club. Karen knew who was responsible.

"It's the two Irish boys," she told the men, drawing her gun.

Duke held a hand out. "Safer to stay in here for a minute."

Duke handed Paul a pistol and said he would be back shortly.

* * *

It was one o'clock. Carrick pulled the grenade launcher onto his shoulder and aimed. Whoosh! The grenade hurtled towards the door. Tricky, the Den Club's doorman, was lucky to see the flash from the window opposite, shouted a warning, took two steps and dived back into the club. The grenade exploded right in the entrance, causing huge damage and creating lots of smoke, which was the plan.

Carrick dropped the launcher and ran down the stairs and careered across the road, shooting his rifle into the smoke at the entrance. Two of the doormen were cut down in a hail of bullets, while Carrick charged through the smoke, still firing, but he had not reckoned on the second door being closed and locked. He stopped and concentrated his fire on the lock of the door, on the other side of which Tricky was standing, and ordering people around. He had sent for reinforcements and there were now three of them waiting, pressed against the walls, with guns at the ready. The door was being ripped to pieces by gunfire and smoke was seeping underneath it.

Aedan fired his grenade a second after Carrick had launched his. The other Irishman then fired his automatic weapon at the goods delivery entrance and obliterated it, then he charged straight into the smoke-filled entrance, shooting as he ran. He knew where the offices were and headed straight towards them. What he didn't realise was that there were four guards in the office area who were all well-armed.

Carla had heard the explosion and immediately hid underneath the boardroom table in Paul's office, along with a secretary and an office junior whose job

The Final Act

included making the tea. Meanwhile the guards ran towards the explosion with no care or forethought, but they paid for their stupidity with their lives. Aedan stood, legs apart, aiming his AK-47 at the smoke and as the guards appeared he gunned them down without mercy.

Aedan then followed the corridors to the offices, shot the locks off the security doors, and was soon very close to Paul's office. He was exhilarated and felt like Superman, and as he kicked Paul's office door open and entered, he fired a short burst around the room.

"Fuck!" he yelled loudly. He looked around and saw the group of people hiding under the table.

"Get up from there now," he ordered, aiming at them, and the three of them crawled out and stood up. Paul Bolton, however, was not amongst them.

"Where's Bolton?" Aedan asked.

Nobody answered.

"OK, I'll give you one last chance," he said, taking aim at the young lad.

"They're having lunch on the first floor," shouted Carla.

Aedan took aim. But just as he was about to shoot them he changed his mind, left the room and headed back to some steps he had seen.

Carrick knew there were guards on the other side of the door waiting for him, and he continued firing at the door and eventually one side sprang open. That was what he had been waiting for, and he rolled a grenade through the gap and curled up into a ball on the floor, waiting for the explosion.

Tricky saw the grenade and screamed a warning, then he leapt forward and kicked the grenade back through the door where it landed next to Carrick and nestled close to his stomach. The Irish killer opened his eyes and saw the grenade and went for it but was too late. The grenade exploded and literally blew what had been Carrick into a cloud of mush and tiny pieces of skin and bone. The entrance to the club was covered in blood and gore and the man that had once been Carrick was no more.

Aedan ran up the small flight of stairs but stopped just before cresting the landing. He strained his head up and around the corner to see if there was anyone there. But it was clear, so he jumped up the final three stairs and stopped. He crouched down and held his AK-47 at the ready to fire. He studied the layout ahead of him: four rooms and he could see a small kitchen at the end of the corridor.

So he tiptoed to the first door and stuck his ear against it: he heard nothing. Then he then picked up shouting and turned back to the stairs—guards were coming. Tricky had found out where Paul was and was racing with two others to help in the battle. Aedan waited till he saw the first man come round the corner of the stairs, then he let rip a burst of fire and the man's face disintegrated and his body fell. The Irishman heard the others retreat back down the stairs.

Aedan was now convinced that he would die in this place and accepted the inevitable as he made for the second door. Again he could hear nothing, so he went to the third and found that all was quiet. Then he made a decision and ran to the forth door, kicked it open, and stormed in firing. He briefly caught a glimpse of bodies in front of him. There were flashes, then just pain and blackness.

Paul, Duke and Karen were crouched opposite the door, and all three were aiming their weapons at the door, waiting. The atmosphere was electric, and they could hear gunfire and explosions from various locations in the club. Karen was sweating, and the gun was getting heavy, so she adjusted her arms and then went back to her position. Paul whispered: "As soon as the door moves start shooting." Then there was an unreal sort of tranquillity in the room: each of them could hear the others breathing slowly, deeply and deliberately.

Then it happened quickly.

A rush of feet. And when the door smashed open they all fired. Aedan must have taken ten shots all over his body. He had stood no chance, and lay slumped on the floor with blood oozing out of multiple wounds. Neither Paul, Duke nor Karen moved, knowing there could be others. Then they heard a voice shouting from the corridor, calling out, "Paul are you there?"

"Yes in the last room," he called back. They still didn't move or lower their guns. Then a man appeared in the doorway—it was Tricky.

"We think we've got them," he told them. "But best stay here till we're sure." The three of them lowered their weapons and relaxed back against the wall.

Karen was the first to speak: "That was some fucking lunch, so please don't invite me again thanks." She laughed and Paul, Duke and Tricky joined in. Soon more guards appeared at the door and declared the situation completely under control. Ten minutes later police had closed Kingly Street and were swarming over the club, declaring it to be a major crime scene.

The fact that Karen was at the club having lunch raised more than a few eyebrows among the officers who arrived at the scene—she explained it away by saying that it was all part of a current investigation and left it at that.

Paul and Karen took a stroll through the devastated club. It would take months to refit, which would cost the insurers a fortune. They found Carla and her team in shock, being given tea by a kindly police officer. Six employees had been killed and two injured. Terrible though the losses were, it had been a miracle that it hadn't been a lot worse.

Paul accompanied Karen to what was left of the entrance area.

"I owe you again Karen," he told her.

Karen was confused. "What for?"

"You saved my life."

"No I didn't."

"If you hadn't come to lunch that killer would have found me in my office. The outcome could have been very different. Anyway, listen Karen, I said it before and I'm saying it again—if you ever need my help just ask, OK?"

"Sure Paul, see you soon." And with that Karen walked towards a police car for a lift back to Rotherhithe.

Paul stood on the pavement for a minute thinking that if things had been different he would love to have worked with Karen.

* * *

Tony was pacing the lounge at the flat in Harlesden. It was four o'clock and there was still no word. He sat down and accepted that it had not gone according to plan and that probably Carrick and Aedan would not be coming back. He flicked on the BBC news on TV and jumped as he saw a picture of the Den Club entrance blown to smithereens.

The Final Act

"We understand that several people have been killed and injured," said the reporter. "Reports at the moment suggest two terrorists attacked the club and that both are dead as a result of gunshot wounds. We do not know who the intended target was, but we can report that a high-ranking Metropolitan police officer was present at the club at the time of the attack."

Tony felt sick. He was watching the screen as more pictures of the club appeared, then he was suddenly transfixed. On the screen he could see Paul talking to a woman police officer, and he thought that could only be, what was her name? Foster. Yes, it was Karen Foster from Rotherhithe. He stared at her face intently and spoke to the screen:

"You are now on my list bitch. You and that cunt Paul will both pay, believe me I'm going to enjoy killing you both." He stood up and turned the TV off, then went to the kitchen and poured himself a large whisky and knocked it back in one.

CHAPTER 31

A few weeks previously Chau had been shocked when Karen had said she wanted to go back to work. Karen had just come off the phone to Michael, the head of CID at Rotherhithe Nick.

"Jeff's been shot," Karen explained to her. "It's very serious—he's in a coma."

"Oh my God. I so sorry Miss Karen. Where was he when it happen?"

"In McDonald's down the Old Kent Road."

"What! People go McDonald's for burger! Not to get shot. Me telling you people crazy, everything crazy!"

"I'm going back to work to find who did it."

"You mad. You want get shot like him? Miss Karen, you no well enough really you're not."

"I'm OK. It's something I have to do."

"OK, OK, you go. When you come back shot I take care of you. Go, go, go!"

Chau didn't try to dissuade her again, as she knew Karen had made her mind up and that was that. But Chau was unhappy. Every time her lover left the house she was terrified that she would get shot or maimed or raped. She tried to keep busy keeping the flat tidy and cooking her famously scrumptious meals, but it was a stressful time.

Chau had begun to make enquires herself. She found out it was possible to transfer from one station to another within the Metropolitan Police. She also found out it would be relatively easy for Karen to join another police force somewhere else in the country. Chau was particularly interested to discover that, as she had guessed, it would be safer to be in a police force that was away from London.

When Chau had seen the club-bombing on the news she had prayed that Karen had not been there. Karen was not about to tell her she had been involved, and it was fortuitous that she had not seen her with Paul Bolton on the TV news.

The Final Act

Karen had talked to Chau and explained that she had to close the case with Tony Bolton, for only then could she relax. They agreed that once that was achieved they would take a long holiday somewhere hot—maybe in the Caribbean.

Two days after the club devastation staff at the NCP Car Park in Brewer Street contacted the police about a silver Ford Focus that had been left at the nearby car park just before the club bombing. The staff had no idea if it was connected or not, but they wanted to find out. Karen and a team including crime scene investigators duly turned up and located the car.

They firstly checked the registration and found it to be a Hertz car which had been hired from Mayfair in London. Officers were immediately suspicious and took every precaution with the vehicle. The doors were opened and the car given a preliminary search. Later it was taken to a specialist police workshop to be completely dismantled.

However they found nothing useful in the car, absolutely nothing: no sweet wrapper, no tissue, no dropped pound coin and after further investigations, no fingerprints or any DNA traces. It was one of the cleanest cars the Met workshops had ever seen. Karen followed up the lead, checking the paperwork at Hertz to see who had hired the car, and what home address had been given. Apparently a Mr Robert Stanton had hired the car and he lived in Fulham. Karen had the address checked but it was fake.

* * *

It was mid-morning. Julie was in the kitchen in her rented flat in Manor Gardens, Holloway, making a coffee. She heard the doorbell and assumed it was the postman. She immediately thought it would be another load of bloody bills. She opened the door with a smile, which disappeared as soon as she saw who it was.

"Hello Julie how are you?" Karen asked.

"Detective Foster. So nice to see you, what can I do for you?"

"I need to talk to you. We can do it here or down at—"

Julie opened the door and stepped to the side.

Karen walked into the flat. "Thanks. Look, there's no need for us to be enemies Julie."

"Coffee?"

"Love one."

Karen followed Julie into the kitchen and sat down at the small table.

"So what can I do for you?" Julie asked.

"Well you know what happened to Richard. He didn't want to go back inside—he knew he would never have come out."

"Yeah I know. He got away in the end."

Karen thought for a second. "Yes I suppose he did. Look I want to talk about the two Irish boys, Aedan and Carrick."

Julie immediately thought about the sex session she had enjoyed with the two boys in Harlesden, and how nice they had seemed.

"Couple of very nice boys," Julie commented. "I hope they haven't got into trouble have they?"

"I think bombing a club in Soho and killing six people could reasonably be called trouble."

Julie couldn't believe it. "No! Those nice boys? Terrible, how terrible." She was shaking her head in disbelief.

"We've asked you this before, Julie. What contact, if any, did you have with the two of them?"

"As I said before, none. Richard did all that."

Karen was just staring at Julie, trying to work out if she was lying or not.

"How are the boys?" Julie asked. "I expect they're back in Ireland are they?"

Karen detected some sort of relationship or intimacy in the way Julie spoke about them.

Karen took a flyer. "They were two handsome, young, fit boys. Which one did you fancy the most?"

"Fancy them? I never even met them for God's sake!"

"Julie you can't fool me. You do realise the more you help, the more I can help you?"

"What do you mean?"

"You are up for a number of charges Julie. If you help me I can put a good word in for you with the CPS."

Julie had been told she was looking at a year or two custodial sentence for aiding and abetting Richard Philips.

"I reckon I could get any sentence suspended so you wouldn't have to do any time at all," Karen said.

"Can you promise me that?"

"Ninety-nine per cent I can."

Julie took a sip of her coffee. "Don't stitch me up here."

"I won't, I promise." Karen thought she was on the brink of getting something and her pulse quickened: her womanly intuition was telling her something else.

"Which one did you sleep with?"

Julie laughed out loud. "Clever detective. Both of them actually. At the same time."

Now it was Karen's turn to laugh. "Sounds like fun."

"Yes it was." Julie hadn't wanted to ask but she had to. "And the boys? They're—"

"They're both dead."

"Shame. A real shame. They were so young."

"Play with fire you get burnt," Karen had no sympathy in her voice. "They killed six people while trying to execute Paul Bolton at his club."

"Why does everybody hate Paul Bolton?" Julie asked. "Richard loathed him and Tony, Jesus, he wants him dead more than anything."

"I'll tell you why. It's because they see Paul as having everything: a beautiful girlfriend, a child on the way, he wants to take the business legit. Richard was and Tony is, jealous beyond all reason. So what do you say, Julie?"

"The two boys were staying at a house in Harlesden. All Souls Avenue."

"Number?"

The Final Act

Julie hesitated for a moment "Don't let me down please Karen. Forty-five."

"Good. Do you think Tony may have gone there?"

"I have no idea. He left us in the lurch at the warehouse, and I haven't seen or spoken to him since, and I don't want to."

Karen got up. She had plenty to do. "Thanks Julie. I'll see you again." She made for the door.

"Karen you don't think he'll come after me, do you?"

"Tony's got enough problems. Don't worry he has no idea where you live, relax."

"Yeah, OK."

Karen rushed to her car and radioed in. She spoke to Michael and gave him the news. She asked for firearms units to be sent to a location near the property where she would meet them. Michael organised the venue, and told Karen they were taking over the the Elmwood Lawn Tennis Club, which was on the corner of Holland Road and All Souls Avenue, about three hundred yards from number forty-five.

She arrived at the tennis club to find a mini army: ten firearms officers and fifteen others. The first thing she did was to close all Souls Avenue at the junctions of Holland Road and Herbert Gardens. The adjoining houses were evacuated so that number forty-five would be isolated. The house was a small detached three-bedroom place with room for a car directly in front of the property. Karen had been driven past in an unmarked car twice but had not seen any signs of life. Officers were at the back of the property: if Tony Bolton was inside they had him. Karen and the firearms officers crept along the Avenue, hugging the bushes and any other foliage for protection. Officers were on both sides of the house at the front and quickly moved to the front door.

Tony Bolton was in his local Co-op store in Lushington Road just round the corner from All Souls Avenue. He had bought three frozen chicken curry ready-meals, two bottles of Johnny Walker, a pint of milk and three packets of assorted biscuits. He left the shop and walked along Lushington Road and turned right into Holland Road.

He was casually strolling down the road and was almost at the junction with All Souls Avenue when something absolutely incredible happened. It happened so quickly that Tony had no time to react which, when he thought about it later, was a godsend. The police officer appeared from nowhere—he was standing in a house driveway keeping out of sight. He put his hand up in front of Tony.

"Sorry sir," the policeman told him. "Please turn around. There is a police operation in this area and you cannot go any further."

Tony said, "Yes officer" and turned round and walked back down the road. It was a scary minute and Tony was waiting for the shout but it never came. He continued down Holland Road and took a left into Furness Road, crossed over Wrottesley Road and ten minutes later was at Willesden Junction Railway Station.

He was feeling physically sick. He had nowhere to go and had now lost his car as well, which really pissed him off. He got on the first train heading into central London. He went five stops and got out at Finchley Road Station, he withdrew money from the cash point, and then walked up Finchley Road until he found a very small and dingy flat-letting agency.

Tony Bolton went in and paid six months' rent on a furnished one-bedroom flat five hundred yards up the road above a newsagent's. Once inside, he sat in the tiny lounge on a sofa that smelt of cat pee and drank straight from one of his bottles of Johnny Walker. This was the end of the road for him, he decided. He wouldn't live like this much longer, Karen Foster and his brother Paul would pay for what they'd done and then he would move on.

* * *

Karen was listening intently but couldn't hear a thing. She motioned with her hand, signalling the officers to go in. Two of them approached the front door and gripped the handle: they could not believe it when it turned and the door opened. They slipped inside, followed by five officers and Karen, firearms at the ready. They all stopped in the hall and listened again: nothing.

She was already sure that he was not there but they had to check. Officers searched all the rooms in the house and found them to be clear. They did however find a handgun, two thousand pounds in cash, a slightly warm kettle and six empty Johnny Walker bottles. Clearly someone had been in there very recently. They declared the house a crime scene and Karen moved back to the front of the house.

The Final Act

The officer in Holland Road was stood down and was walking across the road to the house. He put his hand in his pocket and took out a packet of polo mints, and as he did so a piece of paper fell out onto the road. He picked it up—it was the handout from the morning briefing, featuring the picture of Tony Bolton. He glanced at the face and stopped breathing, and felt a chill run down his back: it was the same man he turned away from the scene fifteen minutes earlier. He thought about his twelve years of service, his future prospects, and then he crumpled the paper up and stuffed it back in his pocket.

CHAPTER 32

The Den Club in Soho was covered in scaffolding and workmen had already started cleaning up the mess. Paul had moved to the Starlight Club while the refit was carried out. The good news was that the insurers were picking up the tab and Paul would have a new club with several design change improvements. It was Christmas Eve and Lexi had decorated the flat in Chelsea and it looked fantastic: a huge Christmas tree was the focal point, and it had flashing coloured lights, baubles and every other type of decoration money could buy. Christmas carols came from the CD player and the turkey was ready to go in the oven.

* * *

Karen was spending most of her time at Rotherhithe Nick. The hunt for Tony Bolton had come to a standstill once again with no apparent road to take. Chau was delighted as Karen left home at eight-forty-five in the morning and returned at a quarter past five. Karen was back on her regime of ten cups of coffee and eight visits to the loo daily. Chau had decorated the flat and it positively heaved with all types of bunting and decoration, and a lovely small Christmas tree with silver lights was in the lounge, flashing warmly.

* * *

Tony had eaten a good steak in Bradleys Café down the road for dinner and had drunk far too much whisky, as usual. He returned to the flat at ten p.m. and found that it was dark, cold and miserable. He switched the lights on, took off his coat, went to the kitchen cupboard and took out a new bottle of Johnny Walker whisky. He poured himself an extra-large glassful, turned the TV on and sat on the smelly sofa. He took a huge gulp of the whisky and shuddered as it burnt his throat.

He looked at the TV. It had no volume, so he played around with the remote but couldn't fix it. He had another gulp of whisky, got up from the sofa, picked up the TV and smashed it onto the floor. Now there was not only no volume there was no picture either. He sat back down and drank, and before he passed out he swore that neither Paul nor Karen Foster would see the new year.

* * *

The Final Act

Jeff Swan was still in St Thomas' Hospital in a coma. Nurses turned him every three hours and checked for bedsores. Rose Cotton was on duty in the morning and went into Jeff's room at ten-thirty. She tidied up the flowers which were still being sent and moved them around the room. She was putting a vase onto the windowsill when she thought she heard a faint groan. Rose quickly turned and looked at Jeff, looked at him for a few seconds, but found he was exactly as he was when she had come in. She then turned back, thinking she had been mistaken and he had not made a sound.

The injured detective constable had actually opened his eyes and saw a shadow of a person moving by the window. He opened his mouth and groaned and then went straight back into the sleep of his coma.

* * *

Michael, the head of CID at Rotherhithe Nick, almost lived at the place. He lived on his own and had all his meals in the canteen, which saved him cooking in his one-bedroom flat in Catford. He had made an effort to put up a few decorations there, even though he was going to Spain for the New Year.

* * *

Sharon had been moved around and was in a safe house in Leeds. She had a weekly amount of money paid into her bank account that was sufficient to buy food but not much else. She had bought a cheap small Asda plastic Christmas tree, and it promised to be a very miserable Christmas for her.

* * *

Julie had moved out of her friend's flat and had rented a cheap place prior to buying somewhere with the money Richard had given her. She hadn't bothered spending money on decorations, but had splashed out on tons of good food and wine. She liked her own company and was happy to spend her time pottering around the flat and going shopping.

CHAPTER 32

Tony opened his eyes and wondered where he was. He looked around and remembered he was in the dingy rented flat in the Finchley Road. It was the 29th of December, and he rubbed his itchy eyes and ran his hands through his hair. He could barely remember anything about Christmas at all. He had been in a drunken stupor for a week, and he hadn't bathed, shaved or changed his clothes. Although he was unaware of it, he stunk of stale sweat, booze and urine. He had peed himself at least twice, soaking his trousers, but the fabric had dried over time.

He got off the sofa and went to the kitchen and opened the cupboard where he kept his whisky: it was empty. His head was throbbing and he had a pain in his knee when he walked, which was as a result of falling down in the bathroom when he had been rushing to have a pee. He looked at himself in the mirror and was shocked: he looked like someone who slept rough every night under a bridge in London.

The vicious killer was hungry and went to the fridge: inside there was only half a loaf of stale bread, some fungus-covered cheese, a curdled pint of milk and one egg—nothing else. He slammed the fridge door, causing the appliance to shake, and he heard the contents crashing around and shook his head in despair. He stood upright and questioned himself. For goodness' sake, he reasoned, he was a millionaire living like a dosser; he had to sort himself out and do it quickly.

First of all he had a long soak in the bath and washed his lank greasy hair, then he had a close shave. He felt better already, the more so when he put on some new grey corduroy trousers, a white cotton shirt and a blue jumper that he had bought before Christmas. He felt alive again, and he went out to the local café and had a full English breakfast with extra toast and orange marmalade and three cups of tea.

He left the café, walked down the road to the local supermarket and bought bread, milk, marmalade, butter, whisky and ten chicken curry ready-meals. Then he went back to his flat and tidied up: there were empty bottles in every room and discarded ready-meal packaging littered all over the flat. It may not have been a comprehensive tidy-up, but he had made an effort.

Once he had finished all his chores he picked up a dirty glass and washed it, opened the whisky and poured a large glassful. He lifted it to his mouth and was about to drink, then he stopped. Doing so was hard. He held the glass there for seconds and his hands began to shake; the whisky was in danger of spilling over, and he put the drink down on the table and looked at it.

If he was going to function he had to stop drinking. If he was going to get even with the copper and Paul he had to lay off the juice. He did something that shocked him: he picked the glass up, went to the sink and poured it down the plughole. The smell hit his nostrils and he reeled back in horror. He made himself a cup of tea and sat on the kitchen chair. His next project was to work out how he was going to capture, torture and eventually kill Karen Foster and his brother Paul. He rubbed his hands together and started laughing hysterically. "I just love it when a plan comes together!" he said loudly to no one.

Tony stole a C 200 blue Mercedes and changed the number plates. He was happy to have wheels again and now he could get about without restrictions. He hadn't had a drink in two days and although he had the shakes he was feeling much better. He decided he could not sort Foster and his brother out before the new year and was happy to gain strength by eating well and laying off the booze.

Paul Bolton's mad brother ate out on New Year's Eve and allowed himself the luxury of a bottle of wine. He was much happier now, he kept the fridge fully stocked and was putting on a few pounds, which he needed. He pondered on how remarkable it is how quickly the human body responds to some love and attention. Tony felt himself to be living proof of this as he began to look and feel much much better than he had for some time.

* * *

It was the first week in January. Everybody was broke, Christmas and New Year celebrations were finished and life was getting back to normal. Karen had gone back to work, as had Paul.

Rotherhithe Nick was quiet. It seemed that all the villains had taken Christmas off as well. Karen didn't have to worry about Michael: he had returned from Spain that same morning and was stuck in his office with the door shut. So it was come late in, drink coffee and an early finish for a few days.

The Final Act

It was Thursday 8th January and Karen had strolled in at nine-thirty. All was quiet apart from a couple of drunks in the cells sleeping it off. Karen spent most of the day chatting to various colleagues, who also had nothing better to do. She had a healthy salad for lunch in the canteen and then sat at her desk twiddling her thumbs. The afternoon seemed to drag on forever until at last it was four o'clock. She got her stuff together and was about to leave when her desk phone rang.

"Hello," she answered the call in a cheerful voice.

"Don't talk, just listen," said the voice in her ear. "I understand you're looking for Tony Bolton."

Karen was suddenly more than interested. "Yes I am. What can you tell me?"

"Well first of all, is there a reward for information leading to an arrest?"

Everybody wants a slice of the pie thought Karen. "There is a fifty-thousand pound reward for exactly that."

"OK. So that you will know me again I am 'Chicken Gravy'. Have you got that?"

"Yes. So where is he?"

"Where else would he be other than Bermondsey?"

Karen bit her lip until it was hurting so much she had to stop. "Come on then. Where exactly?"

"13, Bombay Street. It's a block of flats called Alfred Court. He's in number ten. I know he's out today but he should be back about 7 p.m. When do I get my money?"

"When we've arrested him." Karen replaced the phone's receiver. She was shaking inside, and she shouted out to no one in particular: "Anyone know where Bombay Street is?"

"Calcutta," came the jokey reply.

"Very funny. Come on, does anyone know?"

"Back of the Blue Anchor," someone else answered. "I used to take my car to Mick's garage in Bombay Street for its MOT."

Karen rushed out of the office and was soon in animated conversation with Michael.

213

The Final Act

Detective Sergeant Karen Foster was talking too much. She knew it was to accommodate her stress levels, which had gone through the roof. This was the moment she had been waiting for: Richard Philips had been taken care of and now it was Tony Bolton's turn. It was quarter–past-four and Bolton would be back at the address at about seven p.m, meaning they had less than three hours to prepare.

Michael had taken the decision that he would be in charge of the operation, which slightly pissed Karen off but it was a case of all hands on deck. Firearms units were called in from various locations in London and would be briefed at five o'clock, it was going to be a massive operation. Twenty officers were involved and all had to be firearms trained because Bolton was considered so dangerous. Michael was calmness personified and radiated strength, and Karen was surprised. Of course, she would have preferred Jeff to be with her, but she was still pleased that Michael would be by her side.

Weapons and bulletproof vests were drawn, checked and rechecked. The officers started arriving and were directed to the large CID room where coffee and biscuits had been provided in large flasks. Michael took the briefing with some backup from Karen, who gave a short history of Bolton's crimes to emphasise how extremely dangerous he was. The men were to be split into five teams. The first team of two officers would park up in Drummond Road near the Trispace Gallery. It was unlikely that they would see action but every eventuality had to be covered. The second team of three officers would be at the junction of Blue Anchor Lane and Bombay Street. The third team, consisting of three officers, would be at the junction of Bombay Street and Southwark Park Road.

Karen was to be stationed on the fourth floor, one level above flat 11, along with three officers. Michael and the remaining nine would be at pavement level waiting for an ID on Bolton. Everybody was in plain clothes and in unmarked cars, and were in situ at six p.m. Karen was nervous beyond belief but Michael had changed dramatically: it seemed that getting out on an operation was his real forte rather than sitting behind a desk.

The time was flying by. It was five-thirty and the teams were ready to leave Rotherhithe. Even though it was too early, Michael gave the OK to go. Just as Karen was getting in her designated car her mobile rang. She looked at the name and knew she shouldn't answer it, but she did, saying, "Hello, I can't talk now but we are on our way to pick up the missing package."

"Where?"

Karen knew she was entering dangerous waters. "Bombay Street. But keep away."

The police cars travelled the short distance to Bombay Street very quickly and were in place at five-forty-five. Two of the officers at the junction of Bombay Street and Southward Park Road crossed over the road and sat at a window table in the Pop In Café. The officers at Blue Anchor Lane made sure they were far enough away from the junction not to be seen if Bolton drove up Bombay Street that way.

Time was moving on and soon it was six p.m. Karen was talking to Michael through her headset, which all the other officers could also hear, but they were not allowed to break radio silence except in an emergency. The clock was ticking, and it became six-thirty. Officers were now very alert, as Bolton could turn up at any moment.

"Karen, are you alright?" Michael asked.

"Yes. I'm just praying he turns up."

Michael wanted to give Karen some reassurance. "I've got a good feeling that he'll turn up. And we'll get him, don't worry."

The seconds ticked away. It was six-forty-five.

The car engines were off and, apart from the two officers in the café, everybody was freezing cold.

Suddenly Karen's earpiece crackled with the message: "Karen we have him! He's entering the main door now."

Karen gripped her pistol and nodded to her team.

The well-built man in a long coat went to the lift and got in. He got out at the second floor and went into flat number six.

"False alarm. He went into six," said the voice in Karen's ear.

Karen relaxed again and found that she needed a pee.

It was now seven p.m.

Every minute seemed like hours, and it was soon seven-fifteen.

The Final Act

Karen was saying a prayer for him to turn up.

Then it was seven-thirty.

Karen spoke to Michael: "I think it's a no-show."

"We'll give it till eight o'clock," he replied.

The officers had been through similar situations a hundred times. Tired, cold and pissed off, and no one thought he was going to turn up.

It was eight o'clock.

Karen was back on the radio, saying, "Are we standing down?"

Michael replied quickly. "No. I'll tell you when."

The officers were nodding off because of the cold, it was freezing outside and even colder in the cars.

Eight-thirty came and went.

Michael took another decision. "All officers stand down. Karen, come and join me."

The car engines started quicker than Usain Bolt from the starting blocks, and they quickly disappeared from the scene. Karen came down from the flats and met Michael.

"I want to stay for another hour," Michael told her.

Karen didn't think he would turn up but someone else had to stay. "Sure. He could turn up."

Michael and Karen were standing on the pavement talking.

Across the road next to Mick's Garage was a disused building. It had small windows covered in steel mesh along the length of it, and some of these were broken. Tony Bolton had been sitting in the corner since four p.m. He was wearing a black ski suit with gloves, and he also had a flask of coffee with a drop of whisky in it.

He had watched it all: the police teams arriving, being deployed, the bitch Foster posing like a fucking queen and the man in charge who he didn't know. He had bided his time, he hadn't wanted to shoot earlier, for he could never have got away with so many police officers around. He had watched with great

The Final Act

anticipation when Foster had come down from the flats and then the officers with her disappeared.

There appeared to be just the two of them left: Foster and the boss copper, so now was the time. He lifted up the long bag from the floor and pulled the zip. He took out a British L42A1 WW2 sniper rifle and felt the weight—it was reassuringly substantial; Patrick had supplied a damned old but terrifyingly efficient weapon. He loaded the rifle, lifted it up and rested it on the broken window frame. He looked through the sight and zeroed in on Michael and Karen; he moved the rifle slightly and tucked it into his shoulder, then he moved the gun again and concentrated on Karen. He had her fully in his sights, and he moved for the last time and the telescopic sight was zeroed in on Karen's forehead. He took the glove off his right hand and gently gripped the trigger. He squeezed slowly: it was nearly time. He felt an overwhelming sensation of happiness envelop him, as he squeezed gently again.

He fired.

Michael was talking to his detective sergeant. "Karen you know I've never forgotten that night, I still feel—"

"Please don't Michael," she replied. "It was a long time ago, and things have changed."

Michael leaned forward. "I still look at you and feel the—"

The bullet hit him on the top of his head, carrying away a piece of his scalp, which then hit Karen in the face, accompanied by a fountain of blood that splashed all over. Michael slumped onto the pavement, his head striking the hard surface with a sickening thud.

Karen stood in shock for half a second and then dived for the ground, scratching her hands badly. She made a grab for her gun and looked across the road. The street lighting was poor and it was so dark, she was straining her eyes to see. *Where was the shooter*, she wondered? Of course it was not just a shooter it was that bastard Bolton.

Karen's head was swimming. Jeff and now Michael—it was almost too much to bear. She pulled herself together and checked Michael's body: he seemed to be gone. Karen continued to scan across the road, and then suddenly there was a roar as a Mondeo screamed out of Mick's garage and turned left. She leapt up, aimed, and started firing her pistol but the car was at the corner in

The Final Act

two seconds and she knew it would be gone in a flash. She pumped her legs as fast as she could in hot pursuit and continued firing.

Bolton turned the corner and Karen kept going. He was doing sixty and nearly at the junction with Southwark Park Road. Karen kept firing and then one of the Mondeo tyres exploded, the car swerved. The killer couldn't turn the car and it hurtled across the road into Ambrose Street. He lost control and mounted the pavement, and saw the Elite Fish Bar and ploughed into the front of it, smashing all the huge windows.

Tony Bolton hadn't planned this. He jumped out of the car and began to run towards Trappes House, the block of flats at the end of the road. Karen was hurtling across Southwark Park Road, still shooting—bullets were hitting the parked cars as Tony ran for his life.

Suddenly Tony heard his name called. Was he dreaming, he wondered? He looked over to where he thought it had come from. It was a man, but he couldn't see properly as it was so dark. The man called to him again: "Tony this way!" Tony didn't care who it was. He increased his speed and ran towards him. The man turned and started walking and Tony followed. He caught up with him and could hardly speak as he was gasping for breath. "Who are you?" he asked.

"Don't talk," said his saviour. "Just follow me." He turned to the left and approached a black saloon car that had melted into the night. He opened the back door, Tony jumped in, the man followed and the car sped straight down Anchor Street and turned right onto Southward Park Road.

The man in the front passenger seat turned round.

"Hello Tony. We seem to have arrived in the nick of time."

"Paul?" Tony was shocked. "How did you—"

"A little birdie," Paul said with a smile.

Karen was at the end of Ambrose Street. She had stopped shooting but still held her pistol at the ready, and she slowed to a walk. She was sure he was hiding somewhere, and she got straight on the radio:

"Officer down. Need ambulance and immediate armed backup to Ambrose Street, Bermondsey."

The Final Act

She walked slowly towards the large block of flats: Trappes House. If he's gone in there, this could get very tricky indeed she thought. Within ten minutes the whole area was swamped with police. One of the Met police helicopters was scrambled and was overhead searching with heat detection sensors. There was no trace, so he had to be in the flats and that could mean hostages.

Michael was rushed to St Thomas' Hospital but pronounced dead on arrival, there was nothing they could do to help him.

Karen organised a thorough search of Trappes House by armed teams, who examined every single room in every flat and found nothing. Police dogs combed the entire estate and came up blank. Karen was mystified. She had been only a few seconds behind him and he appeared to have vanished into thin air. She couldn't give up.

"Keep searching," she told them. "He must be here."

* * *

Tony didn't know what to say. He was relieved to be safe but wasn't sure what would happen next.

"So where do we go from here?" the fugitive asked.

Paul spoke without turning around: "You're my brother. I'm going to look after you."

Tony wasn't altogether comforted by those words but sat back and relaxed: he had survived another very close call.

Chapter 33

Tony was now living in a private suite at the Starlight Club. Paul had told him in no uncertain terms that he had to lay low and for once in his life Tony was doing what he was told. The dangerous killer was not allowed out of the suite and Paul had placed guards on the door to ensure he didn't try to leave.

It wasn't all bad for Tony: he had excellent meals provided and an endless supply of whisky, which he was fast becoming addicted to once more. Paul had dinner with him on the first night and they discussed what Tony was going to do. The former told him it was impossible for him to stay in London, and it might be not even be possible to stay in the country.

Tony ummed and ahhed about needing to stay in Bermondsey, while Paul laughed and told him if he stayed in London he would get caught, no question. Tony understood that and said he wanted to leave the country as soon as possible and that Spain was his preferred choice of destination. Paul told him he would arrange everything, but it would take a bit of time.

Paul was busy so wasn't obliged to see Tony that often and in truth he didn't want to. The club owner wanted to throw Karen Foster off the scent, so the day after Tony arrived at the club he placed a call.

"Karen Foster," Karen replied.

Paul was very serious as he spoke into the phone. "Karen what the hell's happening? I was expecting to get a call from you?"

"Don't ask me. We had him and he fucking disappeared. I still don't understand it."

"Disappeared? What does that mean?"

"We'll get him," she reassured him. "It's just going to take a little longer. Any word from your end?"

"Nothing. Which was why I called you."

"Yeah, well, if you hear anything you know where I am."

"Sure Karen. Good luck."

He pressed the 'end call' button and redialled a speed number.

The Final Act

"Dave how you getting on?" he said into the phone.

"We're making progress but it's not easy," Dave replied.

"What's happening with the other teams?"

"Same, but I'm still confident we can get it done on schedule."

"You'd better. Tony won't sit around for ever, so push everybody hard. I'll be away for a couple of days doing my bit so I want everybody here Sunday. This is important Dave. It's the final act. Do you understand?"

"Yes. It's going to go according to plan—don't worry."

"I'll see you back here on Sunday, ten a.m." And with that Paul pressed 'end call'.

He had two days to get his part done—he just prayed he could pull it off; it would not be easy.

Tony was back on the booze big time and couldn't wait to get away. He had decided he would arrange the killing of Sharon Travis as soon as he became settled in Spain. She was obviously on the Witness Protection Scheme but there was always a way if you had enough money.

Paul got back late on the Saturday night, his mission accomplished. Dave arrived even later than Paul, but it had worked and everything was in place for the next day.

It started early on the Sunday morning. Dave was up early and left for the Z hotel in Moor Street, where he collected the packages and made his way straight back to the club.

One of the private dining rooms had been changed on the Saturday and was ready. Tony woke at nine, had some breakfast and a shower and got dressed. Four guards entered the suite at ten-thirty and handcuffed his hands behind his back. Tony was incensed.

"What the fuck are you bastards doing?" he demanded. "Wait till I get out of these, you'll fucking pay for this. Where's Paul? What the fuck is going on here?"

"We're taking you to see Paul now," was the reply.

That confused Tony even more. The guards escorted him along a corridor and up a small flight of stairs and then into the dining room. Most of the tables had been removed and it now resembled something like a courthouse. Tony looked around and saw about ten or so people sitting in two rows of chairs on one side with a single table and chair on the other. He then saw a chair in the middle of the room which was the one they took him to, and strapped him into it, using leather belts.

The killer was looking around trying to understand what was happening. It hit him suddenly. *This is like a trial*, he thought, *a fucking trial!* He started shouting: "What shit is this? Where the fuck is Paul?"

The answer arrived a few seconds later, as Paul entered the room, flanked by Duke and Dave.

"What the fuck is going on here Paul?" Tony yelled, but Paul ignored him.

"Paul you cunt I'm talking to you!" continued the seated man. "You're supposedly my fucking blood! My fucking brother!"

Paul sat on a chair and placed a file in front of him on the table. Paul nodded at Duke and Dave who then approached Tony.

Duke whispered in his ear: "Keep quiet or we will gag you. Do you understand that?"

Tony looked at Duke with deep loathing. "For the moment, cunt, yes."

There was complete silence in the room. Everybody was waiting for Paul to speak.

Paul looked around the room.

"Thank you for coming." He looked around the room again and paused. "This is not a social occasion I wish it was. We are here today to judge my brother Tony Bolton for his crimes."

Tony shouted: "What sort of shit is this Paul? Let me go for God's sake!"

"QUIET!" Paul screamed at Tony.

The accused man was looking at the group of people and thought he recognised one or two but didn't know where from.

The Final Act

"Tony this group of people have travelled from all over the UK to be here today," Paul explained. "And now I am going to introduce them to you."

"Starting at the back on the left-hand side," Paul went on, "the first gentleman is Konstantinios Papadikis. He is the brother of Timius Papadikis who you shot through the eye and murdered while committing the robbery at Arrow Logistics. He was also the brother of Artan Papadikis, whom you shot and killed along with Bashkim Amiti at their house in Totteridge in North London.

"Next is Alison Morgan. She is the wife of Chris Morgan, the police officer you shot while he was sitting in his car in Tower Bridge Road. He has left two young children."

Tony could not believe what he was hearing. What the fuck was Paul doing, he wondered?

"Next is Ryder's father and stepson," Paul went on. "You buried Ryder alive in cement in Millwall Park."

Paul raised his voice in volume as he introduced each new person:

"Next is Gillian Jones, wife of the football referee Cyril Jones and her son James. You shot and killed Cyril Jones at the Royal Lancaster Hotel in London."

"Next—"

Every time Paul said *next* Tony shuddered: it seemed to be going on for ever.

"—Is Philip Taylor, bother of Steve Taylor who you tortured with a screwdriver. He was the man who hit Dave on the head with a bottle in the Tower Tandoori, Tower Bridge Road. He was in hospital for six months and will never work again.

"Next is the father of the guard you assaulted at Broadmoor who has undergone numerous plastic surgery operations since you cut his face to pieces.

"NEXT—"

Tony interrupted, shouting, "That bastard deserved it he—"

"You will be quiet Tony!" Paul shouted "You will have your chance to speak shortly." He paused for a moment.

The Final Act

"NEXT is the son of Paul Carter, who you stabbed to death while escaping from Broadmoor Psychiatric Hospital.

"Next," Paul couldn't help himself from speeding up, the tension was now incredible: tears were streaming down Paul's cheeks. "Tony you were responsible for the deaths of Fifi Miller, a sweet fifteen-year-old girl who had all her life in front of her, and also of Emma Miller, my fiancée and our unborn baby. God help you for your sins. Present today are Peter and Mary Miller, Emma and Fifi's parents.

Tony was in shock and was scared: the atmosphere was electric, and the men and woman of the makeshift 'jury' were staring at him with hatred in their eyes.

The killer defended himself, saying, "I didn't mean to—"

"—Didn't mean to?" Paul screamed at Tony. "Shut up or you will be gagged."

Paul gathered his thoughts. "We are unable to contact and bring relatives of your latest crimes here because they were so recent, but we will have an announcement of the crimes committed."

Paul went on: "And now there's one more witness and for various reasons they will be in disguise."

A person entered the room and stood next to the desk Paul was sitting at. You could have heard a pin drop. The man or woman was wearing a balaclava covering their whole face. The jury and Tony were staring at the person. It certainly appeared to be a woman, but that was about all you could tell.

The witness pointed at Tony and spoke in a loud commanding voice: "I accuse that man Tony Bolton of murdering one Michael Terry, better known as Micky. He was an old overweight man who could not defend himself, and you kicked him to death. This was in the Angel pub in Bermondsey Wall East."

The witness took a deep breath. "I also accuse him of murdering a Mr Andrew Parr in the Mayflower pub Bermondsey. He was a businessman who had simply had a couple of drinks more than he should have done."

There was a long pause as the witness looked at the faces of the jury. "I accuse him," the witness was pointing at Tony again, "of torturing and murdering Roddy Ferguson, who was found in a warehouse in Bermondsey. Roddy was a harmless accountant who was merely doing his job."

The Final Act

The witness then went quiet, took a step back and left the room.

Paul stood up and spoke very deliberately: "Lastly I accuse that man of torturing my fiancée, Lexi, who at the time was pregnant."

Tony started shouting again. "I didn't know Paul! If I'd known I wouldn't have laid a hand on her, I swear it!"

Paul turned to the jury "I will ask each of you in turn is he innocent or guilty and that is how you should reply. I would now ask the ladies to vacate the room."

Alison Morgan, Gillian Jones and Mary Miller stood up and left the room.

Paul started asking each person around the room and the replies were all the same: "Guilty, Guilty, Guilty," and so on.

Tony was now in such a state of shock that he couldn't collect his thoughts. What the hell was going to happen next, he wondered? It didn't take long for him to find out.

"You, Tony Bolton," Paul announced, "are sentenced to immediate death."

Tony started shouting: "Is this a joke Paul? Paul we're brothers! We can sort this out. Please Paul, for God's sake we—"

"Gag him."

Dave had been wanting to do it for a long time. He cut some grey sticky packing tape with his teeth and stuck it over Tony's mouth. Tony was looking at Paul, shaking his head and was pleading with his eyes.

The jury all stood up and approached the desk. Paul pulled out a box from underneath it. Each person leant over and took a sharp hunting knife out of the box. Tony was now frantic. He was trying to rock the chair backwards but he couldn't move it. He saw the knives and his eyes were almost jumping out of their sockets.

The group crowded round Tony.

Tony started to mumble in panic.

The first stab took him in the shoulder, the second in the upper back. Pain coursed through Tony's body and that was the second when he knew he was going to die.

225

The Final Act

The stabbing became frenzied: there were wounds to his chest, neck and legs, he lost count of the number. Blood was flying in all directions and the repellent squelching noise of knives plunging in and being pulled out of muscle and tissue was sickening, and the pain was out over his whole body. And then it all stopped. Tony must have had twenty wounds and was bleeding to death.

Then the jury stood back. Paul came to the front, followed by the person wearing the balaclava. They both brandished knives and lifted them above their heads. They plunged down and both of them entered Tony's neck. Paul cut and slashed with his knife until Tony's whole throat was in shreds—the blood loss was incredible, pouring down his body like a river.

"That's for Michael and all the others. Die you bastard!" shouted the person in the balaclava as they rammed the knife repeatedly into Tony's torso.

Paul and his accomplice backed off. Tony was gurgling and bubbles had appeared at his mouth. He gurgled one last long time and stopped breathing: he was dead at last.

Paul took a deep breath. It was over at last. He hugged the figure in the balaclava and the jury began to leave the room, each of them shaking his hand as they left. Finally he was left with the person who'd helped him finally extinguish his brother's life.

"Thanks for coming," Paul said.

"I wouldn't have missed it," was the reply. "See you around." And with that the person left.

CHAPTER 34

Paul was sitting at his desk writing up some reports when the phone rang.

"Yes?" he answered.

It was Carla. "It's your wife Mr Bolton."

"Put her through please."

"Hi darling. How did it go?" he asked.

"Oh not too bad. George was very brave—he cried a bit but soon got over it," Lexi replied.

Paul chuckled. "Good. He's a tough little thing isn't he?"

"Takes after you I guess."

"No I hate injections. The sight of a needle and I'm in pieces."

Lexi laughed. "What time will you be home?"

"Couple of things to do but I won't be late, love you and give George a big hug and kiss for me."

"I will see you soon, I love you Paul."

"I love you too."

Paul put the phone down and redialled.

"CID Rotherhithe," came the reply.

"Karen Foster please."

"Hold on a second." There was a pause and someone else came on the line. "Who's speaking, please?"

"Paul Bolton."

"Paul," Karen replied. "Good to hear from you. How's things?"

"Good thank you. I hope you can make George's christening?"

"Try and keep me away."

"And I hope you're bringing Chau?"

"Of course—she loves a party."

* * *

Karen was sitting at her desk in the CID office at Rotherhithe Nick.

The phone rang and she answered, saying eventually, "Oh fantastic. Thanks for letting me know. I'll be right out."

The whole station had turned out and were in the car park, looking towards the entrance. Karen joined them and moved to the front of the crowd.

Suddenly it went very quiet as a silver Audi drove through the barrier into the car park. It stopped alongside Karen and the back door opened. Jeff Swan got out and the crowd burst into clapping and shouting. Karen couldn't contain herself—tears were streaming down her cheeks as she lunged and threw her arms around Jeff. They hugged tightly for what seemed an age and then they heard the banter:

"Put him down you don't know where he's been!"

"Lazy sod, 'bout time he came back and did some bloody work."

"Skiving git's been off ages with a bloody cold."

Jeff was a bit doddery but would recover fully in a matter of weeks.

Karen couldn't stop crying and between sobs exclaimed: "How about a nice Latte then?"

"Love one I'll give you an IOU."

"This one's on me Jeff!"

They strolled back into the station and headed to the canteen.

The End

The Best Selling Bermondsey Gangster Trilogy

1. **Bermondsey Trifle**   http://amzn.to/1l3B3up
   Published in June 2014
2. **Bermondsey Prosecco**   http://tinyurl.com/nebwtys
   Published in August 2014
3. **Bermondsey The Final Act**
   Published in January 2015

Available in Paperback and Kindle versions from Amazon.co.uk

Look out for the next exciting Novel from Chris Ward. Karen Foster from CID Rotherhithe moves to Surrey Police in Epsom to escape from the madness and killings of Bermondsey. She has had a promotion to Detective Inspector and expects to be chasing bicycle thieves and shoplifters, but how wrong could she be? It's action all the way as Karen's world is turned upside down when a killer strikes.

"SERIAL KILLER" Due for Publication early 2015

The Final Act